FIGHTING
for your
LOVE

NIKKI ASH

True love is always worth fighting for.

To my children,

who show me every day the true meaning of love.

Prologue

ASHLEY

Six Years Ago

"SHUT THAT FUCKING KID UP! ALL HE DOES IS CRY!"

"He's a baby. Please stop yelling. You're only making it worse! Your yelling isn't helping at all. It's only scaring him."

"Then make him shut the hell up!"

"I will if you move out of my—" *Whack!* My face jerks to the side at the impact of his hand hitting me straight across my cheek. It stings like a bitch, but I don't dare show it. I'm not about to let him know he's gotten to me. I get right in his face because I've had enough of his shit.

"You don't even want to be here anymore. Why don't you just leave?"

He laughs in my face like it's the funniest thing he's ever heard. If I knew I could do any damage, I would punch him in the face.

"You wouldn't even be able to survive without me. You're nothing more than a no-good little bitch."

I want to stand up to him, tell him that I think I'll survive just fine without him, but the fear of being smacked again forces me to keep my mouth shut and silently pray he'll walk out that door. I refuse to let him bully me anymore. Tonight is the last night he'll ever touch me again. I can't have Tristan growing up with him as a role model, and if that means I have to leave then that's what I'll do. I only pray he'll leave instead.

"You want me gone? Okay...I'm gone. I never wanted this fucking life anyway."

I watch him walk to our bedroom not believing for a second he'll actually leave. He threatens to leave every other day. I head into the nursery to check on my sweet baby boy. Tristan has already stopped crying and is sleeping soundly in his crib. He's only six months old and has learned quickly how to sleep through the screaming that's been a part of his life since the day he was born. I'm hoping with him being so young he won't remember any of this. I know something needs to change, but I've been with Tyler for so long I don't remember how to *not* be with him. I pick Tristan up and cradle him to my chest, giving him small kisses on his forehead and breathing in his precious baby scent. "I love you, little man." I vow here and now that if Tyler doesn't leave, I'm going to. I'm going to get away from him and find a way to provide a safe and loving home on my own with my son.

I set him back down in his crib, cover him with his blanket, and head back out to the kitchen to make dinner. As I'm crossing through the living room, I see Tyler with a bag in each hand. While he threatens to leave quite often, he's never actually packed a bag. I stop halfway into the living room, watching him stalk through the house, and then without giving a backward glance, he's out the door and slamming it shut. The sound reverberates throughout the house and I hold my breath, hoping it doesn't wake Tristan up. After a few seconds and no sound of him crying I know it didn't. I let out a breath of relief I didn't know I was holding in. Could he really be gone for good?

I continue into the kitchen, grabbing the chicken from the fridge and the potatoes from the counter, when the phone rings.

"Hello."

"Good evening, this is Chase card services calling to speak with... Ashley Myers regarding a personal matter. Is this Ashley Myers?

"Umm...yes, it is. Can I help you?"

After confirming my name, social security number, mailing address, and the best contact number, he says, "We're calling today because you are ninety days behind on your credit card payment and we would like to help you make payment arrangements before it gets moved into collections."

What the hell?

"I'm sorry. I don't know what you're talking about."

"Your balance on your Chase credit card is eight thousand five hundred and fifty-three dollars, and according to our records, you haven't made a payment in over ninety days. Before we send it to collections, we're asking if you would like to work out a payment plan."

Holy fucking shit! The small hairs on the back of my neck rises and chills run down my spine. This can't be happening.

"I need to call you back."

"Ma'am..."

I don't even listen to what he's saying. I hang up and run into my bedroom to the desk where all the bills are kept. I pull all my credit cards and bills out of the file Tyler keeps them all in and start calling the numbers on the back of each card.

Reached its limit.

Payment overdue.

Maxed out.

Ninety days behind on the phone bill.

Thirty days behind on the electric bill.

Two payments behind on the mortgage!

WHAT. THE. FUCK!

I drop the cards and papers on top of the desk and stare at the beige wall in front of me having no idea where to go from here. I trusted him. Sure, it wasn't always rainbows and sunshine, but I fucking trusted him. While I've been busting my ass to make the money to pay the bills, he's been gambling with my money instead of paying them. I always knew he had issues with gambling, but he had promised he would stop. Not only did he not stop, he used all our money and savings to do it.

I hear a noise coming from the nursery and will myself to shake off the tears that I feel prickling in my eyes before I go to get my little man. I look down into his crib, and he's lying on his back crying, ready for some dinner.

"Come here, little man." He immediately stops crying, smiling up at me while his arms reach up and his little legs stretch out as he kicks excitedly for me to pick him up.

"I don't know how, but Mommy is going to handle this, baby boy."

I look at my sweet baby and know it's up to me to make sure something changes. I can't just sit back and wait for Tyler to return.

After throwing the chicken back in the fridge, I grab my car keys and diaper bag. With Tristan in tow, I purchase new locks for the house. Once we get home, I install the locks then grab everything that belongs to Tyler and put it all by the road for the garbage men to pick up.

The only way that motherfucker is getting back inside my house again is over my dead body.

KADEN

Eleven Years Ago

"PLEASE, GABS, I'M BEGGING YOU WITH EVERYTHING IN ME not to leave me. Please! I'm so sorry!"

I'm kneeling in front of my wife, begging.

Begging her not to leave me.

Begging God not to let her leave me.

Knowing my begging will do no good.

But still begging.

"Please, Gabs! I love you. Please, baby! Don't leave me."

Placing my hand into hers, I entwine our fingers and squeeze gently, but she doesn't squeeze my hand back. I know, no matter how much I beg and plead, she won't squeeze back. She's leaving me and there's not a goddamn thing I can do to change it. The truth is, while she's right here in front of me, she's already left.

I promised to always protect her and I broke that promise.

One

KADEN

Present Day

"LEFT JAB...RIGHT JAB...BLOCK...BLOCK...BLOCK!"

"Motherfucker, I am blocking!"

I throw a punch to his face and it hits him square in the eye. I probably shouldn't have hit him so hard, but the guy isn't fucking blocking.

"How the fuck do you plan to fight in six months if you can't even block!"

"I was fucking shot! I will have this shit under control by the time the fight gets here!"

I'm standing in the middle of the octagon in Cooper's Fight Club training one of my best friends, Caleb Michaels, for an upcoming UFC fight. No, I don't really expect him to be fighting up to par only five months after being shot, but as his trainer, it's my job to push him, especially when I see how badly he wants to come back. I refuse to allow him to hold back. When the UFC called with an opportunity for him, I told him he should turn it down, not to push himself, but he insisted he would be ready. So, as his trainer, it's my job to ensure he is.

"Maybe if you're fighting at the upcoming kids' tournament..."

"Fuck you, bro."

I laugh softly knowing that even though I'm pissing him off, it's also pushing him, which is exactly what I wanted to do, so I continue to push his buttons, getting him worked up.

"Maybe that would be a good idea. We could bring Bella, Tristan, and Marco in, and have them spar with you. You'll probably be able to take the two little ones, but I'm not sure if you would beat Marco."

Caleb growls and throws a punch to my gut, hoping to catch me off guard. Of course, it doesn't work. If he hadn't been shot while saving Marco from some drug dealers last winter, he probably would have stood a chance, but with him having been shot in the chest and shoulder, he's just not fast enough.

I jump back right before his fist connects with my stomach and laugh harder.

"Let me at him," Bella yells, jumping over the ropes. We both look over at the cute three-foot nothing, brown-haired, six-year-old jumping up and down in her fighter stance ready to kick some ass. She's the perfect mixture of her parents, Liam and Lizbeth Cooper. They also have an almost one-year-old son, Nathan. Liam, who goes by Cooper, is the owner of the gym. His father, who is deceased, is the one who hired me several years ago, back in Colorado.

I spent four years working at the gym, living with Bentley and Cooper, until I couldn't handle living in Colorado anymore and decided to make the move to Las Vegas with all the guys, including Caleb, who was moving here hoping for his big break. It paid off. I spent almost ten years training Cooper and Bentley, who were both in the UFC, but the last couple years they've both taken a step back. Cooper is running the gyms with his wife, Liz, and Bentley is staying home with his daughters, Chloe and Faith. His wife, Kayla, is the physical therapist here at the gym.

With the two of them out of the UFC, I've taken on Caleb, and Alex, who is another fighter at the gym, full time, aside from the personal training sessions I do with several other up and coming fighters. Caleb was well on his way to the top until he was injured. Long story short, Marco had a druggie mom who owed some guys money and Marco was selling drugs for them. He and his mom got in over their heads and Caleb came to the rescue. He saved Marco and his little sister Chloe, but couldn't save Marco's mom who overdosed and died that night. Caleb and Hayley—who is our onsite doctor—were married a couple months ago. Hayley adopted Marco while Bentley and Kayla adopted Chloe. If all goes well Caleb will legally be Marco's father soon. Not that it makes any difference, he's already like a father to Marco, and Marco calls him Dad.

The four of us have gotten together and are currently building a sports complex for latchkey kids. It's still in the planning stages, but once it's done, it will be a place for kids to go, where they can play all types of sports, instead of going home alone.

"I said let me at him!" Bella yells again, one of the guys holding her back. I can't help laughing. She's so tiny yet so full of life. She is UFC obsessed and will definitely be a woman's division champion one day.

"Okay, but you need to go easy on Caleb. He's still not at one hundred percent yet. I don't even think he's at ten percent," I add under my breath, laughing. That comment earns me a punch to my arm.

"Not Caleb! You!" Bella glares at me.

"Me? What did I do to you?" I look at her in shock.

"You called me little!" Her hands fist at her sides, and if possible, her glare gets meaner.

"Oh, don't let him get to you, sweetie." Hayley comes walking over with Marco. "You know what they say...those who can't do, teach."

Caleb throws his head back and laughs before grabbing Hayley and giving her a kiss.

"Ha ha, funny, Hayley. At the rate your husband is going, he'll have to resort to teaching the kids' classes for the rest of his life." That earns me another punch to my arm.

"I'm sorry, Bella. I didn't mean anything by it." The guy holding her back, let's go of her.

She glares at me for a few more seconds, letting me sweat it out. She's been hanging out with these women for too damn long.

"I guess I accept your apology. Marco, want to go spar?"

"Sure." They both head over to the kid's area of the gym.

"How was your doctor's appointment?" Caleb asks Hayley, rubbing the bump on her belly.

I know it sounds bad, but I tend to tune that shit out. While I'm happy for all my friends, it's hard watching each of them get married and go through all that family shit.

My phone goes off and I walk over to check it.

Ashley: I can't hang out tonight. Gotta work.

Me: Again? I thought you were only working two nights a week...

Ashley: I took on more shifts. Don't worry about me.

I shake my head in frustration. Ashley Myers just might be the death of me. I met her a couple years ago through our friends. She's good friends with Kayla, Liz, and Hayley, and has a son, Tristan, who is the same age as Bella. We became fast friends and our friendship has grown over time. She is without a doubt my best friend. She is also the most strong-willed, independent woman I've ever met. It's funny because the characteristics I love most about her are the same ones that frustrate the fuck out of me on a daily basis.

I decide not to text her back and instead go to her house. She tends to argue less when she doesn't have a cell phone to hide behind.

"I'm out of here," I say, packing up my shit.

"See ya, man." Caleb gives me a fist bump and Hayley waves.

I get into my black on black four-door sexy-as-fuck Aston Martin Rapide S. She was given to me for my thirty-fifth birthday last month, courtesy of my parents. Yes, that's right, I'm one of those trust fund rich kids, only I'm without the trust fund. My parents firmly believe I should earn my own way in this world and I'm happy to say I'm doing a good job at it. The only money they've ever given me was a million dollars for my twenty-first birthday. Any other money I get, will be in my parents' and grandparents' will. As a trainer for the UFC full time, I make a very comfortable living, so I took that money and put it into a couple investment accounts and haven't touched any of it. Upon moving to Las Vegas, I purchased a decent sized four bedroom, three and a half bath, two-story home on the outskirts of Las Vegas on a nice piece of property. Many epic parties have been held there around the bonfire in my backyard.

My parents' gift is more of a bribe. Since I have moved to Vegas, I've only been back to visit them once and they want me to come home soon. They're hoping by buying me the car of my dreams, it'll guilt me into coming home for a visit. They know why I don't want to go home, but they feel enough time has passed. It's been almost eleven years since my wife left me, taking our son with her, and while I've moved on, the truth is even after all this time, it still hurts like hell to go home. Memories of our life together are in every nook and crevice of that town. After they left me, I lasted about four years living in that town, but the minute Cooper asked if I wanted to move, I jumped at the chance to get the fuck out of there and start a fresh life.

The guys know I was once married and that when they met me I was no longer married, but I've chosen to keep the details to myself. I don't want or need anybody's pity. I've spent the last several years having one-night stands to try to fill a void that can't be filled. Well, that is up until six months ago. It's not that I can't go out and find a woman to get into bed—I just haven't felt like it. Call it a dry spell if you wish, I'm just not feeling it.

"Incoming call from Mom," comes across my Bluetooth. I want to press ignore on the touchscreen but know better. Sandra Scott is not a person who does well with being ignored.

"Hello, Mom."

"Hello, Kaden. How are you?"

"I'm good. Just heading to Ashley's to hang out."

"Oh, Ashley. I would really love to see her and her son again."

"She's just a friend, Mom."

"I know that, Kaden. I know that because she would never behave like all those women you have non-committal sexual relations with. I could tell that about her from the one time I met her when we visited."

I can't help but groan at my mom's comment about Ashley. It reminds that she was the last person that I...Nope! I'm not going to think about that night. It will do no good to think about the night Ashley and I almost...Fuck! I'm not thinking about that shit! She's my friend. My best damn friend.

"Mom, I'm almost to Ashley's house. Is there some other reason you called?"

"Can't a mother call her son to say hello?"

Most moms, probably—my mom, no way.

"Absolutely. Hello. Love you. Gotta go."

"Wait! Kaden...your grandfather would like to talk to you about something. He has a proposition for you."

And there's the reason for her call...

"Okay, well can we talk later?"

"Hello, Kaden. It's Grandfather. How are you, son?"

She seriously put him on the phone?

"I'm good, Grandfather. How are you?"

"Not good. Your grandmother's eightieth birthday is coming up and she wants you here for her party."

Of course, she does. They have used every possible excuse to get me to come back to Colorado over the years. This excuse shouldn't surprise me.

"Look, Grandfather..."

"And she wants you to come back with a fiancée..."

Has he lost his damn mind? I can't help the laugh that escapes. Is he going senile?

"Are you out of your..."

"And once you're married we will relinquish your inheritance early and double it."

The shock of his words almost causes me to run off the road. Luckily, I'm about to pull into Ashley's driveway. I gather myself together, pull in, and put my baby in park.

"Double it?"

"Yes, if you come to Colorado, engaged, for your grandmother's birthday and get married before the year is over we will sign over your inheritance early and double it. You will receive ten million dollars as a wedding gift."

I always knew I was going to inherit a large amount of money once my grandparents passed away, but I had no idea it was that much and for them to double it? What's their end game?

"Why is my getting married so important to you guys? I was already married once. You bought us a house."

"Your grandmother wants to see you happy. She wants to see you married and settled down. You are thirty-five years old, Kaden. You're the only grandchild and you're off getting your dick wet instead of settling down and giving us a great-grandchild."

I did give you one, is on the tip of my tongue, but I don't say the words. I know he isn't trying to be insensitive. My parents and grandparents love me, and it breaks their hearts that I went from being married and having a baby to single and fucking every available woman with no chance of ever committing to a single one of them. While my family can be a bit stuffy at times, they really are good people, and surprisingly not at all stuck up even though they are worth millions.

"How do you know I won't just find a woman to marry and divorce her the minute I get my hands on the money?"

Grandfather breathes a heavy sigh into the phone. "Because I know you would never marry a woman unless you loved her. I saw you with Gabrielle all those years ago and you wouldn't say those vows again unless it was for real. And I also know you would *never* do that to your mother and grandmother."

Fuck! He's right. There's no way I could stand in front of my family and God and vow to love and cherish a woman, until death do us part, unless I meant every word I was saying. The problem is when I made those vows to Gabby, they were supposed to be the only time I would ever make them. She was supposed to be my one and only, my one true love.

"Grandfather, I appreciate your offer, but unless a woman I can magically fall in love with, falls out of the sky and right into my lap, I don't think it will be possible."

And just as I'm saying these words, out walks Ashley, looking hot as hell, staring daggers my way as she walks past my car to her mailbox to check the mail. Long, straight, caramel-colored hair that flows down her back with matching hazel eyes. On a good day, they're mixed with green, but on a bad day they're mixed with gold, which is how they look now. Her hair and eyes are what you notice first, but it doesn't end there. Because as you run your gaze over her body, you notice her perfect-sized tits that I can attest to, fit quite perfectly into the palms of my hands, only spilling out a little. Then when you go a bit farther, you see the soft but flat stomach and amazingly toned tanned legs, which seem to go on for miles from the years of exercising and pole dancing classes she has taken at the girly gym she goes to. She almost didn't renew her membership this year, so I renewed it for her as a Christmas present. She's wearing her cocktail waitress uniform, which consists of a tight, low-cut black tank top that reads Double D's across the front in bright orange lettering—the name of the sleazy strip club she waitresses at—and tiny black booty shorts. And to finish off the outfit, she struts back up the driveway in black heels that have got to be a good five inches tall, showing off her toned calf muscles.

Since my windows are tinted, when she gets near my car, I roll down the window so she can see me wink at her, and when I do, she flips me the bird. I laugh as I watch her ass sway back into the house, and then remember I'm still on the phone with my grandfather.

"Kaden, are you there?"

"Yeah, I'm here. Sorry."

"Your grandmother wants you married and I will do whatever it takes to make sure it's done. She's not getting any younger and her one wish is to see you settle down and give her some great grandkids. What will it take, fifteen million?"

Holy shit! He's dead serious about this. You would think my grandmother was on her deathbed...

"Hold up, is Grandmother sick? Is there something you aren't telling me?"

He doesn't reply for a second, and when he does, he says, "Please just think about it. It would make her happy, Kaden."

It doesn't go over my head he didn't answer my question.

"Okay, I'll think about it. Regardless, I will be there for her birthday this year."

I might not be able to give her a great granddaughter-in-law or great grandkids, but I can at least go back for a visit for her eightieth birthday. What if she's sick and I don't go? That wouldn't be good at all. I live with enough regrets—I don't need to add any more.

"Thank you, Kaden."

And with that, he hangs up.

I turn my car off and head up to Ashley's front door. It's a small two-bedroom house in a rougher neighborhood. Not as bad as some parts of Las Vegas, but it's not the kind of neighborhood you let your kids play outside by themselves in. She said she bought it when she was pregnant with Tristan when she was fresh out of college. I don't hear much about her deadbeat ex-boyfriend also known as Tristan's sperm donor, but I do know he left her in pretty bad shape financially, hence the reason why she works part-time as a cocktail waitress. I've begged her to let me help her out, but she refuses. Stubborn ass woman.

"Honey, I'm home!" I yell out as I walk into the house without knocking in search of Ashley. She doesn't respond and the only thing I hear is music blaring from somewhere in the house. I head through the living room, following the sound of the music, and then into the kitchen, where I find her.

When I get there, the sight in front of me almost knocks me on my ass. Ashley is stirring what looks like spaghetti in a pot, and while doing that, she's shaking her ass to the song *Closer* by the Chainsmokers. She has a wooden spoon in one hand, which she's using as a microphone, while her other hand holds onto the oven door handle. Then she drops her body halfway to the floor, her ass sticking out and then slowly moves her body back up like the goddamned stove is an actual person. Is it weird that I wish I was a fucking stove right now? I'm instantly hard and have to adjust my pants before I make a fool out of myself. I clear my throat and she turns around still singing the song.

She's now allowed my body to take the place of the stove as she approaches me, almost too close for comfort, and then drops to the floor like she did a minute ago, only to come back up slowly. If I was hard a minute ago, my dick is now rock fucking solid. I step back a foot and clap at her performance.

"Nice. Good to know those pole dancing lessons are being used, even if it's in the kitchen cooking pasta."

"Hey now, you never know...Maybe I'm just working on building up my confidence before I take my moves to a real club." She takes the boiling pot over to the sink and pours the pasta into the strainer.

"Aren't you just full of jokes," I say dryly while searching for some food to taste. Ashley can cook something fierce.

"You still mad at me?" I ask, looking across the counter to find something to munch on. Fresh rolls out of the oven. Score! I pop one in my mouth.

"You know I hate it when you question my work schedule." She grabs the basket of rolls and moves them to the other side of the counter thinking it'll stop me from grabbing more.

"I get it. I'm sorry. I just hate that you work so much when it isn't necessary." I move to the stove to see what's cooking over there.

"It's very necessary. Anyway, I told you I have to work tonight. What are you doing here?" she asks, pouring the pasta back into the big pot and then looking down at her phone.

"Well, I'm here anyway. Need any help?" I lift the lid to the smaller pot, which is holding her delicious meatballs. I grab a fork, but before I can snag one, she snatches the fork from my hand.

"Oh, good! You want to help? You can fold the laundry in the dryer while I try to find a sitter for Tristan." I know she's only kidding about the laundry, but I go to the dryer and grab the clothes to fold them. What kind of best friend would I be if I didn't help her out?

After grabbing the clothes, throwing them onto the couch, and turning the NBA finals on, I yell back to her in the kitchen, "Britni canceled again? I can watch Tristan." I grab a couple articles of clothing to fold and see a bright pink thong. *Fuck!* I throw that shit to the side. I'll figure out how to fold those later.

Ashley comes out of the kitchen frowning down at her phone and then looks up at me folding the clothes and smiles. I love that smile. I would do anything to keep it on her face. There isn't anyone I've ever known besides Gabrielle whose smile can light up an entire room.

"Are you sure? I put a text into Hayley and Liz. I don't want to take you away from any plans you might have."

"Tristan!" I call out. It's a small house, so it doesn't take much for someone to hear you. I hear him running down the short hallway, and a few seconds later, he throws himself on the couch next to me.

"Want to chill with me tonight while your mom goes to work?"

"Yeah!"

"There you go. We're good to go. You staying to eat first or do you need to run?"

"I really need to run. I'm hoping to meet with Don to beg for some extra days." She's now running around the house grabbing her purse and coat and keys. She really is the most unorganized woman. Most of the time it's the guys who leave shit everywhere, not the women, but Ashley is the exception. She is forever misplacing her debit card and keys. One time she found them in the washing machine!

She gives Tristan a kiss goodbye, first. Then leans over to give me a kiss on my cheek. "Thank you, Kaden."

Before she can walk away, I grab her wrist, bringing her to a halt. "I can give you some money...even a loan if it makes you feel better. Then you wouldn't need to work at night and you can just focus on Tristan and teaching."

She lets out a heavy sigh, giving me her signature glare while her hand goes to her hip. "We have already had this conversation. I don't want or need your money. Can we please not have this argument again?"

I know there isn't any use in continuing. She's right, we have had this argument, and it always ends the same way, with her telling me no. She is determined to make it on her own. And she is. She has been living on her own, taking care of Tristan and teaching full time as a kindergarten teacher since I met her. She's also been working at Double D's since I met her. It was two days a week for extra money, she said. But recently something has changed. I've seen past due bills on the counter when she's forgotten to put them away and she's been trying to work additional days. She's been doing this same routine for years and now suddenly, she isn't making ends meet? Something isn't right. Unfortunately, until Ashley is ready to talk to me there's no getting any information out of her. She's too damned stubborn for her own good.

"Have a good night at work."

"Thanks! And don't let Tristan stay up past nine, please. It's a school night, even if school is almost over!" she yells as she flies out the door.

"Who do you want to win the finals?" I ask Tristan as I go back to folding the laundry, throwing some of his clothes at him to fold.

"I guess Cleveland," he says, not really caring since his world revolves around the UFC.

"Ugh...C'mon, kid. Don't jump on that bandwagon!" I groan.

"Whatever...Can we play UFC on the PlayStation?"

I look at the game, seeing that Cleveland is destroying Atlanta. It will most likely be a complete blowout.

"Sure, why not?"

"Yes!" He fist pumps into the air before running to the PlayStation

to set the game up.

Two

ASHLEY

I GET TO DOUBLE D'S AND FIND DON, ONE OF THE TWO owners of the club, hence the D in his name, and ask if I can speak to him.

"Sure, honey. What's up?"

"I was wondering if there's any way I could have some more nights."

"Honey, we've talked about this. I don't have any openings. Unless a girl quits or gets fired, I'm maxed out on hours."

"What if I danced? I've taken pole dancing lessons for years."

He shakes his head. "Ashley, I would put you up as a dancer in a heartbeat, but the women who have been dancing here longer get first dibs. If you would have come to me six months ago you know I would have moved you to the stage, but right now my lineup is full."

Yeah, the problem is six months ago I didn't need the money like I do now.

Four months ago

There's a knock on my door. A quick glance at the clock on the microwave showing ten p.m. tells me it's too late for anybody to be coming over. Kaden did leave a little bit ago...he probably forgot something. I swing the door open, immediately going to slam it shut when I see who's standing there. It's definitely not Kaden. What the hell was I thinking not looking out the window to see who was there? His foot catches in the door and then his fingers wrap around the edge, pushing it open.

When he gets inside, I look closely at the man who walked out the door almost six years ago, only he doesn't quite look like the same man. He's a bit skinnier, his clothes are rattier looking, and his eyes are bloodshot like he's high on something. It looks like he has been through hell and back.

"What do you want?" I whisper-yell, not wanting to wake Tristan up.

"I want to see our son."

"He's not our son. He's my son. You gave up your rights the day you walked out."

"That's not what his birth certificate says."

"What the hell do you want, Tyler?"

"I'm broke. I need money and you're going to give it to me."

"Are you fucking serious? Do you not remember what you did to me when you left? All the debt you left me in! I have to work nights on top of teaching all day just to keep up and pay off the maxed-out credit cards you racked up when you pretended to pay the bills, only to use my hard-earned income to feed your gambling addiction!"

He grabs me by my shirt and shoves me roughly up against the wall. "Listen here, you fucking cunt, I have a right to see my son. Either you give me money or I will take him away and you will never see him again." His voice is cold and menacing. What happened to the guy I met in my senior year of college? Who took me on romantic dates and told me he loved me at the top of the Eiffel Tower experience. That guy is clearly gone and I'm starting to wonder if he ever really existed or if it was all just a front.

"Don't do this, please. I don't have any money to give you!"

"I'll sign over my rights to our son for thirty grand."

"Where the hell do you think I'm going to get that kind of money?"

"You live in Las Vegas! There are plenty of loan sharks. Figure it out. I'll be back tomorrow. If you don't have my money, I can promise you our son will disappear. I'm sure a six-year-old boy goes for much more than thirty grand on the black market."

He lets go of my shirt and stalks out the door, slamming it behind him and causing me to jump.

I pull out my phone and text Don. If anybody knows where to find someone to lend me money it would be him. I've overheard all the shady shit he's dealt with over the years.

Me: Where can I go to borrow a large amount of money?

Don: How much we talking?

Me: $30,000

Don: Damn woman! Do I even want to know?

Me: No, you don't.

Don: Go to Giovanni Valentino. He owns a Gentleman's Club about thirty minutes outside of LV. Tell him I sent you. But Ashley, be sure about this. He only takes one kind of collateral...

Me: Which is?

Don: Women

I'm not sure what the hell he means by that, but I need this money, so I'll just have to figure it out. I can't take the chance of Tyler coming back and stealing Tristan from me. I'll deal with any loan shark's demands if it means keeping my son safe.

He texts me the address and I text him back thanking him. After calling in sick for tomorrow, I double check all the locks on the doors and windows. Then grabbing my pillow and blanket, I go to sleep on the floor next to Tristan's bed. I'm not taking any chances.

The next morning after dropping Tristan off at school, I head to the address listed. The GPS says it's a half an hour away, so I use the drive to build up my courage to beg for the money. When I get to the said address I see a beautiful sign that reads "La Stella." As I drive down the long, graveled road, the most exquisite picturesque mansion comes into view. It must be three stories tall made of brick and mortar. While it looks to be generations old, with old-style Church windows throughout and chimneys peeking out in several areas, it also has a certain modern charm to it. It's absolutely breathtaking. I pull up to the large U-shape driveway and see several expensive cars parked along the side. I follow their lead and park on the edge of the drive as well, my beat-up car sticking out like a sore thumb.

Approaching the massive size wooden front door, I take a couple deep breaths, gaining the courage to knock, when the door opens. In front of me is a gentleman, who looks to be only a tad bit older than me, maybe in his thirties, dressed in a three-piece suit and not at all shocked to see me standing in front of the door.

"Good morning, how may I help you?"

"I'm here to see Giovanni Valentino. Don sent me."

"I'll let him know you are here. And your name is?"

"Ashley...Ashley Myers."

He opens the door wider, signaling for me to enter, then leaves me standing in the foyer to, I assume, let Giovanni know I'm here to see him. From what I can see, the inside is even more beautiful than the outside. To my left is a tall brick fireplace that expands from floor to ceiling. The fire is on and crackling giving it a homey vibe. Wood beams run across the ceilings, and in front of the fireplace are a couple of brown leather couches. There is a man sitting on the couch drinking what looks like a scotch and sitting on his lap is a gorgeous woman wearing nothing more than a scrap of lingerie. She must feel my eyes on her because she turns to face me, giving me a small smile, and she's even more beautiful than I originally thought. I give her a small smile back before she turns her attention back to the man she's with.

"How can I help you?" Another man walks over, dressed just as nice as the gentleman who let me in, only this guy runs his piercing blue eyes up and down my body, assessing me.

"I'm here to see Giovanni Valentino. Are you him?"

"I'm his assistant. How can I help you?"

"I need to see him."

He glares at me for a second but nods, walking away. A few minutes later he returns.

"He will see you," the man with the piercing blue eyes says, now signaling for me to follow him. I look for the gentleman who let me in and notice he's back to standing near the door. Is his entire job to open the door?

We head in the opposite direction of the man and woman who were cozying it up near the fireplace. There's a small bar to the right with a younger gentleman wiping down the counter. He gives me a curt nod and I give him a small wave. We reach a long hallway and at the end, the man knocks once and then opens the door.

"Boss, Ashley Myers."

"Thank you. You can close the door behind you."

I walk into the room and am faced with one of the most beautiful men I have ever seen. Brown hair that is gelled to the side with matching dark brown eyes. He has stubble on his face that looks like he hasn't shaved in maybe a day or two. He's dressed in a suit that fits him to perfection with no tie, the top three buttons open showing a hint of a tattoo peeking through. It makes me want to ask him what the tattoo is of.

He stands and I notice he's tall, at least six feet with wide shoulders—he definitely works out. He gestures to the chairs in front of his desk for me to have a seat, his face showing no sign of any type of emotion.

After we both sit, he asks, "How may I help you?" Okay, I guess we're going to bypass all pleasantries and get down to it.

"I need a loan for thirty thousand dollars and was told by Don you could help me." I make sure to sound sure of myself. I don't want this guy to think I am scared shitless.

"Hmm...Did he now. Did he tell you what I accept for collateral?"

"Yes, women," I choke out.

"So, you understand, if at any time, you can't pay me back the set monthly payment you will be required to work it off here at my Gentleman's Club?"

Okay, so I guess that's what he means by women. I wonder what he makes a man do if he doesn't pay him back. Something tells me I don't want to know the answer.

"Yes, I do."

"If Don is sending you to me then I'm sure you're legit, but I will still need to run a background check. Anything you need to tell me?"

"No, I'm in debt, but that's it."

"Okay, as long as your background check comes back okay, I will loan you the money. First, we'll need to sign some paperwork."

"Like a contract? What do you think I'm going to do? Take you to court?"

He chuckles softly and points at me. "You got sass to you. Would you like to work here? I have quite a few guys who would be fond of you. You could make a lot more money than thirty grand in less amount of time." His statement sends chills down my spine.

"No, thank you."

"To answer your question. No, the contract is not for court. It's for my records and for yours. When the loan is paid off, we will both sign off on it."

"Okay."

He types on his phone and a minute later the man who escorted me back here, walks back in.

"Boss."

"Johnny, run Ms. Myers's credit, and if all is clear, put together the paperwork for a loan for thirty thousand with twenty percent interest."

"Oh my God! Twenty percent? It's going to take me forever to pay that off."

"You better hope not because you only have eighteen months to pay it back."

Holy shit! I can't do that kind of math in my head, but I know that *monthly payment is going to require me to get another job.*

"Is that going to be a problem?"

"No." I shake my head. I'll do whatever it takes to make sure Tristan is safe and Tyler is out of our lives for good. "You'll have your money."

Johnny comes back a few minutes later with the paperwork and asks for my driver's license to make a copy of it. After we're done signing all the paperwork and Giovanni lets me know how much I owe by the end of each month, he asks me how I would like the money.

"Um, cash please."

"That's a lot of money to be walking around with. Are you sure you don't want it wired to your account?"

"No, I need it in cash, please," I insist. I need to give Tyler this money so he can be out of my life for good. He gives me a quick nod, a small frown marring his face. It's the first emotion he's shown since I walked in the door, and even upset he really is gorgeous.

"Ashley, please remember you are now dealing with the big boys. You don't pay me back my money and you will belong to me."

"I understand."

Since the day he handed me the thirty thousand dollars, which I then handed over to Tyler, I have done everything in my power to pay back the obscene amount of money every month, but the problem is, in order to pay Giovanni back it means my other bills are going on the back burner. My mortgage is behind, my credit cards I finally got under control are not being paid, and meals like spaghetti and meatballs have become a luxury. But I can't regret my decision because Tyler did in fact sign over his rights to Tristan and walked out the door, once again not looking back.

Now it's the end of May and I'm short on my payment for the month. If I could just pick up a couple extra shifts I know I could make it.

"I have some good news," Don says, pulling me out of my own head. "Charlotte called out. She had several private parties scheduled. You can pick up her shift along with your waitressing shift. You're going to have to bust ass, but you'll make good money tonight."

"Thank you! I will handle it!" I give Don a huge hug causing him to laugh. "Go get ready, Ashley."

The changing room for the dancers is utter chaos at all times. Girls are changing outfits, putting on makeup, doing their hair, and usually bickering with each other over sections and men. It also permanently smells of aerosol and burnt hair, which makes me gag every time I step foot into the room. Since I only waitress, I'm usually in and out in two minutes, simply putting my purse and keys in a locker. I'm not big on makeup and the waitresses are required to wear the standard Double D's tank top and black shorts, so I come in ready to work.

Tonight, however, I'm going to need an outfit for dancing. I'm going through the rack the owners provide and it is severely lacking. The girls who dance on a regular basis bring their own outfits since the ones the club provides are crap. If I had known I would get to work a private party tonight, I would've tried to pick something up on my way in.

I find the best possible outfit and cringe when I hold it up knowing this is my only option. It's an ugly purple body suit that buttons down the front and underneath, and has purple and silver sequins around the neckline. *Gag!*

Just as I'm about to accept I have no choice but to put this horrendous outfit on, clothing is thrown my way, hitting me in the face.

"I heard you're covering for Charlotte tonight." I look over and see Scarlett grinning my way. I met her when I first started waitressing here and we hit it off immediately. She is your cliché stripper, dancing her way through college. She's now going through her master's program, and with the money she makes, she is completely debt free. What I would give to be debt free.

"You are a life saver!" I run over and give her a hug and kiss on the cheek. "You are seriously saving me right now!"

"You're lucky I love you, bitch. Now let's get some makeup on you. We need you looking scandalous so you can bring in some dough tonight."

First, Scarlett straightened my hair, making it pin straight and putting some oil in it to make it shine. Next, she darkened around my eyes with coal, giving me the perfect smoky eyes. Then she applied a couple coats of mascara, giving my lashes extra volume, and finally, she handed me baby pink lip gloss that made my lips look wet and shiny.

Once she was all done making me over, I put on the dress she gave me. It's all white with a black strip going across the chest. It's low up top and short on the bottom and the entire dress from the chest down is completely see through. Underneath I'm wearing black mini-scrunch panties and a matching black lace bra. The bra and panties are mine. Luckily, I put my good ones on tonight.

"Damn, Ash! You look hot tonight," Desiree, another dancer, says, smacking my ass playfully. I look in the mirror and she's right, I do look hot. Between the professional looking makeup, sleeked hair, and the beautiful black and white seamless net dress, I look damn good.

"Thanks! Let's hope I look good enough to make some money."

"Ladies, club is open! Let's go," the bouncer calls into the dressing room.

All the women file out and head to their destinations. When the women who dance aren't on stage, they walk around and offer lap dances to the men sitting at the tables. Some guys will buy a dance and some will go a step further and ask for a private room. Dances and private rooms are where the money is at. This club, like most other clubs, don't allow guys to put cash on the stage like it is depicted in the movies.

We get to the floor and a Britney jam is beating through the speakers. You won't find a strip club that doesn't play her at some point or another—the woman makes music that is meant to be danced to. I go to my section and greet my assigned tables asking them what they would like to drink since I have to work my waitressing shift on top of Charlotte's shift. After bringing their orders back to the table, I head to my first private party of the night.

IT'S ELEVEN P.M., AND MY FEET ARE KILLING ME, BUT I HAVE made more money in the last couple hours than I did during my last few shifts combined. And I still have one more private party to do.

"Ashley, your private party is in room five," Dean, the other half of Double D's, says.

"Thank you."

A private party is exactly what it sounds like— a group of guys who pay extra money to have a stripper dance privately for them instead of them sitting at a table and watching on the main stage. I never thought my pole dancing lessons would come in handy but they have. People assume pole dancing is just wrapping your legs around a pole and grinding on it, and while for some that's what happens, but here, you need to know what you're doing to be hired as a dancer. Don and Dean won't hire amateurs.

Now don't get me wrong, is this place upscale and classy? Hell no. The guys are sleazy and there are no real rules other than not being allowed to touch the dancer on stage, and that's only because it would cause fights to break out. But in Las Vegas you need to know what you're doing because otherwise every girl who has seen *Showgirls* will think they can just show up here, grind on a pole, and have tons of money thrown at them. The truth is, if you can't dance properly, the men and other women will eat you alive, so you better know what the hell you're doing.

After switching on *Body Party* by Ciara, I walk into the room using the backdoor which leads to the mini stage. The lights are turned down and the low light above the stage is just bright enough to focus on the dancer and allow me to dance without seeing who is watching. It helps me pretend I'm dancing in one of my classes for fun as opposed to dancing in front of a bunch of horny men for money. The only difference is, here my clothes end up coming off, whereas in my class, they stay on.

I make my way to the pole, and after walking once around it, hook the inside of my arm around it. Then I hook the inside of my leg around the front and, with a little hop, begin my routine with a front hook spin. I slowly come down and shift into a knee bridge, which is what it sounds like—my knees are both on the ground while my back arches into a bridge. Pretending the men aren't looking at my thong covered lady parts, I push back into a shoulder bridge by lifting my ass up into the air and bringing my shoulders down. From there, I roll backward and end up back on the bar.

As I continue my choreographed moves on and around the pole, little by little my clothing is removed. First, it's my top, then my bra. Finally, the last article of clothing removed is my shorts. While many strippers choose to remove all their clothes, including their panties, I've made the choice not to. I'm sure if I did, it would earn me more money, but I just can't bring myself to do it. Only one man has seen that private area of my body and it's Tristan's father. The next man to see it will hopefully be making love to me. I just can't bring myself to let some horny strangers see me completely vulnerable like that.

When the song ends, along with the routine, I gather up my bra and put it back on, leaving the dress off. Then I walk down the steps leading to the tables situated in front of the small stage. There are several men in their thirties sitting together and clapping. I make sure to add an extra sway to my hips as I approach the men.

"And who is the man of the hour?" I ask, attempting to add an extra little bit of sexiness to my voice.

One guy raises his hand. "It's my birthday, darling."

I walk over to him, sit down on his lap sideways, and give him a wink. "Happy Birthday, handsome. What can I get you gentleman to drink, tonight?" They each give me their order one by one and when I get to the last guy, I notice he's assessing me harsher than the others, like he's confused about something.

"What can I get for you?"

"Do you teach at Old Creek Elementary?"

My pen falls out of my hand as I scramble off the gentleman's lap, so I'm standing.

"You're my son's teacher," he adds.

"Yes, I do," I say softly. He stands and, taking me gently by my arm, walks me to the corner of the room.

"I'm thinking, by the look of shock you gave me, the school district doesn't know one of their teachers is a stripper."

"I don't usually strip. I'm filling in for someone tonight, and I would appreciate it if you wouldn't tell anyone."

"Absolutely, on one condition...you give me a private show."

Is this guy serious right now? Of course, it would be my luck I would run into a father of one of my students on the one night I'm doing more than waitressing.

"Okay, let me get everybody their drinks and I'll see which private room is available."

I put my order into the bar and then seek out Eddie. He is the bouncer tonight and oversees the rooms.

"Hey Eddie, do you have a private room available? I only need it for like ten minutes."

He gives me a questioning look. He's known me for years and not once have I ever asked for a private room.

"Room four is available."

"Thanks."

After going back to the bar to grab the guys' drinks, I let the guy who asked for the private dance know he can meet me in room four in five minutes, I just need to check on my other tables.

Once I walk into the room, I spot him sitting on the couch ready for me. I put *Here I am* by Rick Ross on the speakers and begin the lap dance without saying a word. My moves are robotic and stiff, yet still sexual as I circle around the couch dancing. Once I get back in front of him, I rub against his body then sit on his lap finishing the dance. He doesn't once try to touch me, which kind of surprises me, but makes it more bearable. When the song is over, the room goes silent as I climb off him.

"My name is Eric, Chris's dad." I think for a moment and know I have met Chris's mom. I also know she is married to Chris's dad.

"Nice to meet you. I appreciate you not saying anything about my working here."

I flick the switch to the iPod dock off. "You ready to head back to your friends?"

"Who said we were done here?"

"You asked for a private show and I gave you one."

"Did you really think when I said private show I meant you dancing for me? I meant I want to fuck you."

I let out a soft gasp. "I don't do that. I'm sorry."

I walk to the door and open it, silently making it clear he needs to leave.

"You sure about that?" The question sounds more like a threat.

"Yes, I am."

He nods once, stands, and walks out the door. When he gets to the room where his friends are, he says, "I suggest you rethink your stance on my offer before the end of the night. You might regret it if you don't."

I don't rethink his offer, and as their party comes to a close, I see the silent threat Eric gives me. I have to hope it's an empty threat.

IT'S TWO IN THE MORNING AND I'M MORE THAN READY TO go home. After changing out of Scarlett's borrowed outfit and giving it back to her, I count my money. I've made almost enough to pay Giovanni this month's payment.

My house is dark when I walk through the door, aside from the faint light glowing under the microwave. I see Kaden on the couch, sleeping with the remote in his hand. The TV is still on and it casts a light on him. He looks beautiful. But what makes him beautiful isn't just his looks. He's beautiful on the inside and out. Black hair that is just long enough you can run your fingers through it and mess it up, and his hair always looks like it's a perfect mess. His eyes are currently closed, but when they're open, they are the most amazing shade of bright green. They remind me of my birthstone—emerald. They pop against his lightly tanned skin. His body is ripped; I am talking six pack of abs, ripped. Not overly muscular, but healthy and fit. And he's my best friend. He's been there for me this last year, providing me a shoulder to cry on, as well as an ear to listen without judgement. He can be a total goof, but he can also be downright sweet and serious when he needs to be. Him and Tristan have grown close these last several months, and I'm thankful Kaden can provide a good, male role model for my son.

"Hey there." I softly touch his cheek, causing him to stir awake.

"Hey," he answers groggily, stretching out. His voice is raspy from sleep and I can imagine him saying my name in that same voice...

Abort! Abort! No thinking about how my name sounds coming out of Kaden's mouth.

"I'm home. Thank you for watching Tristan. Was he good?"

Kaden grabs my arm and pulls me into his side, giving my temple a quick kiss. "He's always good. Although, he did kick my ass in the UFC fighter game on his PlayStation. How was work?"

"It was good." I lean in closer to Kaden, enjoying for a second the safety I feel when I'm close to him.

"Are you getting the extra hours you were hoping for?"

"No, I'm not, but a girl called out, so I got to take over her tables. I made some extra money. It was a good night."

"That's good, Ash." Kaden stands, then taking my hands in his, pulls me into a standing position as well.

"You spending the night?"

He gives me a look that tells me I'm an idiot for even asking. "Of course, I am. Don't I always?"

"Well, I don't know what you had planned. Maybe you had to put off plans with one of your black book girls to babysit Tristan for me last minute."

He just shakes his head and laughs, as he guides me down my hallway. We stop at Tristan's room and I walk in to give him a quick kiss and pull up his blanket. "Love you, little man."

After changing into my pajamas, we get into bed, and within minutes, Kaden is back to sleep. I watch him for a little while, thanking God for him being in my life. He and Tristan are without a doubt the bright lights in the darkness I'm surrounded by these days. I don't know what I would do without Kaden in our life, and I don't ever want to find out.

Three

KADEN

IT'S SUNDAY AFTERNOON AND EVERYBODY IS OVER AT Bentley and Kayla's house hanging by the pool. While Bentley and Caleb are manning the grill, everybody else either has a drink in their hand lounging in a chair or are swimming with the kids. I'm one of the people swimming with the kids along with Cooper, Alex, and Alex's new girlfriend, Jessica. All the other women are laying out in the lounge chairs holding babies with fruity drinks within reaching distance. I look over and see Ashley in her skimpy fucking little yellow bikini, holding Kayla's daughter Chloe in her lap while she laughs at whatever Hayley is saying.

It's times like this I think about how different my life would have been if Gabby was still in my life. How much I miss her and wish she and our son were both here with me. I look around and guilt overcomes me for the happiness I feel surrounded by my friends. It feels wrong to be happy while my wife and son aren't here to experience even an ounce of the happiness I feel.

"Kaden!" Bella shouts, waving her arms in the air to get my attention. I'm on one end of the pool, while Tristan and Bella are on the opposite end trying to explain some game to me they're insisting I play with them.

"Explain this game to me again. And please tell me why the heck it's called Toothpaste."

Bella and Tristan both laugh. "I don't know why it's called Toothpaste. It just is! Focus Uncle Kaden!" Bella glares at me and Tristan shakes his head in amusement at her.

"You name a category like favorite color or favorite food. Once one of us guesses correctly, we race from one end of the pool to the other and the first person to touch the wall and yell 'Toothpaste' wins."

"Thank you, Tristan, for patiently explaining the game to me once again."

Bella huffs and rolls her eyes. "Can we play now?"

"Okay, the category is..." I tap my chin, thinking, and take an extra-long time just to aggravate Bella, who acts like she's six going on sixteen. Marco comes from inside the house and sits on the edge of the pool, laughing, knowing exactly what I'm doing.

"Can I play?" he asks.

"Sure! You can be on my team." He jumps into the pool and swims over to join me.

"Oh, my God! Can you please pick a category?" Bella screeches.

"Bella Cooper!" Cooper yells out in his dad voice, pointing the spatula in her direction. "Don't be rude."

"I'm not, but Uncle Kaden is purposely not picking a category. I need to beat these boys!"

She looks back over at me and glares once again, causing me to chuckle.

"Okay, okay! The category is favorite food."

"Pizza."

"Chicken nuggets."

"Grilled cheese."

"Spaghetti and Meatballs."

When Tristan says, "Lasagna," I confirm he's correct and the four of us take off across the pool. When I get to the middle and see Bella about to pass me, I scoop her up, causing her to shriek. With both hands, I throw her into the air, and her body hits the water with a splash.

"Throw me, too!" Tristan yells. So, I pick him up and throw him into the deep end as well.

Bella swims to the end of the pool and steps out wiping the hair out of her eyes. "I give up," she says before running and jumping into the water cannonball-style right next to me to get my face soaked.

"Kaden," Ashley calls to me. "Your phone just went off with a text from your mom asking if you booked your plane tickets yet. Do you want me to respond?"

I grab Bella and chuck her across the pool once again. "Yeah, just tell her I'll do it tonight."

"Okay... Oh, you just got another text. It's Sabrina. She said she thought she saw you last night at Club Eleven."

Tristan swims over to me, lifting his arms up, so I throw him again.

Then I swim to the edge of the pool and get out. "Just text her back, 'I'm sorry I missed you.'"

"Okay."

I get over to the chairs and look over her shoulder, dripping water all over her. I watch the droplets of water run down her chest and get lost between her tits before taking a look at what my cell phone says.

Me: I'm Sorry. I missed you. <insert smiley face emoji>

"Ashley! You can't put a damn period in there! You just changed the entire sentence! And you put a smiley face emoji at the end. Jesus, woman! She is going to think I actually missed her!"

"What?" She looks down at the phone as it dings.

Sabrina: Aww <insert heart filled eyes emoji> I miss you too!

"See? That's just great!"

"Sorry! I didn't mean to..."

Suddenly my phone is ringing and, before I can stop her, Ashley hits answer to the FaceTime call.

"Hey Kaden, what are you up to?" Sabrina's annoying voice comes over the speaker.

"Nice, Kaden! You gonna hit that?" Bentley laughs, earning him a hit to the chest courtesy of his wife.

"Oh! She's live! Like on the phone right now." Ashley's eyes bug out, not realizing she was answering a video call.

"Hey, Sabrina. It's Ashley, Kaden's friend. I didn't mean to answer the call...or is this a video? Sorry! I don't have one of those techy phones."

"Excuse me, I was trying to reach Kaden. He just texted me."

"Oh! That was actually me...Sorry!" Everyone around us is laughing while Ashley looks confused as shit and Sabrina looks like she wants to reach through the phone and rip Ashley's head from her body.

"Can you just give the phone to Kaden?" Sabrina spits out.

After drying my hands, I grab the phone and quickly tell Sabrina I'll call her later before ending the video chat and putting my phone on silent. I throw it onto the table and pick Ashley up, sitting her on my lap to get her all wet.

"Kaden!" she shrieks, batting me away. I hold her to me, shaking my hair like a dog and getting her soaked.

"Let me up! I'm getting all wet!"

"You deserve it! You just made some annoying chick think I want to hook up with her. You're lucky I don't throw your ass in the pool."

She stops fighting me and turns around. "You wouldn't dare. And mistakenly telling one of your many floozies you missed her is hardly a crime bad enough to be thrown into the water."

"Oh, it's definitely enough to throw your ass in the water. And just because you told me I wouldn't, I'm going to."

I pick her up bridal style and carry her toward the deep end, hanging her over the water. Everybody starts chanting to throw her in.

"Don't freaking do it, Kaden," Ashley demands.

But I do it anyway. Only I jump in with her. We both sink to the bottom of the pool and when we come up to the surface everyone is laughing and cheering.

"I can't believe you did that!" Ashley laughs, wiping the water out of her eyes then splashing water at me. Her hair is all over her face and she looks breathtakingly gorgeous. She's bobbing in the deep end, so I swim to her and grab her sides, bringing her body to mine to hold her up. She wraps her legs around my waist, so she can use her hands to move her hair out of her face.

"Thank you," she says softly. "I must look like a drowned cat."

"You definitely don't look like a drowned cat. You look beautiful."

"Burgers are ready!" Cooper announces. I swim us to the shallow end, then reluctantly let her go.

"Just not beautiful enough for you," she says under her breath.

She walks away and I know exactly what she's talking about—the night when we almost hooked up and I put a stop to it. She thinks it's because she isn't good enough or pretty enough for me. I know I should correct her and tell her she's completely wrong, but then I would have to explain why I'm not capable of giving a woman anything more than one night. Ashley is my best friend and I can't imagine my life without her, but I can't be with anyone. If she remains my best friend, I never have to let her go. It's selfish of me, but I need her in my life, even if it's only as a friend.

Four

ASHLEY

Three Months Ago

"OH MY GOODNESS! I SWEAR EVERY SINGLE TIME I DRINK those Bahama Breeze's I get drunk. They are so fruity and delicious and I always forget they are filled with alcohol. It just sneaks up on me."

I plop onto my couch and Kaden sits next to me. He takes my feet into his lap and, after throwing my heels onto the floor, begins massaging one foot and then the other.

"Ohh, that feels so good. Between working at Double D's and teaching all day, my feet are taking a beating."

I close my eyes for a second, and when I open them, Kaden is staring at me like he wants to devour me whole. The way he looks at me gives me the confidence to do what I'm about to do. Moving my feet out of his hold, I straddle him, putting my thighs on either side of him. His hands move to my hips to hold me in place as my hands run through his messy hair.

"Ashley...what are you doing?"

The truth is, I'm not sure. I know it's the alcohol talking, and if I wasn't drunk, I wouldn't have the courage to make my move. But I also know if I was sober I would still want this man. He's my best friend and I love him. I'm aware he doesn't do commitment and I don't do one-night stands, but what I feel for him is so strong maybe it would be worth it to have one night with Kaden, even if that means I would be left broken in the morning.

"I want you." Kaden slowly shakes his head. I can't handle the rejection right now. I grab his hands and bring them to my chest. "Please."

I let go of his hands, and for a second, think he's going to move them from my breasts, but he doesn't. Instead he not only keeps them there but he begins to massage them.

I let out a small moan at his touch and it gets him riled up. He grabs my shirt and throws it over my head. Then he pulls his up and over his head.

His mouth goes to my left breast as he pulls my bra cup down and takes my pebbled nipple in between his lips and sucks. Then he moves to the other one and does the same thing. His touch causes my legs to tense up and tighten around him.

And then my phone rings.

Kaden's hands go to my ass, pulling me in closer to him. I can feel his erection through his jeans.

And my damn phone rings again!

This time Kaden removes his mouth and hands from my body, setting me on the couch next to him. He gets up and grabs my phone from my purse.

"It says it's Giovanni and he's calling you *Bellissima*. Who's that and what the fuck does *Bellissima* mean?"

Fuck! How do I explain who Giovanni is without telling him I owe a loan shark thirty grand?

"He's just a friend of mine. *Bellissima* is just an Italian word."

Kaden grabs his phone. "Siri, what does *Bellissima* mean in Italian?"

Oh jeez! "Hmm...According to Siri, it means gorgeous. Why the hell is some guy texting you saying you're gorgeous?"

"You're my friend! You don't think I'm gorgeous?"

"I didn't say that..."

"It's not what you say, it's how you say it, Kaden."

"Are you trying to change the subject?"

He looks down at the phone when another text message comes through.

"He wants to know if you're coming by tomorrow?"

I snatch the phone out of his hand. "Thanks, I'll text him back later."

"Ashley, are you seeing someone?"

It's a legitimate question, but one I can't explain, so I get defensive instead. "No, I'm not. It's nothing. Don't worry about it."

He gives me a questioning look and then closes the distance between us. It's then I notice the small tattoo on his left pec. I've seen it before but not close enough to read the words.

Gabrielle y bebe,

mi mundo

I don't know what it says since it's not written in English, but I do see the name Gabrielle.

"Who's Gabrielle?"

Kaden glances down at his chest, but instead of answering my question, he walks to the couch to grab his shirt.

"Who's Gabrielle?" I repeat.

"Who's Giovanni?" he counters.

"Nobody."

"Ditto."

I grab my shirt from the floor and throw it on. "I'm tired. I'm going to bed. Are you staying over or grabbing a cab?"

"It's after three in the morning. I'll stay over if that's okay."

"You know it is."

"Look, Ash…"

"You don't have to say anything. I get it."

"You're my best friend. I don't want to ever lose you. If there's a guy, I'll understand, but I just don't get why you would be meeting him somewhere and be so adamant about hiding it from me."

"Do you want to explain who Gabrielle is?"

"No."

"Then let's drop this and pretend tonight never happened."

I walk down the hall to my bedroom without waiting for his response.

Present Day

"ASH! YOUR PHONE IS GOING OFF," KADEN SAYS, HANDING me a huge plate of food. My stomach growls in anticipation. The last few months have been rough moneywise. Tristan is always fed, but sometimes if I'm short on money, which seems to be more often than not lately, I'll skip a meal to ensure he'll get fed.

"Thanks."

I check my phone and see it's an email from work.

> From: Wilcox, Margaret
> To: Myers, Ashley
> Subject: Meeting requested
> Good evening,
> Please plan to meet me tomorrow morning before school at 7:30 a.m. I have a matter that needs to be discussed with you.
> Thank you,
> Margaret Wilcox
> Principal
> Old Creak Elementary

A lump forms in my throat and I pray this email is not about what I think it's about. I email her back confirming I will meet her in the morning. The rest of the evening goes by like a blur. I can't remember anything anybody says. My only thoughts are on my upcoming meeting tomorrow morning.

"MORNING, LITTLE MAN," I SAY, TURNING THE LIGHT ON IN Tristan's room. "It's the last week of school. Are you excited?"

"Yeah, I can't wait to spend the summer practicing at the gym. I don't know why I even have to go to school. I'm going to be in the UFC one day anyway."

"The same reason football and basketball players stay in school. You need an education. Plus, if they get hurt, they will still be okay because they went to school."

"Yeah, yeah." He pouts, throwing his covers off him.

"Get ready for school, please. We need to leave early this morning. I have a meeting before school."

"Okay."

When we get to school I have Tristan hangout with Megan, a teacher friend of mine, while I go speak with Mrs. Wilcox.

"Ashley, please have a seat. I know we already met earlier this month for your evaluation. Unfortunately, a situation has been brought to my attention. Before I go any further, I will ask you if what I have heard is true. Do you work at a strip club?"

I could lie, but there's no point. She already knows I do, and she could easily find out if I'm lying.

"Yes, I do. I am a waitress there."

"And if that were the truth, we wouldn't be having this conversation."

"I did do a private party one time, but it won't be happening again. I was just filling in for someone."

"Ashley, as an educator you agree to uphold yourself to certain standards. I am sorry, but at this time, after this week of school is over, I will not be able to rehire you."

"Can I get a job at another school?"

"I suppose you could, but due to the notes on your record, I would suggest you wait a few years for it to blow over. I don't believe you will be hired in this county."

"Okay."

"I am sorry, Ashley."

"I understand."

After grabbing Tristan from Megan, I bring him back to my classroom while I finish grading some papers I wanted to give back before school lets out. I look around and realize after this week I'll not only no longer be a teacher, which was my dream since I was a little girl, but I will be short a huge chunk of money since I won't be teaching summer school. Everything is spiraling out of control and I have no idea how to fix any of it.

Five

KADEN

"SHIT! THAT HURT!" I LEAN OVER HOLDING ONTO MY GUT. I'm completely off my game and deserve that kick to my stomach.

"What's going on with you?" Alex grabs a couple towels from the rack and throws one at me. I catch it and lie down on my back, wiping the sweat off my face and neck in the middle of the octagon while staring at the fan whirring around.

"Just got a lot on my mind. I'm sorry. You deserve better than that."

"It's all good, bro. We all have our off days."

"You're going to be ready for this fight. You're kicking ass. You have gotten quicker and stronger these last several months."

"It would be nice to win, that's for sure. I'm hoping if I win I can use some of the money to pay for our honeymoon. I can't believe Jessica actually said yes to marrying me." He laughs at himself.

I sit up and throw my towel at him. "I can't believe it either. I can't believe you asked her to marry you!"

"Not all of us can be bachelors for life like you. Do you think I'm making a mistake?"

I look at Alex for a second. He's not much older than I was when I married Gabrielle. I can see the love clearly in his eyes. I would recognize that look anywhere because I once had the same look before I lost it all. But instead of feeling the usual hurt, my mind switches to Ashley and how much I miss her.

"No, you aren't making a mistake. Bachelorhood isn't all it's cracked up to be."

"Do you ever think about settling down?" The first images that pop into my head are of Ashley and Tristan. Ashley making dinner. Me and Tristan playing video games. Helping Tristan with his homework. Ashley and I watching television together. Kissing her goodbye before I head to the gym. Then my thoughts go to Gabrielle. Loving her. Losing her. Missing her. My heart aches, and if I'm honest, I feel guilty I thought of Ashley and Tristan first.

"No, that ship has sailed for me." I get up and grab Alex's hand, pulling him up as well.

"Hold on to your woman. Never let her go. Don't waste time fighting over stupid shit. Love the fuck out of her and cherish every moment with her."

I can tell he wants to ask me where this is coming from, but he doesn't.

I grab my bag and pull my phone out of it while I walk up to the front counter. Not a single text from Ashley, so I send her one.

Me: Hello

Me: I miss my best friend.

Me: Tristan had class today and wasn't there.

Me: Okay...I'm coming by your house.

Me: See you soon

I slam my phone on the counter and will myself to stay calm. I don't know what is going on with Ashley, but these last few weeks she has completely checked out. She doesn't call or text and she flat out ignores me when I text or call her. She hasn't been by the gym in weeks either, not even to drop Tristan off for class. My phone dings and I quickly pick it up.

Mom: Did you get your plane ticket yet?

This is the tenth time she has asked me this since I told my grandfather I would be at the birthday party. It's not even for a couple months, but she's hoping if I book my flight now, I won't change my mind.

Me: I will.

Mom: How many tickets?

Real subtle mom...I don't even bother to respond to that.

"Hey Kaden!" Marco says as he runs by me through the gym with Hayley and Kayla coming in after him. Hayley has her hand on her belly and is absentmindedly rubbing it. It's Hayley and Caleb's first time having a baby and they're due to find out the sex in the next week or so. It reminds me of when Gabrielle and I found out the sex of our baby. We both said we just wanted a healthy baby, but secretly I was excited to have a little boy I could teach MMA to.

"Ladies."

"Are you coming to Marco's Birthday?" Hayley asks.

"Of course. Do you know if Ashley will be there by any chance?"

"Aren't you two attached at the hip?" Kayla jokes.

"She hasn't returned my phone calls in a while. She's used every excuse not to see me. First, she was cleaning up her classroom for the summer. Then she said she picked up extra shifts at the club she works at. Another excuse she gave me was she was visiting her parents for a few days. I've been busy training Alex since he has a fight coming up next month so I keep letting it go. I'm about to go by her house right now, though."

"She said she would be at the party," Hayley says. "Now that I think about it, she hasn't responded to me much at all lately."

"Who?" Liz asks, coming out of her office with her purse, most likely heading to Caleb's club *Assets*. He inherited a strip club from his father who passed away last year, and after shutting it down and remodeling it, he turned it into one of the most sought out clubs in Las Vegas. Downstairs is a restaurant with stages in both corners that lead up to a main one in the middle. Upstairs is a bar with a large stage. There are also several private and VIP rooms. It was even on the top fifty best restaurants list as well as having received a best chef award.

"Ashley," Hayley says.

Liz frowns. "I was just renewing the kids' memberships for summer and fall, and when I didn't see her renewal, I called her. She said they'll be too busy this summer so she isn't renewing Tristan's membership."

"Are you serious? What is she so busy doing that she isn't letting Tristan do MMA all summer? There's no way Tristan is okay with that. The kid lives and breathes fighting."

"I know, Kaden. I honestly think she doesn't have the money but doesn't want to say anything. Since she didn't come out and say it, I couldn't offer her the financial aid form. And I'm not sure I would have. Ashley has too much pride to ask for help. When we met years ago in the mom group we were both part of, her ex had just left her and she was so scared but would never let anybody know. She made it look so easy raising Tristan on her own, while I was barely doing it with Kayla by my side."

"Oh, stop your crap," Kayla says. "You were and are a great mother! She had already graduated college. We were just starting out. We were babies. But I agree, she is a strong woman and full of pride. She would never admit if something was wrong."

"You can go ahead and renew Tristan's membership. Just take it out of my account. I'm going to her house now. I'll deal with this shit."

I slam the gym door behind me. I have no idea what is going through Ashley's head, but I'm going to get to the bottom of this shit. I arrive at her house in half the time it usually takes me, and when I pull up, I see an electric blue Rolls-Royce Phantom sitting in her driveway leaving me no room to park as well. Instead, I have to park along the side of the grass.

In a different circumstance, I would stop and check out the beast of a car, but right now I'm more concerned with who she's associating with that can afford this car.

As I walk up the driveway, I notice Ashley, standing outside her door on her front porch, talking to a big fucker. He's got to be six-foot-four at least and probably two hundred pounds of solid muscle. He has his hand on her shoulder like he's comforting her, which pisses me off. When I get closer, I see she's crying. What the fuck!

"Everything okay here?"

Six

ASHLEY

"TRISTAN, I KNOW YOU'RE UPSET, BUT I HAVE TO WORK THIS summer and Nana and Papa will be able to watch you while I work."

"I want to stay with you and go to MMA camp with Bella and all my other friends. This sucks!"

"Hey! Don't say sucks. I promise I'll come and visit you whenever I can. One summer without MMA will not kill you."

It's taking everything in me not to cry right now. After being forced out of my job, I spent the week cleaning out my classroom knowing I wouldn't be returning. The next week I spent wallowing in self-pity. Then I got myself together and remembered I don't have time for self-pity or to wallow for that matter. I need to make money and fast. My mortgage is several months behind and they've sent me a foreclosure notice. If I don't get caught up with the payments and pay the fees they're going to force us out at the end of July.

I called my mom and asked if she had any money she could lend me to pay my mortgage. She offered to take some money from my father's retirement fund, but I couldn't allow her to do that, so I played it off like it wasn't a big deal. Then I asked her if she could take Tristan for the summer. She's a teacher like me and was more than happy to have Tristan come and visit for the summer.

I give Tristan a kiss goodbye, but he doesn't kiss me back or acknowledge me. He's mad and I get that, but it still hurts. I've tried so hard to keep him from being affected by my money problems so he doesn't understand why I'm being forced to leave him with my mom and dad. What he doesn't get is that it's killing me to leave him with them. I would love more than anything to enjoy my summer with Tristan, but sometimes life isn't fair and it doesn't work in our favor. I just hate that he's having to learn that lesson so young.

"Thank you for taking him." I give my mom a hug.

"Is everything okay, Ashley? I feel like I haven't seen you much since Christmas."

"I'm sorry I've been distant these last few months. I just have a lot going on."

"Okay, sweetie. If you need anything, your dad and I are here. I love you."

"I love you too, Mom."

When I get back to my house, I turn on the computer to find local clubs I can call around to, to see if they're hiring, but my internet is down. Shit! I didn't pay that bill.

There's a knock on my door and I look out the window to see who it is. Yeah, you didn't really think I would ever open the door without looking again, did you?

It's Giovanni standing at the door. He knocks again. "Ashley, I know you are home. I saw you look out your window."

Damn it! I open the door slowly trying to prolong this conversation. I step outside, closing the door behind me, and he hands me a piece of paper.

> 30-DAY
> PERSONAL PROPERTY
> NOTICE
> Pursuant to the foreclosure sale conducted on June 22nd, 2016, Las Vegas Community Bank is now the owner of this property. You must remove all personal property, including all furniture immediately.
> On July 22nd, 2016, the doors will be locked and any items still in home will be forfeited.

"You're about to get kicked out of your home."

"Yeah, I stopped paying in January."

"Why did you borrow all that money and not pay your mortgage?" He looks at me incredulously.

"I borrowed the money to pay off my ex. He was threatening to take my son and said he would hand over his rights for thirty thousand dollars. I kept putting off paying the mortgage to pay you. I just couldn't get caught up in time."

Suddenly it all is just too damn much. The tears start falling and I can't stop them.

"I lost my job teaching a few weeks ago. I've been trying to find another job, but I haven't found anything yet."

"Oh, *Bellissima*, do you have *any* of my money this month?" Giovanni takes my chin between his fingers and raises my face, forcing me to look at him.

"I have a little bit of it. If you could just give me a little more time..."

"Beautiful, if I give you more time then I have to give everyone else more time. If I let everyone pay whenever they *could*, I wouldn't be the businessman I am. Nobody would take me seriously."

He places his hand on my shoulder, and for a minute, I let him comfort me—if that's what this even is.

"How about this? You come to work for me at my club for six months and I will wipe your debt clean."

The tears flow harder. The idea of having sex for money makes me feel sick. I get that there are women who can do it, but I just can't. I don't know how to fix this, though. I have a feeling Giovanni is trying to be nice about this, but he's really letting me know I don't have a choice. I made a deal and I couldn't hold up my end of it. I figure it'll be easier to go willingly at this point. "I guess I don't..."

"Everything okay here?"

I look around Giovanni to see Kaden standing in front of my porch.

"Everything is all good," Giovanni says.

"What's going on?" Kaden asks.

Giovanni is the one to answer. "Ashley and I were just discussing a business opportunity that has arose I think she might be interested in."

"Ashley, what the hell is going on? Who is this guy?" Kaden ignores Giovanni completely, focusing on me.

"This is Giovanni. He's a friend of Don's, my boss at Double D's. I owe him some money."

Kaden's eyebrows shoot up recognizing the name from the night Giovanni texted me. He walks up and joins us on the porch. My tiny porch suddenly feels extremely claustrophobic with these two large guys both crowding me in.

"How much does she owe you?" Kaden directs this question to Giovanni, but before he can say twenty-two thousand, I say, "four thousand." Thankfully Giovanni doesn't give anything away.

"Why do you owe him so much money?"

"I borrowed it from him to pay off some bills."

"I'm assuming you aren't going to accept a check, so why don't you follow me to the bank and I'll give you the money she owes you."

Giovanni looks to me. "You good with that?"

I want to say no. The last thing I want is to owe yet another man, but I would be a fool to say no right now.

"Yeah."

Giovanni puts his hand out to shake mine and I look at him quizzically. The foreclosure notice is exchanged from his hand to mine. He holds my hand for a moment before he says, "If you change your mind, you know where to find me." And then softly so only I can hear he adds, "Please don't be late next month."

Both men take off and I go inside to stress clean. I don't even know why I bother. In thirty days, this will no longer be my home. Hell, technically right now this is no longer my home. I'm only allowed here to remove my belongings. I take a moment to walk down the hallway and look at the pictures hanging on the wall. They start off with Tristan as a baby. Then move to him in preschool. One of him in Kindergarten. Another of him at his first MMA tournament last year. There's one of us during Christmas last year. Kaden is in the picture as well. We were at my parents' house before Tyler came through like a tornado destroying everything in his wake.

I hear the door slam shut and tentatively go down the hall to see who's there. Kaden is sitting on the couch with his hands in his hair, his face down. I can tell by his actions he's trying to calm himself down.

"Hey," I say quietly. Kaden has never yelled at me or hurt me so I don't know why I'm nervous.

"Hey," he says back, patting the couch for me to join him.

"Thank you for paying him. I'll pay you back."

Kaden shakes his head. "I don't care about the money, Ash. What's going on? Liz said Tristan isn't going to Cooper's Gym anymore."

"He's spending the summer at my parents."

"You know he loves MMA. Why would you do that? If it's the money, you don't need to worry about that. I paid his membership in full for the year."

"What the hell, Kaden! I didn't ask you to do that!"

"You're right, you didn't ask. You never ask for anything. You're my best friend, and I can see you're struggling, but you won't let me in. Let me in, please."

Now would be the perfect time to tell him the entire truth, but I can't make this his problem. I can't count on another man.

"I appreciate you paying for his MMA, but he's spending the summer with my parents. And as for me, I am fine. I will pay you back as soon as I can."

He assesses me for a moment and I can tell he doesn't believe a word I'm saying, but instead of calling me out on it, he simply nods.

"Okay, let's do something fun tonight. I miss my best friend." Kaden throws his arm over my shoulder and pulls me into him, giving me a kiss to my temple. To him, it's nothing more than a friend being affectionate, but unfortunately, my body and heart don't see it that way at all, and the butterflies in my belly prove that.

"What do you want to do?"

"How about we go to dinner and go watch the fountains at Bellagio. We can take a walk on the strip."

"Okay, that sounds good. Let me get dressed."

And just like that the tension between us is gone.

"MORNING." I ROLL OVER AND SEE KADEN LYING NEXT TO ME in my bed. We had a blast last night. We ate dinner at a delicious steakhouse and then walked down the strip acting like tourists going in and out of all the little shops. We stopped at the fountains and watched two of the shows before heading home to watch a few episodes of *House* on DVD. It's one of my favorite shows and months ago I insisted Kaden watch them with me. Now he's as addicted as I am to the crazy doctor. We eventually fell asleep watching one of the episodes.

"Caleb texted asking if we want to go to breakfast with everyone. I guess they were all kidless last night and are going to breakfast before going to pick them up."

"Sure, I'm going to jump in the shower."

"Sounds good. I'll take one after you."

We get to the diner that Hayley always insists we eat at and everyone is already there. Hayley and Caleb are sitting across from Liz and Cooper, and Kayla and Bentley are sitting across from Alex and his fiancée, Jessica. Toward the back there are two seats open across from Stephen and whatever girl he woke up next to this morning. We say hello to everyone and make our way to the two empty seats.

After everyone has ordered, the conversation flows and eventually moves to Alex and Jessica's upcoming wedding. "Caleb, we should do Alex's bachelor party at your club," Stephen suggests.

"Does it bother you that your husband owns a strip club?" Stephen's date asks. *Rude much?*

If her question bothers Hayley at all, she doesn't show it. "No, not at all. Plus, Liz works there several days a week, so I'm sure she keeps him in check." She winks at Caleb and he laughs, leaning over to give her a kiss.

"I'm not planning to be there as often as I have been. I'm still getting things situated, but once it's all under control, I'm planning to train someone to manage the place."

"Before you do that you need to hire a dancer," Liz says. "Shayla got married and left last week."

"Yeah, I know. Any chance you can set me up a couple interviews? Weed out the crazy chicks..."

Liz laughs. "Already done."

"So...what about the bachelor party?" Stephen asks again.

"Yeah, I don't see why not. Just let me know the date and I'll make sure I put it down so you're taken care of."

"Nice, dude!"

Kaden's phone goes off and he checks it, frowns, and puts it back in his pocket.

"Everything okay?" I ask.

He leans over and gives me a kiss on my temple like he always does, and as usual the butterflies appear.

Hayley catches my eye, waggling her eyebrows, and I roll my eyes at her. Things between Kaden and I will never be more than friends, and I have accepted that. Whatever it is he is looking for isn't me.

"My mom is asking again about my flight to Colorado. It's my grandma's eightieth birthday coming up at the end of August. Any chance you and Tristan would want to join me? I know they would love to see you guys."

"Tristan goes back to school at the end of August. As long as we're back before he starts school, we should be good to go."

"Yeah? Awesome. I'll book our tickets tonight. You and Tristan joining me will definitely make this trip better."

The waitress delivers our food and it all looks delicious. I ordered pancakes, while Kaden ordered bacon, eggs, and potatoes. He is forever eating healthy, except for when I cook for him. Then he gives in to the temptation of the delicious carbs.

I try to snatch a piece of bacon from his plate, but I'm rejected when he blocks my hand.

"Hey! I just want a small piece," I say with a pout. He laughs, knowing I'm a faker. I'll eat all his bacon if he turns away for too long.

"A small piece to you is the entire strip." He rips off a piece of the bacon and places it up to my mouth. I part my lips and snatch the piece with my teeth, biting the tips of his fingers in the process.

"Oops, sorry."

"Yeah, I bet you are." He feeds me another bite, and I take it this time without nipping at him.

"Let's go get Tristan," he says.

"Huh?"

"Let's bring him back. I paid for his membership. I don't want him missing class. If you need to work I can watch him. Please. I miss him."

His comment makes my stomach do somersaults. For so long it's just been Tristan and me. It's weird to have someone else care about him aside from my parents.

"Okay."

"Good, we can go get him together. I haven't seen your parents in a while."

He puts another piece of bacon up to my mouth, smiling when I bite his fingers, completely missing the bacon.

Seven

KADEN

TONIGHT IS THE NIGHT OF ALEX'S BACHELOR PARTY, AND while I should be excited to see some T and A, the idea of hanging out with these guys while watching some naked women shake their ass on stage does nothing for me. I would much rather be hanging out with Ashley and Tristan. Ever since she took on more hours at *Double D's* she rarely has time to hang out, and as much as I love hanging out with Tristan while she's at work, I miss hanging out with Ashley. Tonight just happens to be her night off and while she's at home, I'm stuck going out.

Instead of lounging around her house watching one of her crazy shows, I'm in a limo on my way to *Assets,* Caleb's strip club, to party with Alex and the other guys before he gets married in a couple weeks. The bachelor party was originally scheduled for next weekend, but when the promotions manager of the UFC said they need him in New York to do a photo shoot for his upcoming fight we all got a text last minute letting us know it's happening tonight.

After getting dropped off at the front, we walk up to the hostess stand. Caleb greets her and lets her know we're going to be using private room C. She marks something off on her paper and tells us to enjoy ourselves.

Once inside, I can see why this club is ridiculously popular. Scanning the room, I see the walls are all a matted black with shiny marble flooring. There's blood red accenting the dark room, making it look seductive yet romantic—it's all tastefully done. The booths and tables are high quality, black, distressed wood with plush black leather seats throughout. Everything is clean looking. If it wasn't for the women currently dancing on the stages in the back of the restaurant you wouldn't even know it's a strip club.

We walk past the bar, which has mirrored walls behind it going up two floors with black glass covering the bar tops, to the steps leading to the second floor.

"Damn, Caleb. This place looks great," I tell him. I know he's been hard at work turning this club around while he couldn't fight, and it shows.

"Thanks, you know I wasn't keen on the idea of owning a strip club. It seems like living in Vegas, the term stripper is given a bad name. But once I started working on the one in Colorado, I realized I could make them classy. I had no idea they would blow up to be this big, though. I just sold the one in Colorado for way more than I thought I would be able to get for it, and the guy is considering buying this one as well."

"You should be proud of this place."

"Thanks, man."

Upstairs, the music is a bit faster unlike downstairs where the music is slower and quieter. There are two girls dancing, one on each side of the stage, and the place is packed with guys sitting at the bar and tables that are surrounding the two circular stages.

We get to the end of the area and there's a narrow hallway filled with several doors on each side. Each door has a small letter on it. When we get to the letter C, Caleb opens the door and the club's red and black theme continues. The room is obviously smaller than the open areas, but it doesn't look any different. It's just a smaller version of the same setup. We have a seat at the tables surrounding the stage and I can hear the faint sound of music playing in the background.

There are about a dozen of us here celebrating the end of Alex's bachelorhood. Most of the guys are from the gym, but there are a few others I was introduced to but don't know. A couple of them are his brothers and one is his future brother-in-law. I think there's also a couple guys he knows from high school.

I sit at the table with Caleb, Bentley, Cooper, and Stephen. We aren't even sitting a few seconds when the stage lights turn on and *Black Widow* by Iggy Azalea comes across the surround sound.

At the same time, a woman wearing a tight red tank top that has Assets written across her tits in black appears handing us menus.

"What can I get you fellas?" She smiles seductively at me, and it should probably do something to me, turn me on in some way, but it does absolutely nothing. Not too long ago, I would have found this woman attractive and would have been figuring out where I could take her to fuck her. Now, while I'm not blind and know a beautiful woman when I see one, the only woman on my mind is Ashley.

I decide to keep it simple. "I'll take a Jack and Coke."

"Sure thing, handsome."

She moves on to the other guys and I take the opportunity to check my phone. I have a couple new texts from Ashley. They were sent a couple hours ago.

Ashley: Hey can you watch Tristan tonight? I got called into work.

Thirty minutes later.

Ashley: Okay, you must be busy. Tristan is spending the night at Hayley's. If you want to come over later I should be home around 2.

Me: Alex's bachelor party got moved to tonight. I'll come over when it's over.

She doesn't keep her phone on her while she's at work, so I stick my phone back in my pocket without waiting for a reply, then look up to see the curtain opening and a woman walking out onto the stage. It's too dark to see her at first, but once she gets to the center of the stage where the pole is located, I can see her clearly.

Caramel-colored brown hair pin straight down her back and light eye makeup making her hazel eyes pop are just the beginning. She's wearing a black lacy top that is just not see-through with her perfect-sized tits peeking out enough to tease me. My eyes trail down her toned stomach and land on black silky-looking shorts. Her legs are long and toned and she's wearing black fuck-me heels.

She walks to the pole but doesn't stop until she's standing in front of it. Raising her hands above her head she grabs the pole behind her with both hands and drops her body almost all the way to the ground, allowing her back and ass to glide down the front of the pole. She is without a doubt fucking stunning.

Lowering herself a little farther to the ground, she bends backward, causing her shorts to stretch, and giving the entire room a sneak peak of what's underneath. The sight of her body on display shakes me out of my frozen state of shock and it hits me. The stunning woman isn't just any woman—it's fucking Ashley! What in the actual fuck!

I look around at the guys gauging their reactions. The ones who know Ashley are all sitting in silence unsure of what to do. The ones who don't know her are making comments about her body and how they would love to have her beneath them. Caleb looks over at me with wide eyes, and I realize he isn't shocked to see Ashley on stage. He's shocked that I'm seeing her on stage.

Without thinking, I get out of my seat, knocking it over in the process, and jump onto the stage. With her back to the tables, she doesn't see me coming, but the instant I grab her by her torso and fling her over my shoulder, she screams, not knowing what is going on. She starts hitting and kicking me, trying to get me to let go of her and put her down, but I'm not having it.

"Don't fucking move!"

"Kaden?" She stops trying to break free when she realizes it's me carrying her.

"Yeah."

I'm not even sure where I'm going at this point, but I know I need somewhere quiet to calm down. I find a door open at the end of the hall and walk into it, slamming the door behind us. There's a couch up against the wall and a mini stage in front of it. I drop her onto the couch then back up, needing to take a minute to breathe.

"Kaden..."

I turn around and Ashley is no longer sitting on the couch. She's standing up and walking over to me. She places a hand on my arm. "I don't want to argue about this."

"Argue about what? About the fact that you aren't really a fucking cocktail waitress at *Double D's*? About the fact that you are a goddamned stripper! Or how about we *don't* argue about the fact that you would rather take your fucking clothes off for money instead of just letting me help you! What the hell, Ash! How the fuck did I not know that you were stripping at Caleb's club?"

Her hand goes to her hip and her head tilts to the side slightly—her telltale sign of her defenses going up.

"You didn't need to know! It's my business. I needed the job and Caleb gave it to me. It has nothing to do with you."

"When the fuck did you start working for Caleb anyway? How long have you been lying every time you leave for work while I watch Tristan for you?"

Eight

ASHLEY

Three Weeks Ago

I WALK INTO CALEB'S RECENTLY ACQUIRED RESTAURANT and strip club *Assets* for the first time and it's gorgeous! What he's done to this place is nothing short of amazing. It's only four in the afternoon so the place is deserted and quiet. I'm assuming someone is here or the door wouldn't be open.

"Hey, Ashley! What are you doing here?" Liz walks down the steps to greet me, giving me a hug.

"Do you guys just let anybody walk in?" I ask, stepping back to check out the place.

"No, there's a silent bell that rings in our offices. I unlocked the door because Caleb has a couple interviews today."

"That's actually why I'm here."

"You have an interview?"

"Umm...No, I don't, but I was hoping I could apply for the dancing position."

Her eyebrows raise slightly. "Ashley, you know if you need any help with money..."

"Liz, I love you for offering, but you know I won't accept any money from you or from anyone for that matter."

Liz gives me another hug, holding me tightly. "I know, but I had to try."

"And I appreciate it."

She releases me from her embrace. "I'll let Caleb know you're here to see him."

"Thank you...and Liz..."

"Yeah?"

"Can you please not tell anybody I'm here?"

"My lips are sealed...but if you need anything...."

"I know. You got my back. Thank you."

I follow her up the stairs and down the hallway, until we get to the last door on the left.

"Why don't you give me a minute to let him know you're here?"

"Okay."

A few minutes later she comes out, giving me a small smile.

"Are you sure you want to do this?"

"Yes, I'm sure."

She nods. "Just knock before you go in."

I walk over to his door and give it a small knock.

"Come in."

Caleb is looking down at something on his desk, but once I enter, he looks up. Then he stands and tells me to have a seat.

"Is everything okay?"

I close my eyes and swallow thickly, trying to work up the courage I need. When I open my eyes, I take a deep breath and say, "I need your help, Caleb. Please. I am begging you."

"What's going on?"

"You said you were hiring a dancer. I would like to apply for the position. I have taken pole dancing lessons for several years and I'm good. Actually, I'm more than good. I worked at *Double D's* for close to six years so I know how this business works. I can work the bar when needed, waitress, work private parties, whatever you need."

He stares at me in shock but quickly snaps out of it. "Why do you need this job so badly?"

"I was let go from my teaching job and *Double D's* doesn't have the availability to give me the hours I need. Plus, dancing means getting the lap dances and private parties, which means bringing in more money. And I need the money. Waitressing isn't enough."

"If you need money, I can..."

"No, stop, please. Liz already offered. Kaden has offered over a dozen times. I am not taking a dime of anybody else's money. I just need a job, please."

"Does Kaden know you're here?"

"Kaden has nothing to do with this and I need you to promise not to say anything. He can't know. He would be so pissed I chose to strip instead of taking money from him. Nobody can know I work here, please."

He scrubs his hands over his face. "Ashley, Kaden is going to be pissed if he finds out."

"That's between me and him. I need this job. I'm begging you. If you need to tell Hayley, I understand. I wouldn't ask you to hide it from her."

"How about this? I'm looking for a manager. I could train you to take over. You said you know the business."

"I don't want preferential treatment. I'm just asking to dance here. You wouldn't hire anyone else who came in here for the dancer position, to be a manager."

Caleb takes a deep breath. I can tell he's torn as to what to do, and I know I'm making this hard on him, but this is my last chance.

"How about you start as a dancer and slowly I'll show you the ropes so you can eventually take over as manager? You would be helping me out. I'd like to have someone managing this place before the baby comes, so I only have to be here a couple days a week."

"Okay, I can agree to that. Thank you."

"No problem. But if anything changes I can help…"

I shake my head to stop him. "No, this is perfect, thank you!"

"When can you start?"

"Would tonight work?"

"That will work."

"Thank you so much, Caleb!"

Present Day

"YOU'VE BEEN WORKING FOR HIM EVER SINCE WE ALL MET

for breakfast? That was weeks ago! Why didn't you say something?"

"I knew you wouldn't understand why I'm dancing instead of waitressing. I need the money."

"Damn right I don't understand and you're not dancing! You're stripping! There's a big fucking difference. You should have told me. If money is that bad, I can lend it to you."

"I was embarrassed."

"Well, now that I know, you can quit." Kaden closes the distance between us, putting his hands on my hips and tugging me close to him. Then he pulls me into a hug, nuzzling his face into my hair.

"Whatever money you need, I will give it to you."

"I know you will, but I don't want you to. I need to handle this on my own. I can't depend on anybody but myself."

He backs up and raises a brow. "Ashley, you are quitting," he says slowly.

I make it a point to say it back the same way. "No, I'm not."

"Are you fucking serious right now? I'm not letting you strip at a club for other men."

"You aren't the boss of me, Kaden. You are my friend. You don't control my choices."

He nods his head slowly. "Okay, we'll see about that. You're my best friend and it's my job to look out for you." He takes me by my hand and heads to the door.

"Where are we going?"

"To speak to Caleb about this."

"No! You can't do that. He might be your friend, but he's my boss.

Can we please just go to my house? I've been embarrassed enough. Just be my friend tonight and take me home, please?"

He stops in his tracks, his eyes running down my body. I can see when he gives in temporarily. His jaw goes slack and shoulders slouch a little, telling me he's finally calming down. "Okay, do you have clothes so you don't have to walk out like this?"

"Yeah, in the dressing room. It's right over there."

We go to the dressing room and I change back into the clothes I came to work in. Then we head outside through the back, so Kaden can't accidently run into Caleb. Since he didn't come in his car, we take my car back to my house.

"I'm going to wash this makeup off and change into pajamas. Want to order a pizza and watch a movie?"

"Sure."

Kaden follows me into my room, grabbing a pair of sweats and a shirt from the drawer of clothes he keeps here for the nights he ends up staying over.

After he orders the pizza, we plop onto the couch. Kaden goes to grab the remote, but I remember I don't have working cable. "Want to watch a DVD?"

"What's wrong with your cable?"

"I'm not sure," I lie. I'm not about to tell him I'm three months behind so they canceled my service until I get caught up with the overdue balance. That will just lead to another fight over money.

He scrutinizes me for a moment but lets it go. We decide on one of the Fast and Furious movies and after popping it in, we snuggle up like we always do.

"I'm assuming you didn't know who was in the room you were working in tonight," Kaden says after a few minutes.

"No, I didn't. Caleb didn't mark it down on the sheet in the back that the bachelor party got moved up a week. I wasn't even supposed to work tonight. One of the girls called out and I agreed to cover her shift. I didn't have time to ask who was there."

Kaden doesn't say anything else. He just pulls me into his side and gives me a kiss on my forehead. We watch the movie in silence...not necessarily uncomfortable, but not exactly comfortable either. I know Kaden isn't going to let this all go, but living in denial can be a great thing.

Nine

KADEN

I WAKE UP AND ROLL OVER ONLY TO FIND ASHLEY'S SIDE OF the bed is empty and the shower running. I roll back over onto my back and stare at the ceiling remembering everything that happened last night: The bachelor party. Ashley being the stripper. Hearing the guys say they wanted to fuck her. Me, throwing her over my shoulder and then demanding she quit stripping. Her, refusing to quit stripping. Me, realizing that I'm falling for my best friend.

Yep, you heard me right. I'm falling for Ashley, and I know what you're thinking, how the fuck did I not realize this sooner? It's called denial. Don't act like you've never experienced it. The problem is, I have absolutely no intention of acting on my newfound feelings. She deserves better than what I'm capable of giving her and Tristan. My heart split in half and was taken with my wife and son eleven years ago. Ashley deserves more than the broken man that's left of me.

I rub my hands repeatedly up and down my face hoping last night was a bad dream, but knowing it wasn't. I don't know how to handle this whole situation with Ashley. She is stubborn as hell and is refusing to quit stripping. Thinking about this is just pissing me off, so I get up and throw on my workout gear. I need to head to the gym to train with Alex and Caleb today. Fucking Caleb! I can't believe he hired Ashley as a goddamned stripper. I don't know what the hell he was thinking.

I go into the kitchen and open the cabinet to find something to eat and notice every cabinet is about empty. I open the fridge and it's empty as well. What the hell are she and Tristan eating? I scour through the drawers hoping to find a K cup to make myself a cup of coffee at least but only find a stack of papers. They're similar to the bills I found a few months ago which Ashley insisted were being handled. The only difference is those were first notices and these are final notices. I flip through the papers and find one that says notice of foreclosure. The date is scheduled for July twenty-second, which is a week away.

I hear her footsteps coming down the hall, so I quickly throw all the papers back in the drawer and walk out to the living room.

"Morning."

"Morning, were you looking for coffee in there? Sorry, I haven't had time to go grocery shopping."

"No problem, why don't we grab coffee and breakfast out?"

"Okay, cool. I need to go to the gym anyway to get Tristan. Hayley is meeting me there with him."

After stopping at a small diner for coffee and a bagel, we head straight to the gym. As we're walking up to the door, Hayley, Marco, and Tristan are walking up at the same time.

"I'm going to go catch up with her," Ashley says.

I walk to the locker room and throw my gym bag and phone into a locker. Then I head to the octagon to go find Alex. Before I can make it out of the locker room, I hear Stephen and a couple of other fighters talking.

"Bro, you should have seen her! She looked smoking fucking hot. I would sink my dick into her in a damn heartbeat."

"Fuck yeah, man! And that outfit...Goddamn! That shit ended too quickly when Kaden threw her over his shoulder and..."

I walk up to the group of them, and grabbing the kid who just commented on her outfit, throw him up against the wall. "Say another fucking word about Ashley and I will knock your teeth out. That goes for all of you. Got it?"

They all start apologizing, but I don't even stop to listen. There's one person responsible for this shit and he and I are about to have some words. I stalk out to the main floor and look for Caleb. I spot him laughing with Cooper on the mat next to the octagon...and I snap.

Without even thinking, I grab him by his shoulder to spin him toward me and deck him in the face, sending him flying backward. Yeah, it was a sucker punch at its finest, but I don't give a fuck.

"What the fuck!" he shouts at me, his fingers touching his bloody lip.

"What the fuck were you thinking hiring Ashley to work at your fucking strip club! And on top of that not telling me!"

"Kaden, it wasn't my place to say anything." He shakes his head.

"Caleb!" Hayley comes running over and gets in his face, and judging by the tone in her voice, I have a feeling I wasn't the only one he kept this secret from.

"Is it true? Is what Kaden saying true? Did you hire Ashley as a dancer?"

"Hayles…"

"Oh no! Don't you 'Hayles' me! What were you thinking?"

Caleb glares at me, pissed I just got him in the doghouse. Well, good! He deserves it.

"Hayles, can we not do this here, please?"

"Fine, we'll talk about this at home." She pokes him in the chest with her finger and then stomps off.

I turn my attention back to Caleb. "You're firing her."

Caleb doesn't even think about it before he says, "No, I'm not."

I see red and go to deck him again. But before I can, Cooper and Alex jump in front of me to hold me back.

"Kaden, you need to walk away right now. Go for a walk, bro. Cool the fuck down. You aren't doing this shit here. Not in my gym." Cooper signals to the front door.

I shrug their hands off me and walk out the door, slamming it behind me. Once I get outside, I keep walking. I have no idea where I am going, but Cooper was right, I need to calm down before I do something I'll regret.

"Kaden!" I hear someone calling my name, so I look behind me to see who it is and spot Tristan running after me to catch up. I slow down to wait for him.

"Everything okay?"

"Yeah, I saw you punch Caleb and yell at him. I heard what you said. You told him to fire my mom."

Oh fuck!

"You can't have my mom fired. If you have her fired then she'll have no job at all."

"Listen buddy, I shouldn't have said all that in front of you. It's not your job to worry about grownup problems. Plus, your mom does have a job. She's a teacher, remember?"

He shakes his head. "No, she's not. I heard her tell Nana she was fired from work. And she packed up all her stuff from her classroom. She never packs it all up because every summer she teaches, but this summer she isn't teaching."

What the hell is going on? Why was Ashley fired from the school she works at? So much isn't adding up. She's been making ends meet for years. Something has changed, and whatever it is, she doesn't want me to know about it. And I have a sneaking suspicion that guy Giovanni is somehow tied to all this as well.

"It's okay, bud. She's not going to get fired from her job."

"You promise?"

"Yeah, I promise. Does your mom know you followed me out here?"

He gives me a sheepish look, which tells me she has no idea.

"Let's head back before your mom freaks out."

Ten

ASHLEY

IT'S BEEN A WEEK SINCE KADEN FOUND OUT I'M A STRIPPER and walked out of the gym pissed when Caleb refused to fire me. To say I was shocked Kaden actually punched Caleb in the face is putting it mildly. I felt so bad, I offered to quit, but Caleb wasn't having it. He said he and Kaden would work it out. I just wish I wouldn't have placed him in the middle of my cluster-fuck.

The day after the fight, Kaden texted me several times asking if he could bring dinner over. When I didn't respond, he showed up with a pizza in his hand asking why I was ignoring him. I realized then my cell phone had gotten shut off because I couldn't pay the bill, but there was no way I was telling him that. Instead, I told him it was broken.

As a result, the next day he showed up after work with a new iPhone. He added it to his plan and told me he got a good deal on it. It's probably the most expensive phone I've ever touched so I seriously doubt he got a deal on it. I tried to refuse it, but he totally played the mom card on me, insisting Tristan might need to get ahold of me while at camp.

He, again, showed up with food, this time Chinese. The three of us watched a movie, and after Tristan went to bed, we caught up on more episodes of *House*. Every morning this week, he has insisted we all go to breakfast before he and Tristan head to the gym. And when he walked into the kitchen as I was packing Tristan a peanut butter and jelly for lunch, he told me the program was buying them all lunch. I didn't remember reading anything about them buying lunch, but I'm not going to look a gift horse in the mouth.

The fact is, Kaden has been a godsend this past week. I don't even know how I would have fed Tristan and me. And just like he promised he would, every night he has watched Tristan on the nights I have had to work. I'm kind of surprised he hasn't once asked me to quit my job, but I'm hoping he has realized my money issues are my problem and it's not his place to tell me where to work.

While Tristan has been at camp all week, I have spent every day in search of another job. I have filled out hundreds of applications, but I haven't gotten a single bite. When I run out of places to apply to each day, I head over to *Assets* to learn more about the club and restaurant business. Caleb has been walking me through all the specifics of running a club, getting me acquainted with the ins and outs of the business, such as scheduling, hiring, and ordering. Liz covers all the payroll, Daniel, the chef, covers the menu items, and Jevon, the bar manager covers the bar ordering, but he wants me to learn it all so I when I take over, I'll be able to know what it is I am supervising.

Now it's July twenty-first and I have less than twenty-four hours to move all mine and Tristan's stuff out, but instead I'm at work. I'm well aware my being in denial is completely irresponsible and stupid, but I don't really know what else to do at this point. This is the first time in my life I feel completely out of control and helpless. Even when Tyler walked out the door, I handled my shit.

Since I'm not sure what's going to happen with the house, or when they'll be showing up to lock me out, I told Kaden I needed to bomb the house for bugs and asked if he could please watch Tristan at his place. He agreed without questioning me.

Before going into work, I moved our clothes and photo albums into my car the best I could until I figure it all out, but I'm at a complete loss as to what choice I should make. If I move to my parents' house, I'm too far to commute to work. If I don't move there, we'll be homeless. I've already told my mom Tristan will be going back to her house for the rest of the summer. She clearly knows something is going on but has learned I need to handle it myself. Thankfully, she always agrees to take Tristan without asking questions.

I've considered asking Caleb if I can sleep on his office couch on the nights I work but decided against it. I have put the poor guy through enough.

What I do know is if all my shit isn't out of the house soon, the doors will be locked and I won't be able to get any of it. Unfortunately, I can't deal with it right now because I'm at work and need to focus on making money.

"Hey boss." I knock once and enter Caleb's office. He's rolling his neck from side to side in a circular motion.

"Everything okay?"

"Oh yeah, it's just great. My very hormonal pregnant wife has decided she's going to hold a grudge for not forcing you to become my manager and has stuck my ass out on the couch for the last week. I think my neck has a permanent kink in it."

"I'm so sorry, Caleb. I can talk to Hayley. She didn't mention it when we were hanging out the other day."

Caleb waves me off. "Don't worry about it. It's all good."

"Okay, well, I was just checking in before I go on the floor. I checked on Daniel's order and realized he forgot to place it. I added it to the calendar so it will alert him every week. He always seems to forget, so hopefully that will help him remember. I also moved some of the girls around because Kora is running late, and Annalise's daughter has the stomach bug, so she might be out for a couple days."

"Thank you, Ashley. Any more thoughts on hanging up your dancing heels and taking over full time?"

"Not yet, but I appreciate your confidence in me."

"This might be a personal question, but I have to ask. Are you going back to teaching in August?"

"No, my teaching career is over."

"Okay, I'm sorry about that, but let's keep working on you managing this place. Hayley is due in November so that only gives me four months to train you fully."

"Okay, sounds good."

"Hey Ashley!" Bianca pokes her head into the office.

I turn around to give her my attention "Yeah?"

"Your shift technically doesn't start for five more minutes, but you have a private dance request."

"Okay, thanks. I'll be out in a minute."

I turn back to Caleb. "Duty calls."

After quickly changing into my dancing costume, since I'll be dancing tonight and not waitressing, I head to find Bianca. She's the hostess and sets up all the private rooms as well as handles all the restaurant's reservations.

"What room number?"

She glances at the sheet. "Room A."

"Thanks, girly. Any requests?"

"Actually, yes. He requested a pole dance and a lap dance."

"Ay, ay, Captain."

I give her a mock salute as I head upstairs to room A, hoping whoever is in this room will be a good tipper. I'm still a little short to pay Giovanni and only have a couple more days until the end of the month. Knowing I already lost my house, I gave up trying to pay my bills and have just been focusing on paying him. The last thing I want is to be owned by a man like Giovanni. I have enough trouble taking my bra and shorts off when I'm stripping, I don't even know how I would handle being required to have sex with strangers.

After picking out the music, I turn the lights up on the stage and down on the floor and then begin my performance. Thanks to the lighting, it's almost impossible to see whoever is sitting there watching me, and to be honest, I prefer it that way. Once I've made it halfway through my performance, I remove my bustier. Then a few moves later, my shorts are removed, leaving me in only my G-string and high heels. The song, and performance, ends, but I don't bother collecting my clothes yet. Bianca said the guy requested a lap dance, so I might as well leave my clothes off and get it over with.

I'm sauntering down the steps of the stage as a new songs transitions, when I notice the guy sitting at the table in one of the chairs is Kaden and he looks delicious. He's wearing dark wash blue jeans and a powder blue button down collared shirt with his sleeves rolled up to his elbows. His hair is still wet like he recently showered and is all messy like always. He's lounging in the chair with his legs spread wide like he doesn't have a worry in the world. His beautiful green eyes are piercing into mine and it causes my breath to catch. I suddenly remember I'm standing in front of him in nothing but a scrap of fabric and heels. Feeling extremely vulnerable, my hands go up to cover my breasts.

"Why are you covering yourself? It's nothing I haven't seen before." *Ouch!*

"I didn't expect to you to be here. Where's Tristan?"

"He's at my house with Kayla."

"Okay..." I'm not sure what Kaden's intentions are, but I'm not going to question it. It's not a secret that while this man is my best friend, I would give almost anything to have one night with him. However, Kaden has made it clear he has no desire for us to be anything more than friends so why he's here is a mystery to me. One I'm sure he will reveal soon.

"Where's my dance?" Kaden places his hands on the curves of my hips and tugs me toward him. Okay...so he really wants a dance from me. The same guy who wanted me to quit stripping...I need to figure out what his end-game is here.

"Nuh-uh," I say, backing away and removing his hands from my body so we're no longer touching. He tilts his head to the side in confusion, and his bottom lip juts out, making himself look adorably sexy.

I move my pointer finger back and forth to push my point. "No touching the dancer. It's the rule."

Kaden gives me a smirk but doesn't argue. The song transitions into *Na Na* by Trey Songz and I begin teasing him. Since he's sitting in a chair, I circle around the back of it, running the tips of my nails across his chest, shoulders, and back, then up his neck. I feel him shiver under my touch, which makes me smile inside. Once I get to the back of the chair, I lean forward so my breasts rub up against his neck as I trail my fingertips up his body, starting from his hard abs that I can feel even through his shirt.

Moving to the side of the chair, but without taking my hands off him, I begin dancing next to him lightly rubbing my body up against his side as I move back around to the front. Once I'm in front of him, I drop to my ass and kick my legs over from one side to the other. He looks down at me on the floor, his eyes widening at the sight of my pussy only being covered by a thin piece of almost completely see-through fabric. I swear I hear a growl come from deep within his chest, and I have to hold back my grin.

I stand, parting my legs just enough so his leg is nestled between mine, and continue to dance. My eyes close, and I get lost in the feel of the music, rubbing against his jean clad thigh. A soft moan escapes from my lips as an orgasm slowly builds. Before I can even open my eyes, I feel Kaden's hands on my hips once again lifting me up onto his lap so I'm straddling him.

I grind down on him, the area between my legs sensitive and wanting. His hands go to my breasts, and my back arches forward, encouraging his touch.

"Fuck, baby," he growls, taking both my breasts into his mouth, one at a time, sucking on each one as I continue my grinding. My fingers are tangled in his hair and I'm pulling his face closer, forcing him to suck harder. Between the sensation his mouth is causing and the grinding of my pussy on him, an orgasm overtakes me, and before I can stop it, my entire body shakes with pleasure.

Kaden, still sucking on my breasts, picks me up and carries me over to the couch. My back hits the cold leather and I remember where we are.

At a strip club.

In a private room.

Where I work.

Where I'm getting paid to dance.

I push him off me and sit up, covering my chest before I quickly walk to the stage to throw on my clothes.

"What's wrong?" Kaden says as I grab my bustier top, then walk to the other side of the stage to grab my shorts. I put them all back on, but I still feel completely underdressed. I walk back over to the couch and sit next to him.

"I can't do this...We can't do this. We got caught up in the moment. This is where I work. I don't do this with guests. You and me...We're friends. You are literally my best friend. I can't become your next one-night stand."

Kaden flinches at my words. "You could never be a one-night stand, Ash. You know that. But you're right, this isn't the time or place to be doing this. I only came here to see you. I was hoping if you saw me here, you wouldn't want to strip and you would agree to quit. The last time I was here at the bachelor party you said it embarrassed you for me to see you. I'm probably grasping at straws, but I just didn't know what else to do. I didn't plan on it going this far. I'm sorry."

I'm stuck on the words *you could never be a one-night stand*. Does that mean he wants more? Does he want to be with me for real? The thought gets me excited until I remember I'm a stripper and I'd never date a guy while working here. It wouldn't be fair to him. I know it's technically not cheating, but I just couldn't do it. It would feel like cheating to me and I care about Kaden too much to disrespect him in that way. Plus, I need him in my life too much to take the chance that after one time he won't dump me like he's done to all the rest of the women he's been with.

"I'm not quitting my job here, so you can leave now, if that's all you came for."

Eleven

KADEN

THE NIGHT I FOUND OUT ASHLEY WAS STRIPPING TO MAKE ends meet, we went back to her house and I started to pay close attention. First red flag, her Wi-Fi wasn't working when I went to get on the internet. Then when we went to watch TV, I noticed her cable wasn't working either. We would only watch DVDs. The next red flag was finding the foreclosure notice while looking for coffee. To solidify my suspicions, when I texted her the next day and she ignored me, only to blame it on a broken phone, I knew I had to take matters into my own hands. I'm not sure what trouble Ashley is in, but I know one thing for sure. She's in over her head.

While she doesn't have the income coming in from teaching anymore, there is no way she isn't making enough to pay her bills working at *Assets*. After I calmed down and spoke with Caleb, he told me how much the girls make on average dancing there, and it's enough to pay her bills.

Every day I made sure Tristan and Ashley were fed, whether it was ordering in, bringing food with me, or asking them to join me. I knew if I tried to give Ashley money, she wasn't going to accept it, so I had to figure a way to go around her. I was hoping sometime this week she would mention having to be out of her house by tomorrow, but she didn't mention it at all. If it wasn't for the notice stating the date and details, I wouldn't even know.

Then my grandfather texted me asking if I had found a potential wife and it was like a light bulb popped up on top of my head like it does in the cartoons. Ashley needs money, and I need a wife. What could be better than fake marrying your best friend? So, I put a plan into motion. I spoke with the guys and their wives, letting them know that Ashley needed to move out of her house and, to make it easy on her, I was going to move everything to my place. They all knew there was more to the story but also knew if I wanted them to know I would have told them.

So, once Ashley left for work, we all began moving her stuff into my garage, minus Caleb since he had to be at the club. After the place was emptied, I texted Caleb to see what time Ashley would be off, and when he said not until two a.m., I decided to go to the club. I needed to talk to Ashley and was hoping maybe if she danced for me, she would get embarrassed and it'd make her want to quit. Also, if I'm honest, I was a little curious to see her in action. Okay, maybe a lot curious. Don't get me wrong, I'm one hundred percent against her stripping, but when we went to the club for the bachelor party, I threw her over my shoulder before I could see her dance. Plus, if she's dancing for me, that means she isn't dancing for somebody else, and since she's refusing to quit, I might as well be the one to reap the benefits.

And holy fucking shit, did I! Watching her ass dance on that stage, the way her body glided with natural grace across that pole, had me painfully hard. And when she removed her clothes I thought I might come in my pants. When the girl asked me if I had any requests, I said I wanted it all hoping to have extra time with Ashley. What I didn't know was 'it all' consisted of her sexy-as-sin body grinding on my own until she fucking came right there on my leg.

The orgasming on my leg part better be a bonus only I get.

If she wouldn't have pulled the brakes, I would have been balls-deep in that woman within seconds of throwing her ass on the couch. When she accused me of simply wanting a one-night stand with her, like I do with other women, I wanted to throw up. How could she ever put herself into the same category as those other women? She's my best friend for God's sake. I love her. And if I was capable of giving my heart to someone, it would without a doubt go to her. She and her son are the two most important people in my life. I will never do anything to lose them, which is why I'm glad she stopped us before anything really happened.

I'm not stupid. I know there's no way I could go into a fake marriage with Ashley objectively after having been inside her. She only orgasmed on my thigh and I just about lost it.

This was not exactly how I planned to bring my proposition up to her. The issue is, if I don't tell her, she's going to leave work and head home to an empty house. So, it looks like I'm going to have to just bite the bullet and throw it all out there for her.

"There's something I need to talk to you about." I look at her and can't help but glance down at her pebbled nipples poking through her practically see-through top. Needing to cover her up so I can focus on what I need to say and not her perky fucking nipples, I unbutton my shirt, which leaves me in just a white undershirt. I hand her the shirt and she puts it on, covering herself without buttoning it up. She faces me on the couch and sits Indian style giving me her full attention.

I need to lay this out in a certain way to reel Ashley in, so she doesn't think I'm trying to save her or some shit. "You know how my grandmother is turning eighty next month?"

She nods.

"Well, I have a feeling she isn't doing so well. My grandfather kind of insinuated she might not live much longer."

"Oh, Kaden. I'm so sorry." *Hook.*

"He asked me for a favor…I guess she has a dying wish, but I don't think I'll be able to grant it for her."

"Is there anything I can do to help?" *Line.*

"Actually, there is…You can marry me." *And sinker.*

Her eyes bug out like marrying me is the worst thing that could happen to her. So, I quickly add, "For pretend, of course."

Her face morphs from concerned to angry in point-two seconds, and I have a feeling I'm about to lose my fish—figuratively speaking— if I don't say the right thing.

"She wants to see me get married before the year is up. And if I do, my grandfather will give me fifteen million dollars. I don't care as much about the money as I do seeing her happy, but I sure as hell won't turn it down. And I'll split it with you. I'll pay you to marry me. To make my grandmother's dying wish come true."

I hold my breath, waiting to see if she's going to take the bait...

And then she storms out of the room.

I guess I lost that one...

I take off after her, down the hallway to the stairs, down the stairs to the restaurant. Holy shit, this woman can haul ass in heels! I almost catch up to her when I see the guy from her porch the other day. *Giovanni?* He's in a three-piece suit that's tailored to fit him. He's clean shaven and his hair looks professionally cut. The guy screams money.

Ashley comes to a screeching halt right in front of him and I'm not completely sure but I think she quickly shakes her head at him. His eyes glance over her shoulder and land on me. He gives her a small nod, as he lets her continue on her way. I want to go after her, but something tells me this guy is who I need to speak with.

"Giovanni, right?"

He gives me a once over, sucking on his teeth like he's trying to decide how to respond. He's clearly sizing me up, and while he may have twenty pounds and a couple inches on me, I would knock this fool across the room in one hit, and if he sucks his teeth at me again, I just might consider it.

His manners win out and he sticks his hand out to shake mine. "Giovanni Valentino," he says with a bit of an Italian accent.

"Kaden Scott. Mind if we have a word?"

He considers it for a moment, then heads over to the hostess to let her know he's decided to sit at the bar. We have a seat and, after ordering drinks—him, a Macallan, me, a Jack and coke—he's the first one to speak.

"What can I do for you?" He takes a sip of his whiskey sounding like he's already bored of this conversation.

"You can tell me why you keep showing up where Ashley is."

"Not that it's your concern, but she and I have a deal. I couldn't get ahold of her, and since her phone wasn't working, I came by here."

"Her phone broke. I bought her a new one. What deal do you have with her?"

He gives me a side glance. "You her boyfriend?"

"She's my best friend. I'm worried about her."

"I normally wouldn't tell someone's business, but I like her, and she's in over her head. She owes me twenty-two grand."

I choke on my whisky. *What the hell, Ashley!*

"Adam," I call to the bartender. "Can you call Caleb down here for me?"

"Sure thing."

I turn back to Giovanni. "If she pays you that amount in full, your business with Ashley would be done?"

"I'm a businessman, Kaden. I just want my money."

"I don't have that kind of money on me, but I'm sure my friend does in his safe. I'm going to give you the money so your deal with Ashley will be over."

Caleb walks over, slapping his hand on my shoulder. "What the fuck happened with Ashley? She got changed and left. Did you tell her you moved all her stuff to your place?"

Fuck! I completely forgot to tell her. She's probably on her way to her empty house.

"I'm assuming you keep money in your safe here for emergencies."

"Yeah, a little bit. What's up?"

"I need you to give Giovanni twenty-two thousand. I'll give it back to you tomorrow after I go to the bank."

Caleb's eyes ask a million questions, but he doesn't voice any of them.

"Right this way."

We follow him to his office and after he gives Giovanni the money, we shake hands.

"It's too bad...I was looking forward to her coming to work for me. She's lucky to have you in her life."

"What do you do for a living?" I ask out of curiosity.

"I own a gentleman's club...El Stella's Bordello."

"A brothel?" Caleb asks.

Giovanni nods. "Yes." He pulls out his business card. "If you gentleman are ever in the need of female companionship, let me know. My club offers different levels of memberships. It was nice doing business with you."

He walks out, leaving Caleb and I stunned stupid.

"I need to go find Ashley."

Caleb just nods slowly having no clue what to even say. *Yeah, man...I know exactly what you mean.*

I text Kayla, Hayley, and Liz asking if they've seen or heard from Ashley. They all respond with a no. She must have gone straight to her house.

I pull up in the driveway next to her car, and my headlights shine on the porch, lighting up Ashely, who is sitting with her head down.

"You okay?" I ask, sitting next to her. She doesn't say anything, but her shoulders silently shake up in down—she's crying.

"Hey, now. Don't cry." I put my arm around her shoulders and pull her into my side.

"Everything is so messed up, Kaden. I've lost everything."

"What? Your house? It's just a house, Ash. I know that's not what you want to hear. but it's all going to be okay."

She looks up at me, her sad eyes connecting with mine, and I use my thumb to wipe away the tears that are falling down her cheeks.

"You know about my house?"

"I know bits and pieces. It's time you tell me the entire story. Why did I just have Caleb give a guy who owns a brothel twenty-two thousand dollars?"

Twelve

ASHLEY

I AM SURPRISINGLY RELIEVED THAT KADEN KNOWS ABOUT me losing my house. It's one less secret I have to tell him, but what shocks me is when he tells me he had Caleb pay Giovanni the twenty-two thousand I still owe him.

"Kaden..." He shakes his head at me, not giving me the chance to argue. "Why, Ashley?"

I let out a long breath and start from the beginning. I tell him about Tyler and how we met in college, how he was sweet and wooed me. How everything was great until he started gambling, and then it was far from great.

"So, you were working full time and he was paying all the bills?" He only asks to understand, and it reminds me why this man is my best friend.

"I was so busy with Tristan and going back to work, I just let him take it all over. When he told me to buy a house when I was pregnant, I thought it was a great idea. I wanted nothing more than to provide my baby with a home like the one my parents gave me growing up. I didn't think about why he didn't want it in his name. I didn't ask questions... I trusted him." The tears come back when I think what my naivety has cost me.

"But this was years ago. Did something happen recently?"

"Yeah, Tyler came back in January, threatening to take Tristan away from me. He said with him having rights he was going to disappear with him before I could even take him to court."

"Motherfucker. Why the hell didn't you come to me?"

"It all happened so fast. He wanted thirty thousand dollars in exchange for signing over his rights and he only gave me less than twenty-four hours to come up with it. I asked Don for a number to a loan shark and he sent me to Giovanni."

"What the fuck...The guy owns a whorehouse."

"I know..."

"You know?"

"I didn't have anything to give him to ensure I would pay back the loan...so...I used myself as collateral."

I close my eyes knowing Kaden is about to freak the hell out, and I'm right. He does. He stands and punches the window behind us. Glass shatters everywhere, and when I rush over to him, I can see his hand is bleeding from the shards of glass. I rush inside my house to grab a towel and remember there's nothing in the house. I have no idea why the door isn't locked, like the bank said it would be, but they emptied out my entire house.

Remembering I have some clothes in my car, I run out to it and grab an old shirt. Taking Kaden's hand in mine, I blot his hand with the shirt. "You shouldn't have done that. We need to run it under cold water to see if there's glass under your skin."

He pulls his hand away. "I don't give a fuck about my hand! You sold yourself to a man who sells women to rich men so they can fuck them?"

"No! I agreed if I didn't pay him back I would go to work for him, but so far I've paid him back…"

Kaden gives me a look. "Well, except when you paid him the four grand I was behind…" He gives me another look. "I almost had enough to pay him this month!"

He lets out a groan and shakes his head, having a seat on the porch swing and patting it for me to join. "I'm assuming Tyler signed over his rights?"

"Yeah. Then he disappeared. Thank God."

"What about your job?"

"How did you know about my job?"

"Tristan overheard you talking to your mom. He was worried."

Talk about failing as a mom.

"A dad from the school I worked at blackmailed me, and when I refused to take him up on his offer, he reported me to the school. The principal pretty much forced me to resign."

"What's his name?"

"Oh no, you aren't going after him. It's over with. Caleb is working on teaching me the insides of the club. I am really loving it. I never imagined running a strip club and restaurant, but I'm finding it to be fun, and I'm good at it."

Kaden and I sit for a few minutes in silence before I speak up. "All my stuff is gone. I thought I had until tomorrow night, but it's all gone. The bank must have taken it all."

"It's all in my garage."

I whip my head around to look at him. "Your garage?"

"I saw the notice the other day. So when you left for work earlier, Cooper, Bentley, and I moved all your stuff to my garage. You and Tristan are moving in with me."

"I'm not even going to argue because I know I have nowhere else to go, but I promise you I will work all the hours Caleb will give me and I'll not only pay you back for you paying off Giovanni, but we will be out of your hair as soon as possible."

"About that...If you marry me, for pretend of course, not only will it make my grandmother happy, but I'll split the fifteen million with you." It doesn't go over my head that he once again makes it clear this marriage isn't real. Of course it's not real. Kaden is sexy and wealthy with a nice job. He has a beautiful house and an expensive car, and that's just the exterior. He is sweet and selfless. He could have anyone he wants, so why would he ever settle for a poor stripper single mom?

Then it hits me what he said.

"Kaden!" I screech. I don't even know what else to say. "I can't take...like...seven million dollars from you! I owe you money, not the other way around."

"Technically after taxes it would only be around four million. The IRS is a bitch like that. But if you don't marry me, I don't get any money and my grandmother will die without ever seeing her only grandson marry and have his happily-ever-after."

Damn, guilt-trip much.

"Okay, I'm going to agree to marry you...for fake." I add it in there just like he did so he knows I'm not going to try to rope him into a real marriage or something. "But I can't accept seven million dollars from you."

"It's non-negotiable." I decide not to argue knowing he's going to just keep at it until I agree with him. When the time comes, I will just refuse the money. Kaden has done so much for Tristan and me, there's no way I am taking his family's money.

"C'mon, Ash. Let's get you home so you can change out of my shirt and those tiny shorts."

I follow Kaden back to his house trying not to think too hard about the fact that Tristan, Kaden, and I will all be living under one roof. Instead I focus on taking in my surroundings. Kaden lives on the outskirts of Las Vegas in one of the wealthier areas like his friends all do. But while his friends, Cooper and Bentley, live in a neighborhood filled with cookie cutter houses with zero land, Kaden is in a gated community where every home is on a nice piece of property. Each home is on a minimum of five acres, so the houses are far apart. A lot of people who live in this community even have horses with barns and such.

We pull up to Kaden's country-style home and the front porch light is on. I'm always blown away by the beauty of his home. He bought it years ago but has renovated it little by little. It's a multistory home with several bedrooms and bathrooms. The outside has been redone and has the cutest wraparound porch with a blood red front door. The red door was my idea. With the different color bricks and the white windows with black shutters, he had to have a red door.

The inside has a spacious, open floor plan. There's a fireplace in the center of the house that can be seen in the living room as well as the dining room. The master bedroom is on the first floor along with a guest bedroom and his office, and on the second floor are two more bedrooms. The kitchen is completely stainless steel and is gorgeous.

We're usually at my house because of convenience. Tristan has all his stuff at my place and I worked right down the street at the elementary school. But occasionally Kaden will throw a party here and I swear I spend the entire time just admiring the house.

"Hey girly!" Kayla comes walking out of the guest room to give me a hug, thankfully ignoring my outfit. "I see Kaden got his way." She gives me a wink and giggles.

I look down in embarrassment. I know she's joking to lighten the mood, but it reminds me I've lost my house. I've lost everything.

"Hey," Kayla says. "Don't do that. Shit happens. I don't know the details as to what's going on with you, but you will work it out, and you have all of us. Please don't shut us out."

Tears well up in my eyes and I lose it. Kayla pulls me into her arms and rocks me softly, not letting go of me until I feel hands on my waist pulling me out of her arms. Kaden puts his arms around me and holds me tight. His warmth makes me feel safe, something I haven't felt in a long time. I breathe in his fresh scent and it feels like home.

There's a knock on the door, but Kaden doesn't let me go. The door closes and he still doesn't let me go. We stand in the middle of his foyer for I don't know how long with him just holding me, letting me cry until I run out of tears.

Thirteen

KADEN

I HOLD HER UNTIL SHE FINALLY STOPS CRYING. THEN AFTER going upstairs to check on Tristan, we go to bed. I know she's physically exhausted from working all night and emotionally exhausted from all this shit. She just needs a good night's sleep and tomorrow will be a fresh start. Lying down in my California King, we have more than enough room, but instead of lying on our own sides, Ashley lays her head on my chest while I play with her hair until she finally passes out.

"ASHLEY," I WHISPER. SHE ROLLS OVER AND GRUNTS FOR ME to shut up. It's five in the morning and I need to get going to the gym. "I'm leaving for work." Another grunt.

I walk out to the kitchen to grab a cup of coffee and see Tristan at the table eating a bowl of sugary cereal for breakfast. I never carry food like that in my home, but knowing Tristan would be living with me, I had Kayla help me out by taking Tristan to the grocery store last night to buy food he likes. Watching him makes me think of my son and everything I'm missing out on not getting to watch him grow up. It pisses me off knowing Tristan's dad signed away his rights for a measly thirty grand. If it were in my control, no amount of money could ever keep me away from my child. Too many people take the important things in life for granted like family and loved ones.

The past couple years Tristan and I have gotten closer. I'm aware he isn't a replacement of my son and I'm not a replacement of the father he's never known, but I love that kid like he's my own. I find myself looking forward to spending time with him, and now with him living with me, I hope our relationship will grow even more. Tristan means a lot to me just like his mom does.

"Morning."

Tristan looks up from the iPad in front of him, the one I bought him for his last birthday. "Morning, are you going to the gym?"

"That I am, want to go?"

His face perks up out of excitement. "Can I?"

"Sure, go get dressed. We'll let your mom sleep in. She's probably exhausted from working late."

I write Ashley a note letting her know I took Tristan with me and leave it on the nightstand, so she doesn't freak out once she wakes up, then take off with Tristan to the gym.

He spends the first hour working out with me, but once Bella and a couple of his friends arrive, he takes off to the kids' area. Cooper decided last year to split the gym into two areas: the smaller part is the kids' area and the larger main area is for the fighters. That way the kids won't hear the cursing and bashing that goes on when you stick a bunch of amped up fighters into the room together. The kids who belong to the fighters always venture into the adult area, but for the most part it works out well, especially for the kids who are only here for the kids' MMA classes.

Alex arrives shortly after seven and we begin training immediately. After an hour of warming up, we start working on some takedown defense moves. His opponent, Gavin 'Stunner' Fitzgerald's strength is submission, while Alex's strength is stand-up—his area of expertise boxing. Most fights, Alex will win with a knockout, but if his opponent gets him to the ground, he'll be in trouble, and that's what we need to prepare for.

"I can't believe you're planning a wedding the month before your big fight. Talk about adding more stress."

"Well, if it helps we're holding off on the honeymoon until after the fight so I won't miss any training other than the day of the wedding... and the day after." He waggles his eyebrows up and down giving me a wink. I use him being distracted to take him down, and before he can even think about his next move, I pull him into a quick arm bar forcing him to tap out.

"Fuck!" he says, standing up, pissed.

"Just don't think about fucking your wife during the fight," I say, patting him on his shoulder. "Oh, by the way, right after the wedding, I have to go visit my family for a few days. My grandmother is turning eighty and is demanding I'm present. I've asked Bentley to train with you. You'll learn some good moves from him. Make sure you work his stay-at-home daddy ass hard."

"Thanks, man! Will do."

I see Ashley walking into the gym out of the corner of my eye, so grabbing a towel, I wipe the sweat off me while heading over to see her.

"What are you doing here?" I ask, giving her a sweaty side hug. She scrunches her nose up in disgust, so I go all in, giving her a bear hug.

"Ewww! Kaden, stop! You are so gross." She laughs, grabbing my towel to dramatically wipe her face and neck off.

"Better get used to it, soon-to-be-Mrs. Scott."

Her smile spreads across her face, but she quickly straightens it out.

"Thank you for letting me sleep in. I definitely needed it."

"No worries. I'm working with Alex right now and Caleb this afternoon. but I'll be home later. Want to order in for dinner?"

"Hey, Kaden!" Stephen comes over. "The guys and I are all going to *The Hideout* tonight, it's ladies' night. You in?"

Before I can answer, Ashley answers for me. "You should go. I'm actually here to pick up Tristan." Then she walks away without even giving me a chance to answer.

"Nah, man. I'm going home after work," I say, my eyes never leaving Ashley's ass as she sashays to the kids' area to get Tristan.

I pull up to my house with Thai takeout and don't see Ashley's piece-of-crap car in the driveway, only the oil stain it left behind. It really does need to get replaced, but she would probably skin me alive if I tried to buy her a vehicle. I got so busy at the gym I didn't have time to text her all day. Hopefully she and Tristan haven't eaten yet.

"Honey, I'm home," I yell out like I do most of the times I enter her house.

"Hey Kaden!" Tristan yells out from the living room, playing my PlayStation.

"You hungry? Where's your mom?" I bring the bag of food into the kitchen.

"She's at work." It's not Tristan who answers this time, but Britni, his babysitter.

"Uhh, hey. What are you doing here?"

She looks at me confused. "I'm babysitting Tristan. Ashley went to work about thirty minutes ago."

Oh. Hell. No.

"You can take off. Do you need a ride home?"

"No, I can have my boyfriend pick me up."

I pull out some money from my wallet to pay her her full amount since it's not her fault I'm sending her home early. Then I shoot a text to Caleb.

Me: Is Ashley working tonight?

Caleb: Yeah...

Then a thought strikes me.

"You know what, Britni? Would you mind watching Tristan? I'll give you some extra money for the mix-up. I need to run an errand."

"No problem, Kaden. I'll let my boyfriend know to pick me up later."

"Thanks! And there's Thai food in the kitchen for you and Tristan."

I take quick shower and get dressed in a pair of nice jeans and a button-down dress shirt. I throw on my shoes and quickly dry off my hair before heading out. On the way, I give Caleb a call.

"Hey man, I need a favor."

"I'm going to assume it has something to do with Ashley working tonight. You know I'm not getting in the middle of that shit. It was bad enough I was stuck on the couch for over a week for not telling Hayley before. I'm finally back in my bed and getting laid again."

"I just need you to book her for a private party for tonight. If she has any other parties, give them to someone else."

"Fuck, Kaden," Caleb groans.

"I'll pay."

"You know damn well it's not about the money. It's about fucking with Ashley. She's good for my business and I'm hoping she'll eventually manage this place. Pissing her off isn't going to help with that."

"Just do it."

He groans louder but agrees.

I arrive at *Assets* a few minutes later and am let in right away. Caleb has us all on his VIP list so we never have to wait to get in. When I walk through the restaurant I don't see her so I head upstairs to the bar area. She's up on the main stage in only a thong barely covering her pussy, as she moves her body up and down the pole. She is breathtakingly beautiful and every man watching her is entranced by the way she dances so gracefully on the stage. Unlike in some of the trashier clubs, *Assets* doesn't allow men to stick bills in the girl's underwear or throw it up on stage. Girls take turns dancing a couple times a night, but it's mostly to advertise themselves. Seeing them on stage is what makes a man want her to perform for him up close. I can't even imagine the amount of men that request Ashley.

Waitresses aren't allowed to give private dances, which is why, according to Caleb, Ashley left Double D's to work here for him. As a dancer, she can make money from the private dances and parties.

Once she's done dancing, the curtains close around her so she can grab her clothes as she heads out back. Caleb sends me a text letting me know which room to go into, so I go straight there to wait for her.

I get comfortable on the couch this time and wait for the music to start for my private performance. A few minutes later, the music begins and she's back to climbing and grinding that pole, only she's in a different outfit this time. A light blue dress with a matching bra and panties. When she's done, I make it a point to clap loud and slow. She looks past the bright lights and sees me sitting there. Throwing her sexy see-through dress back on along the way, she walks toward me until she's standing in front of me.

"What are you doing here? When Caleb said VIP, he didn't mention you."

"The real question is what are you doing here?"

She looks around dramatically mocking my question like I'm an idiot for even asking. "I. Work. Here," she says, slowly enunciating every word.

Grabbing her by her waist I bring her into my lap so she's straddling me. "You're my fiancée. You aren't working as a stripper."

"I'm your *fake* fiancée." She makes sure to emphasize the word fake. "And I have to work so I can pay you back and get a place for Tristan and me."

"We'll discuss that in a moment. Why didn't you have Tristan stay with me?"

"I thought you were going out tonight. I didn't want to cock-block you."

"One, you said I was going out, not me. And two, there's nothing to cock-block, unless you want to deny me yourself."

I don't know what comes over me, maybe it's her accusation that I would rather be out trying to find an easy lay than home with her when the truth is I haven't fucked a single woman in God knows how long, but I bring my hands up to her head and pull her into me, smashing her mouth to mine almost violently. She tenses up at first, but I can feel it when she gives in and starts kissing me back. Her hands slide around my neck as her hot pussy begins to grind against my already hard dick through my jeans causing me to groan into her mouth.

She grinds against me harder and seconds later I'm lifting her dress up and over her head throwing it to the floor. Next, her bra is removed, and then I'm grabbing her ass and changing our positions so her back is on the couch and I'm hovering over her. My lips curl around her taut nipple, sucking it roughly. She grabs my hair, moaning loudly at my assault, spurring me on. I continue to suck her on her tits for several beats before I head farther south.

I place an open-mouthed kiss through her thin panties, and her ass jerks upward, bringing her pussy closer to me. Ripping the thin strip of material, I dive right in to taste her. My tongue hits her clit as my fingers enter her to see if she's ready. She is. She's dripping fucking wet. Sticking one digit in, then another, I fingerfuck her while my tongue continues to lick her clit.

"Kaden...Oh, shit. Kaden!" Ashley's pussy walls tighten around my fingers like a vice. Taking her clit between my teeth, I bite down softly then suck on it. Her back arches up and her hands fist my hair as she grinds her warmth against my mouth trying to fuck my mouth with her pussy. My tongue strokes up and down her clit as she face-fucks me. Her moans get louder and her hands fist my hair tighter. Then her entire body tenses, her thighs clenching around my head. "Oh. My. God!" she screams in pure ecstasy as her orgasm rips through her.

"Holy shit," is all she says when she's finally catches her breath. Moving my fingers out of her pussy, I unbutton my pants and pull them down to my knees, taking my briefs along with them. I line my dick up at her entrance but stop when I look at her wide eyes.

"What's wrong?" She shakes her head, but her pained expression tells me otherwise. "What's wrong?" I repeat.

"We shouldn't be doing this. I keep putting myself in this position with you when I know there's only one way this is all going to end. Badly. This engagement isn't even real. The marriage will be fake. I'm a stripper for God's sake. Men see me naked almost every day. I know we aren't together for real, but it would feel like I was cheating on you if we get together and I continue to work...and I will be continuing to work. I promised myself I would never be with a guy while I'm stripping."

Ashley covers her eyes with her hands. "Jeez, I'm such a freaking tease. This is the third time I've stopped us from having sex. I'm so sorry. If you want to be with someone else, I'll understand. You have needs."

I remove her hands from her face. "What are you talking about?"

"I can't have sex with you. I don't want to lose you."

I pull my jeans and briefs back up, tucking my dick back inside, pissed. Not pissed we didn't have sex, but pissed she would insinuate I would ever be with another woman while being engaged and married to her—real or fake.

I stand from the couch, feeling my blood boiling. I need to walk away. I shouldn't be this hurt by such a simple comment, but I am.

"I can't believe you would think I could ever think so little of you that I would cheat on you. I gotta go."

"Kaden, wait." Ashley jumps up from the couch still completely naked. "Have you ever had sex with a woman more than once."

I want to say yes. I had sex with my wife exclusively for many years, but I don't say that. I can't say that. That would raise too many questions I don't want to answer.

"No." I give her the half-truth. Since my wife left me, I have never spent more than one night with a woman.

"Don't you see? If we have sex, it will change everything. Sure, we're attracted to each other, but you don't do commitment, and even if you stay faithful to me during our fake engagement and marriage, once it's over, you will move on, and where will that leave us? Where will that leave me?"

"I could never just drop you, Ash."

"Kaden, right now I'm your best friend, and our friendship works because sex isn't part of it. There's no commitment. If we step over that imaginary line, there's no going back. I couldn't take it if you stopped talking to me. You can say you would never do that, but your actions speak for themselves. You have never been with a woman more than once. I can't take that chance."

I don't know what to say. She's right to an extent, but it's different with Ashley.

"I'm pretty sure my tongue and fingers in your pussy was us crossing over the line."

"And I don't think we should do that anymore, but if we had sex, it would definitely be crossing the line. We could never come back from that."

Not wanting to continue this argument, I say, "Okay, but can you at least quit dancing? Once we're married, you're going to be rich. You don't need to strip."

"I'm not taking your money, Kaden. I'm going to keep my job and pay you off. I'm not ever going to owe anybody again. I can't take your money. The last time I depended on a man, he nearly destroyed me."

She'll be taking this money, but there's no point in going back and forth with her.

"I'm going to go home and relieve Britni from babysitting."

"Okay."

I start walking out as Ashley calls my name. "Kaden...are we okay?"

I turn around to face her. Her eyes are hooded and her lips are curled down into a frown. Her hands are covering her chest because she never had a chance to put her clothes back on. I ignore her nakedness, closing the distance between us, and wrap my arms around her tight. "We will always be okay." I pull back enough to give her a chaste kiss on her forehead, then I head home to relieve the sitter.

Fourteen

ASHLEY

IT'S BEEN TWO WEEKS SINCE KADEN GAVE ME A MIND-blowing orgasm only to have me stop him once again before we had sex. I still can't believe I stopped him, but I knew it was for the best, especially after these past couple weeks. Kaden is what women call *husband material*. He is selfless in every decision he makes. He picks up dinner on the nights I don't cook, and he doesn't let me spend a dime of my own money on anything. He takes Tristan to the gym with him on the mornings after I work late, and he never complains about the house now being *lived* in. Last weekend, we all took the kids to *Cowabunga Bay*, a waterpark about thirty minutes away, and had a blast. The entire time he focused on Tristan and me, acting like we're really a family.

When everybody looked at us like we're crazy, and Liz got excited thinking we were really a couple, I felt it was best to tell our close friends the engagement and wedding are fake for his grandmother so they wouldn't be confused once we get divorced. Kaden wasn't thrilled about it but reluctantly agreed. That hasn't stopped him; however, from acting like we're together. He holds my hand and kisses me like it's a natural thing. I should probably ask if we can get this marriage over with sooner rather than later because I can already feel it...once our marriage is over, I'm going to be left heartbroken. And the longer we wait, the longer I fall even deeper in love with this perfect specimen of a man who isn't mine for the taking.

It's Saturday night and I have the night off. I can't even remember the last time I was off on a weekend night, but I'm not complaining. Kaden and I are watching a UFC fight in the living room, and Tristan is in bed for the night—he watched a few fights but passed out before the main event. Kaden promised to record it for him so he can watch it tomorrow.

"We need to get you a ring," Kaden says out of nowhere, glancing at his cellphone.

"What made you think of that?" I'm lying on the floor on my stomach, looking at the Cosmo magazine on my phone.

He shows me his screen. It's a picture of Jessica and Alex's engagement pictures on social media. It's a beautiful picture of them smiling into the camera with her hand sticking straight out showing off her engagement ring.

"We can just get wedding bands. I don't want you to waste money on a fake engagement ring." I scroll down and come across an online quiz: **HOW WELL DO YOU KNOW YOUR GIRLFRIEND?**

"We'll see," Kaden says. "Did you get a sitter for their wedding next weekend?"

"My parents asked if they can take him for the week. We leave the following day for your grandmother's birthday party so they wanted to see him before we go." I click on the quiz and the first question pops up. I read through it.

"Ashley? Are you listening?"

He was saying something? "Yeah, sorry. I'm looking at this quiz. It determines how well you know your girlfriend. Want to take it?"

Kaden laughs. "Those quizzes are crap."

I pout. "Please."

Kaden rolls his eyes. "Fine. Hit me with it."

"Yay! Okay, what color are my eyes?" I quickly close my eyes so Kaden can't cheat, and he laughs.

"Seriously? Your eyes are hazel. Sometimes with a hint of green when you're happy or excited. When you're sad, they have more of a gold to them." Well, all right then...I open my eyes.

"That one was easy. Do you know my favorite movie?"

"*Save The Last Dance*. And you cry every time they fight and he walks away." *Damn...*

"Okay, here's a hard one. What are one of my dreams?" There's no way he can answer this question. I don't even know the answer myself.

Kaden gives me a small smile. "To provide a safe and loving home for Tristan. That's the only dream I can think of. Since I met you, you haven't focused on anything else but doing that." His answer makes me choke up, and tears prickle behind my lids. I shake them off and laugh.

"I'll give you credit for that one." I look down at my phone and click yes, bringing up the next question.

"Do you have any other dreams?"

I think about his question for a minute. Growing up I always wanted to be a teacher. I guess it wasn't so much teaching but working with kids.

"I would love to work with kids. Spend my days making a difference in their lives, even if it's not as a teacher. Okay, next question. Do you know who my friends are?"

Kaden looks at me like I have three heads. "Are you serious? We have all the same friends."

I laugh. That's true. "Okay, next. Do you remember how we met?"

"At Cooper's house." Wrong!

"Nope! We met at the gym when I brought Tristan in for a trial class."

"Wrong. We met at Cooper's house. You and the girls showed up drunk and I volunteered to give you a ride home. You passed out halfway to your house and I had to go through your purse to find your address. I carried you both inside and put you to bed."

"Oh, my God! How do I not remember that? Is that how you got my number? I thought you got it off my paperwork at the gym!"

Kaden throws his head back with a laugh. "You gave me your number in the car and told me you weren't against me sending you naked selfies."

I cover my eyes laughing. How do I not remember any of that? I must have been seriously drunk that night.

You know...if you still want a naked selfie of me, I'll gladly send you some." Kaden winks, making me blush.

"Let's move on to the next question, shall we?"

We go from question to question. Kaden's not only able to answer every single one, but on many, he takes it a step further and explains. I hit finish on the quiz, so it can give me his score.

"You did good," I say nonchalantly, trying to play off how well he did. "So, what is it we were talking about before? Alex and Jessica's wedding?"

"Oh no! Give me that phone." Kaden grabs the phone out of my hand and swipes up to pull the screen up with the quiz results.

"One hundred percent. It says 'Boyfriend of the year. Don't let this man go. Chance of you finding someone who knows you that well are slim. Hold on to him and don't let go.'"

Kaden is grinning from ear-to-ear and waggling his eyebrows. "I normally would disagree with anything from the internet, but in this case, I definitely agree." Yeah, if only he meant it the same way the quiz means it.

"Yeah, yeah...give me back my phone." I snatch the phone back from Kaden. "So, what is it you were talking about?"

"I was telling you that I went ahead and booked a room at the hotel the wedding is being held at so we can drink and have fun. Just don't get too drunk. If you ask me for naked selfies again while you're drunk, again, I might just have to give in and send you some."

"Sounds good," I say, refusing to acknowledge his comment about the naked selfies. "You know if you want to get separate rooms so you can..."

"Don't even finish that sentence." Kaden pounces on me, making me fall onto my back on the floor. My phone flies out of my hand, and he pins my hands above my head. His face is holding a mock glare with his beautiful green eyes only being shown through small slits. It makes me laugh before I bring my knee up to his stomach to playfully push him off me. I don't know why I even bother, though. I'm like a hundred and twenty pounds at most, dripping wet, while Kaden is probably double that and all muscle.

He lets me knee him and falls to the floor onto his back dramatically, allowing me to switch our positions so I have his hands pinned down. Because he's so wide, my thighs barely make it around his waist. My knees are barely touching the ground, and my hands are up so high because his arms are so long, it puts my chest right in his face nearly suffocating him.

"Nice view." His voice is muffled, but I can still hear his smile. When I try to move backward out of his reach, he grabs my hands in his, holding me in this position. My sex is grinding against his stomach, and when his knees come up, his dick hits my ass...and it's hard. Heat pools between my legs. I try to move my hands to get off him, but he isn't letting it happen. He starts laughing, knowing he's outmuscling me. I'm on top of him and I can't even get up!

It's clear my hands aren't moving, so I do the first thing I can think of and bite him. Yep! I bite him right on the neck. He jumps in shock, letting go of my hands. I use this opportunity to roll off him, but he's too quick and seconds later he has me pinned under him, his legs pinning me down with both my hands in one of his. His other hand comes down and...he starts tickling me. *Tickling me!*

"Kaden! Stop!" I'm yelling at the top of my lungs, but the tickling is so bad I'm barely getting any words out at all. I can't stop laughing, and if he doesn't stop, I'm going to pee my pants.

"You think you were slick, huh? Biting my neck?"

He continues his tickling assault. His fingers dig into my ribs and I lose it. "Kaden, I'm going to pee in my pants!" I shriek, still laughing because it's completely out of my control.

He laughs but stops tickling me. With his one hand still holding both of mine, the hand that was just tickling me comes up and runs along my cheek. I lean into it, making eye contact with Kaden. I can see it on his face. He is filled with the same lust I feel being in this close of proximity to him.

"Kade..." And then his mouth is on mine. His hand that was just on my cheek comes down to my breast and massages it while his tongue seeks entrance.

"Mom?" Tristan calls out from his room causing us both to part. Kaden quickly adjusts himself and I run up the stairs to see what Tristan needs.

"I had a bad dream," he says, rubbing his eyes. I hear footsteps coming up the stairs. Then Kaden is entering the room, handing Tristan a glass of water.

"Thank you." I give him a small smile of appreciation. "It was just a dream, sweetie. I'll leave your bathroom light on, though. Okay?"

"Okay, Mom."

"I love you." I give him a hug and a kiss on his forehead before pulling his covers back up.

"Love you, too, Mom."

"Goodnight, buddy," Kaden says, leaning over Tristan and ruffling his hair up.

"Goodnight, Kaden. Love you."

Kaden stops and stills. I can hear him swallow, but then he visibly relaxes and gives Tristan a smile. "I love you, too."

I want to ask him why the words *I love you* coming from my son's mouth looked like it caused him physical pain, but I'm afraid of the answer I might get, so I don't.

Fifteen

KADEN

WHEN TRISTAN SAID *I LOVE YOU* TO ME, IT FELT LIKE MY heart, which was buried six feet under, was put back into my chest. Not completely pieced back together, but enough that I could feel it beating again. It warmed me up and scared the shit out of me all at the same time. I realized in that moment, I want more. I want to be somebody's dad. I want to be somebody's husband. But not just anybody—no, a certain somebody. I want to be Tristan's dad and Ashley's husband. But the guilt that came with my sudden realization of feelings made me feel sick to my stomach. The thought of replacing Gabrielle and our son made me feel like the biggest piece-of-shit.

I know Ashley felt something was wrong, but she didn't call me out on it, for which I appreciate. She asked if I wanted to go with her to drop Tristan off at her parents' house, but I said no. She looked disappointed and it broke my heart, but I needed some space. She was right. At the rate we're going, when this is all over, hearts are going to be broken. And we'll be over because I can't marry anyone else. I just can't do it. It doesn't matter how much I love Ashley and Tristan, I can't just replace my wife and son.

Without Tristan around, Ashley and I don't have to put on a happy front—not that we're usually fake, because we aren't. Our friendship has always been an open book. Hasn't it? Well, except for her hiding her violent ex-boyfriend...and the fact that she used herself as collateral to pay him off...and the fact that she has no idea I was ever married with a baby.

Now, that I'm thinking about it, we've kept quite a lot from each other. And now that it's all starting to come to the surface, we aren't handling it very well at all. The tension between us is palpable, and I don't know what to do about it. Well, actually, I do know what to do about it—tell her the truth, which is something I'm not ready to do yet.

Ashley and I have successfully avoided each other all week. It's Saturday, the day of Alex and Jessica's wedding, and the day before we leave for Colorado. Ashley even made it a point to sleep in the downstairs guest room instead of in my bedroom with me. I'm showered and dressed in my suit for the wedding. My luggage is up against the front door, and I'm waiting on Ashley to finish getting ready. We figured since we're going to be spending the night at the JW Marriott, where the wedding and reception are both being held, we might as well bring the luggage for our trip and leave from there to get Tristan and go to the airport.

"You ready to go, Ash?" I call out.

"Ugh! Yes, I think so," she says, huffing and puffing. I turn around and am nearly knocked back by how amazing she looks. Her hair is in waves over her shoulders, her makeup is done lightly, and her thin, light pink, strapless dress is tight in all the right places and loose in others. She's wearing black heels that are delicate and feminine, and her toes and fingers match her dress.

"You look beautiful." Grabbing the two suitcases she's attempting to wheel behind her, I bring them out to the car.

"Thank you," she says shyly. "You look good too."

After hauling the luggage into my car, we head to the wedding. After valet parking, we head straight back to the large gazebo where the ceremony is being held. We find our seats only minutes before the wedding march starts. Once everyone has made it down the aisle, Jessica and Alex begin to say their vows. I try to stay in the present, but my mind goes back to the day Gabby and I said ours...

"Gabrielle, you are my everything. You are my past, my present, and my future. I promise to love and cherish you through good times and bad, in sickness and in health. I promise to always protect you and be by your side. I promise to love you and only you for the rest of our lives."

I slide the wedding band onto Gabby's ring finger. Her eyes are smiling as small tears fall down her cheeks. I reach over to gently wipe them away, trying not to ruin her makeup.

"Kaden, thank you for loving me. This is just beginning for us, and I can't wait to see what is in store for our future. If it's half as amazing as these last five years have been, I will be a very happy woman. I promise to love and cherish you through good times and bad, in sickness and in health. I promise to be a good wife to you and stand by your side. I promise to love you and only

you for the rest of our lives.”

She takes my hand in hers and she slides the ring we picked out for me onto my finger.

“I now pronounce you husband and wife. You may kiss the bride.”

“Kaden?” I look down at my empty ring finger and feel for a second for the indent that has long disappeared.

“Kaden? Are you okay?” Ashley is looking at me worriedly. I glance around and notice the wedding is over and everybody is filing out.

“Yeah, I’m okay.” Her brows scrunch together, and a frown mars her face, but she doesn’t call me out.

Once at the reception, we find the table we’re assigned to. It was obviously done with thought because we’re sitting with all our friends. After the newlywed couple is announced and have their first dance, I take my jacket off and ask Ashley if she would like a drink from the bar.

“Sure, a Bahama Breeze please.”

After grabbing myself a Jack and Coke and her Bahama Breeze, I have a seat. Ashley isn’t sitting where I left her, instead she’s out on the dance floor dancing away with all the women. I don’t bother sitting down. I just stand there like a lovesick fool watching the woman I can never have, laugh and smile, and wish it were me putting that smile on her face.

“Dude, you have it so bad,” Caleb says, slapping my shoulder.

“Yeah, but we both know nothing can come of it.” I have no idea why I say that and immediately wish I could take it back.

“Why? Because you were married once before? Fuck that. It

obviously didn't last for a reason. Maybe Ashley was the reason."

It's not his fault because I've never told him what happened with my wife, and I know he wouldn't be saying what he's saying if he knew the truth, but I don't think about that when I shove him up against the wall. "Don't you ever talk about my wife that way. It's my fault she's gone! Mine! I'm the one who deserves to be alone for the rest of my life."

Caleb's eyes go wide. "Bro, I'm sorry. I don't know what happened, but nobody deserves to be alone. I, of all people, know that shit firsthand."

"I need a drink."

Grabbing my shoulder as I walk away, Caleb turns me around to face him. "I'm sorry. I get you don't want to talk about whatever happened between you and your wife, but regardless, you deserve to be loved, Kaden, and so does Ashley. And if you can't love her, you need to let her go. I've gotten to know her these last couple months and she's a damn good woman. A woman who's been through a lot of shit and deserves to have some good."

"I know."

Picking my drink up, I down it like a shot. Then I head to the bar to order a double. And I spend the rest of the evening drinking my confusion away.

Sixteen

ASHLEY

THE WEDDING IS SO ROMANTIC AND THE RECEPTION IS A blast. I can't even remember how many Bahama Breezes I've had, but it's enough that I'm drunk. Kaden spent the reception moping over God knows what and I'm so over his shit. I'm in too good of a mood to let him bring me down. A wedding should be a joyous occasion, not a reason to brood in a corner alone. Although, now that I'm thinking about it, last year when we were part of Liz and Cooper's wedding, Kaden kind of acted the same way.

The party comes to an end, and after congratulating Jessica and Alex, we all part ways, going to our own rooms. When we get to our room, Kaden goes straight to the mini fridge and pulls out a few mini bottles of liquor, downing two of them after he drops to the couch. I grab the last one out of his hand and down that one.

Putting his head back against the couch, he closes his eyes. We're both trashed and we know it. Only I'm hyper and not ready to pass out quite yet. I notice an iPod dock in the corner of the room, and grabbing my awesome iPhone Kaden got me, plug it in and switch on iTunes, clicking shuffle.

I'm n Luv (wit a stripper) by T-Pain blasts through the small portable speakers, and I crack up laughing at the irony of this song. Kaden's head tilts forward as he glares at me, clearly not finding the humor in it, which makes me laugh even harder. *Well, fuck him!*

Kicking off my heels first, so I don't break my neck (I'm drunk, not stupid), I climb up onto the coffee table and start to dance to the rhythm of the music. I'm staring straight at Kaden, and he's staring back, watching me with the undeniable lust in his eyes. I sway my hips seductively, just like I do on stage, singing the words to the song.

I laugh as my words come out with a slur and definitely not to the beat of the song. Then I drop my ass to the table, spreading my legs, and give Kaden a complete visual of my pussy, since I didn't wear panties to the wedding—can't have panty lines ruining the dress.

His eyes widen at the visual.

"You better be a good tipper. I don't show just anyone my goods."

That gets me a smirk from him. He reaches into his back pocket and pulls out a crisp one-hundred dollar bill from his wallet. I laugh but keep dancing. I roll onto my stomach and then pop back up onto my feet, peeling my dress off me and throwing it at him.

He chuckles lightly and stands, wobbling his drunk ass up to the table. I don't stop dancing, though. I turn around, backing my ass right up to him and shake it. I feel a hand land right on my ass cheek with a smack, causing me to crack up. Once I turn back around, he places the bill in the cup of my bra, letting his hands linger on my body.

He moves them slowly down my sides until they land back on my ass cheeks.

"No no, you know the rules. You don't get to touch the stripper."

Kaden growls...*fucking growls*. Then grabbing my ass with both his hands, lifts me off the couch, and throws me onto the bed.

"You are my fiancée. I can touch you whenever the fuck I want. Got it? This pussy is mine...Mine."

Seventeen

KADEN

FUCK! WHO THE HELL IS BANGING ON THE DOOR? OR IS IT the wall? I open my eyes and realize the banging isn't coming from anywhere. It's my head pulsing so strongly it feels like a constant banging is taking place right behind my eyes, in my head. Scanning my surroundings, I remember I'm in the hotel where Alex got married, and next to me is a naked woman. The blanket is wrapped around her shoulders and head, but from the waist down is nothing but silky smooth skin. I know right away it's Ashley. I would recognize her sexy legs from a mile away. But why is she naked? I try to remember what happened but can't. My head is pounding and the more I try to think about last night, the harder it pounds.

Needing to take a piss, I get out of bed and head to the bathroom. When I go to pull my briefs down, I notice I'm naked too. Fuck! It all comes back to me in flashes.

Her: dancing on the table.

Me: Hauling her over my shoulder.

Then...nothing. I can't remember shit after that! Fuck! Did I have sex with Ashley and was too drunk to even enjoy it? I mean, I'm sure I enjoyed it. But I can't remember how her pussy felt wrapped around my cock. How it felt to be fully inside of her. Damn it! I'm such a fucking idiot.

I shower and get dressed, when I'm done, Ashley is up and floating around the room getting things together to leave.

"I'm going to get in the shower since you're out."

"Ash, wait." I gently grab her wrist. I need to apologize for taking advantage of our inebriated states last night. "I'm sorry..."

She flinches, pulling her arm from me. "There's nothing to apologize for. Let's just pretend last night didn't happen."

Now it's my turn to flinch at her harsh words. I wasn't thinking it was a mistake at all. I was thinking the opposite. But if that's how she feels..."Got it."

We forgo meeting everyone for breakfast, going through a drive-thru instead. The drive to her parents is silent. Ashley is reading a book on her phone. She's so funny when she reads, letting all her emotions show. At a good part, she'll smile or laugh. At a sad part, she'll frown. It's so adorable, especially since she has no idea she's doing it.

After grabbing Tristan, we drive to the airport. My grandma's birthday party isn't until Saturday, but we're staying the week and flying back after the party is over. Tristan starts back at school Tuesday with open house Monday, so Ashley asked if we could be home Sunday so she can get him situated. Ashley's decided to sign him up at the school in my school zone so she filled out all the necessary paperwork.

She said it's a lot nicer and closer and Bella goes there as well, so it makes sense. I like the idea of him going to school here, maybe that'll keep her living here that much longer.

After bringing our bags through security, we make our way to the first class lounge to wait to be called. "Do you want something to drink, bud?" Tristan has been acting weird since we picked him up.

"No," he says, quickly shaking his head.

"Are you okay?" He looks at his mom and then back to me. "What's going on?"

"He's never flown before," Ashley admits, nervously.

"Never?" I ask incredulously.

"Nope," Tristan answers softly.

"Oh, Tristan. We need to get you out more, buddy! This is going to be great. First class is awesome. This trip is short, only around two hours, so no dinner served, but the flight attendant will bring you whatever you want to drink and tons of snacks. There's Wi-Fi available and there are TVs in all the seats to watch movies. Plus, they give you a pillow and blanket and your seat reclines."

Tristan's eyes go wide in excitement, and Ashley smiles at his excitement. They both make my heart melt and I'm already planning where to take them next.

After the short flight to Denver International, we grab our bags and head to the car rental area. I get an Audi SUV so we're comfortable, then we make the thirty-minute drive to my parents' place.

"Welcome to Cherry Hills Village," Ashley says, reading the sign as we enter the community my parents and grandparents live in.

"Is this where you grew up?" Tristan asks in amazement, looking out the window as we pass by the huge homes. Cherry Hills Village is a community within itself just outside of Denver. It gives people country living without having to drive an hour to get to the main city.

"I was born and raised here." Ashley looks at me like I have two heads. The truth is, I once even owned my own home here, until I sold it to have a fresh start away from here. When my parents visited me in Las Vegas they stayed with me but asked numerous times if I'm okay on money and if I need them to buy me a house. I could fit about five of my houses into the house my grandparents purchased for Gabrielle and me for our wedding present.

"There's a golf course! Can we play golf, Kaden?" Tristan shouts enthusiastically.

"Sure, buddy. There's also a community pool and tennis courts, and if you want, my mom can take you for a ride on her horses."

"Wow! I want to ride a horse!"

"Your parents have horses?" Ashley asks.

"Yeah, not in their backyard or anything. They board them at the club."

She nods softly, a frown marring her beautiful face.

"Is something wrong?"

"I just didn't picture her like this when she came to visit with your dad."

"Just because we have money, doesn't mean we're snobs."

"No! I wasn't thinking that..."

I laugh. "Yes, you were, but I get it. I'm a UFC trainer. I make a good living, but nothing like this. I'm lucky. My parents encouraged me to follow my passion. Sure, my father and grandfather would have loved for me to join them in their businesses, but mixed-martial-arts was always my passion."

"That's great, Kaden. I can't imagine you doing anything else."

We pull up to my parents' house and, before the doors are opened, Sandra Scott is running outside waving her arms in excitement with her husband, Stewart, walking slowly behind her shaking his head, laughing.

"Oh, Kaden! You're here!" She gives me a hug not letting go for several seconds. Then she moves on to her next victim, Ashley. "Oh, sweetie! I'm so excited to see you and that precious son of yours." She looks Tristan up and down. "I swear you have grown a foot since the last time I saw you."

"It's wonderful to see you, too, Mrs. Scott," Ashley says.

"Mom, you saw him like seven months ago."

"Oh, hush! And Ashley, if I can't get you to call me Mom, at least call me Sandra, please. Let's go inside. I made cookies. Your grandparents should be over shortly. We're going to go to the club for dinner tonight so we don't have to deal with cooking. Tomorrow, your father has scheduled for you guys to go golfing."

Tristan looks over at me and I give him a wink. "Cool, I'm going to bring Tristan with me, and sometime this week, can you take him to meet Shorty and Copper?"

My mom beams at someone wanting to meet her horses. "Of course! We can go for a ride! Ashley, would you like to join?"

"Sure."

"And I was thinking tomorrow while the boys are golfing, we can go to the club and have a spa day."

Ashley suddenly looks nervous. "Umm...that's okay. I thought I could just hang out by the pool..."

"Nonsense, it's my treat! I'm so excited to spend time with you."

Eighteen

ASHLEY

WE'RE ALL SITTING IN THE BEAUTIFUL FAMILY ROOM. Tristan is eating cookies and playing on his iPad while Kaden's parents play twenty questions with Kaden, trying to catch up on what's going on in his life. He tells them about Alex's fight coming up and about Tristan and me moving in with him. I'm thankful he doesn't tell them the reason why.

"Kaden, honey?" We all look to the door where we see a beautifully-aged woman waving her cane in the air toward Kaden. He gets up, smiling ear-to-ear, and hugs her.

"Grandmother, I've missed you so much!"

"Oh, dear boy. You have grown into such a handsome man. Please don't ever leave for this long again."

Kaden nods, giving her a kiss on her cheek. He hugs his grandfather next, and they exchange a few words as well. It's clear Kaden is loved and wanted here in his hometown. What I don't understand is why he ever left, and why he hasn't wanted to come home. The love surrounding him is so strong. His grandparents are still married and clearly in love, and so are his parents. So why doesn't he want to get married? I remember the name Gabby written on his chest and wonder if maybe he had his heart broken.

"And who do we have here?" His grandmother turns to face Tristan and me.

"This is Ashley Myers and her son, Tristan." Kaden puts his hand in mine, putting on a show for his family.

"Ashley, Tristan, these are my grandparents, Rose and Victor."

"Oh, sweetie. You are gorgeous. And hello there, Tristan. It's wonderful to meet you both. Let's go to dinner and get to know each other. Shall we?" Kaden's grandmother says, heading back toward the foyer.

"Sounds good, my love," his grandfather says, following his wife. Their love is adorable.

"Ready?" Kaden asks.

"Yep, let's do this." Then it hits me. Kaden is going to announce we're engaged and we haven't told Tristan! He's going to be so confused. I didn't even think about him in all this. What kind of mother am I?

"We need to explain this to Tristan!" I say, whisper-yelling after Tristan jumps in to the Audi. "We didn't think about him at all in this. He's going to think we're getting married for real. I can't have him get hurt."

"No, you're right," Kaden says. We get into the car and Kaden turns around to face Tristan. "Hey, bud. When you're in school, do you ever play make believe?"

"Yeah," Tristan says.

"While we're here, your mom and I are going to play make believe. We're going to pretend to be engaged to be married. So, if you hear the grownups talking about it, it's just pretend. Okay?"

Tristan looks at us both skeptically. "Okay, but why can't you get married for real?"

His question stumps us both. Kaden says, "Umm...well...the thing is..."

I jump in to help him out. "Kaden is my best friend."

"So, you can't marry your best friend?" Tristan asks. *Damn kid!*

"Well, I guess you could," Kaden says slowly. "But your mom and I aren't that kind of friends. She's my friend like how you and Bella are friends. My grandmother is really old and she wants to see me get married, so we're going to play pretend to make her happy."

"Well, when I get older, if Bella is still my best friend I would want to marry her for real and not for pretend."

"You would?" I ask.

"Yeah, she's really nice and always spars with me in class. She always shares her Oreos with me and plays UFC with me. She's good at fighting, too. And she's not all girly like the other girls in my class. And if I marry her, I could play with her whenever I want."

Kaden looks at me with a smile in his eyes, clearly trying to hold back his laughter. What I would give to be able to live my life through the eyes of an innocent six-year-old.

"That's very nice of Bella," I say. "But Kaden and I are just going to be friends."

We both hold our breath, waiting to hear what Tristan has to say. "Okay, but if you do want to get married for real, that's okay too," he says, grabbing his iPad ending the conversation.

We both turn around in our seats ,knowing my six-year old is probably the most logical one in the car.

WE'VE BEEN IN COLORADO FOR THE LAST FIVE DAYS AND have all had a blast. Sandra and I had our spa day, one I will never forget. I'm considering taking some of Kaden's inheritance just so I can go to the spa on a weekly basis, after I pay off all my debt of course. The Swedish massage was so relaxing, and the spa pedicure...holy moly! I almost passed out from feeling so stress-free. We had lunch in the club afterward and she introduced me to all her friends.

The next day, Tristan, Kaden, and I went horseback riding through the trails with Sandra. I rode behind Kaden and Tristan rode in front of Sandra. Tristan started begging me to buy him a horse, but Kaden promised him we would come back and visit. Sandra then recommended to Kaden that he should build a barn on his property and purchase a horse. He laughed her off, but it reminded me how different we really are. I'm stripping to make a living while Kaden comes from a wealthy home with horses that are worth more than I make in a year.

Kaden's parents and grandparents are beyond sweet and have welcomed Tristan and me with open arms. There hasn't been any talk about us being engaged, for that I'm thankful, but I know it will come out before we leave.

"Hey," Kaden says, walking into our room. Tristan has his own room next to us with his own bathroom. I tried to insist on separate rooms, but Kaden said they only have two guestrooms right now because the third is filled with stuff they're donating.

"Yeah?" I ask, putting my iPad down. I'm not even concentrating on the book I'm reading anyway.

"I'm going to go meet my grandmother for brunch. When I get back, want to head into town? Go do something fun with Tristan?"

"Sure."

Kaden leans down and gives me a kiss on my nose, and then one to my forehead. "I'm really glad you and Tristan came with me."

"Me, too. We've had a lot of fun."

"I'll text you when I'm on my way back."

"Okay."

After Kaden leaves, I go in search of Tristan and find him in the back of the house throwing stones into the pond. Kaden taught him how to skip rocks last night after dinner and he's become obsessed with seeing how many times he can get his rock to skip.

"Hey sweetie. Want to go to the pool with me after I make us breakfast?"

"Yes!" he yells, throwing one last rock. It skips along the pond three times before disappearing into the water.

"Good job!"

"Kaden can make it skip like six times."

"It takes practice."

WITH OUR BATHING SUITS ON, TRISTAN AND I JUMP INTO the golf cart and head to the club. We park in the designated parking for members and go straight to the pool. Kaden's parents added us to their membership as family, so we can utilize the club while we're here.

As we are walking to the back, I spot Kaden and his grandmother and decide to stop and say hello—I didn't realize they were having brunch at the club. Before I get to them, though, a beautiful Hispanic woman, who looks to be accompanied by her parents, taps Kaden on the shoulder. He stands with a smile, and gives her a hug, then a kiss on her cheek. My heart stills. It's probably just an old friend, but then I think, what if it's Gabby, the name he has inked on him? His grandmother stands up next, hugging each of them. I watch them all for a moment before thinking it would be best not to intrude.

"Mom, there's Kaden," Tristan says a little too loud before I can get us out of the room. Kaden looks over his shoulder hearing his name. His beautiful happy face morphs into...shock? Or is it guilt? I turn to go to the pool, suddenly feeling like an intruder. Only Rose isn't having it.

"Ashley, Tristan, come here you two. I would like for you to meet Juan and Margarita Nievez and their daughter, Danielle. This is Kaden's fiancée, Ashley, and her son, Tristan."

I guess Kaden told her the news.

Mr. and Mrs. Nievez both look shocked and if I'm not mistaken, sad, at the mention of me being his fiancée but both quickly smile.

Danielle, on the other hand, doesn't even try to hide how upset this makes her. Tears well up in her eyes, and she quickly excuses herself.

"I should go find my daughter, but it was nice to meet you. I'm glad Kaden has found someone and was able to move on. He deserves to be happy," Mrs. Nievez says before excusing herself to go after her daughter.

Mr. Nievez watches her walk away, then says, "I agree. I'm glad you have moved on, Kaden." Then he turns to me. "It was lovely to meet you."

After he walks away, we all stand there in silence until Rose speaks up. "Kaden…Please tell me Ashley knows about Gabrielle and Gab…"

"No, she doesn't," Kaden says, cutting her off.

"Oh, sweetheart. Why wouldn't you tell her?"

Kaden doesn't say anything, just shakes his head.

"Why are you guys here?" Kaden asks me, his tone cold enough to freeze hell. This shocks me, because no matter how mad he gets, he's never cold with me.

"We were going to the pool. I'm sorry. I didn't mean to intrude." There's so many questions I have, but now is not the time to ask them, and I'm a bit pissed at the way Kaden just spoke to me. I don't know what is going on, but I didn't ask to be brought here nor did I ask for this fake engagement. This was all him, so he better figure his shit out.

"That's okay, dear," Rose says. "Kaden and I were just finishing up our brunch. I'm going to have my driver take me home. I'm feeling a bit tired. Kaden, you should join them in the pool."

"Yeah, Kaden! Will you come swimming with us, please? You know my mom never gets in unless you throw her in." Tristan bounces up and down, completely oblivious to the adult tension in the air.

"Sure, bud. Let me walk my grandmother out, and then I'll meet you guys at the pool."

"Okay, bye, Grannie," Tristan says. She smiles at his name for her. The first time he called her that I tried to correct him, but she just chuckled and said she loved it.

Nineteen

KADEN

MY PAST AND MY PRESENT ARE COLLIDING AND THE GUILT that's eating away at me is causing bile to rise into my throat. I never imagined in a million years that Ashley and Tristan would be meeting Gabrielle's parents and twin sister, which is stupid seeing as we're all members at the same damn club. I clearly didn't think any of this out properly.

When my grandmother introduced Ashley as my fiancée to Danielle and her parents I felt like a piece-of-shit. I wanted to warn them, but I didn't have time. As I watched Danielle run away, I wanted to chase after her so I could explain it's not real. I didn't want her thinking I would ever hurt her sister like that.

The look Ashley gave me was one that said she knew something was up. I've managed to keep my past separate from my life, but I'm going to have to explain it to her. I owe her that much.

"Why wouldn't you tell that sweet girl about your wife?" my grandmother asks while we wait for her driver to pull up.

"I haven't told anyone."

"Oh, dear! Does she know about your son?"

"No, nobody knows anything."

"They're not your dirty secret, Kaden. What happened was horrible. A horrific tragedy. But that doesn't mean you pretend it didn't happen."

"I'm not pretending it didn't happen. I live with the guilt of what happened every damn day, Grandmother."

"Kaden…" my grandmother takes my hand in hers, giving me a look of sympathy. "It's okay to move on. It's okay to remember your past and still embrace your present, as well as look forward to the future."

When I don't say anything, she takes a box out of her purse. "This is my engagement ring your grandfather bought me. I want you to have it to give to Ashley."

Taking the box from her, I open it up to find a beautiful vintage diamond ring in a simple platinum band. In the center is a large circle diamond and accented on each side are several single cut round diamonds. There are six in total, three on each side. I remember my grandmother wearing this ring years ago. I look down on her hand and see a simple platinum band.

"Why are you giving me this?"

"I'm getting older, Kaden. I haven't worn the ring in many years. I can see the way you love Ashley and her son, and it makes me so happy. I would be honored for her to wear the ring your grandfather gave me sixty-two years ago on my eighteenth birthday."

"The way I love her?" I ask. I know I love Ashley, but she can see it as well?

"The way you look at her, like she's the only person in the room. And the way you treat her son, like he's your own. It's beautiful to watch. I can't wait for the wedding. I hope you will consider having it here, so I can attend. I'm not sure I'll be able to handle flying. I'm not the young woman I once was."

"Of course we'll have the wedding here." I give her a kiss on her cheek, helping her into the car. Then I jump into my rental and head to the first place that comes into mind. My brain is foggy and my heart is pounding. I love Ashley. I've always known it, but I've refused to accept or acknowledge it, because loving Ashley would mean replacing my wife with her and I can't do that.

"She's not here," Margarita says when she opens the door. "Why don't you come in?"

"Thanks, I just wanted to apologize. There's something you guys need to know. I should have warned you. I didn't think my visit through and how it would affect you and your husband...and Danielle."

We sit on the couch, Juan joining us. "Kaden, you don't have to feel bad for moving on."

"That's just it, I didn't. I wouldn't do that to Gabrielle. My grandmother is getting older and my grandfather asked for me to marry to make her happy. It's all fake. I would never marry again, I swear."

I hear a gasp come from the side and turn to see Danielle standing in the doorway. "What do you mean it's fake? What is wrong with you?"

I'm taken back by the tone of her voice. I thought this would make them all feel better. "Of course it's fake. I would never disrespect your sister by marrying again. I promised her forever. I promised to protect her. I messed it all up."

"Oh no, Kaden." Danielle sits next to me on the couch and takes my hands in hers. "Sure, it hurts to see you move forward knowing my sister never will, but don't you ever for a second think anything that happened was your fault. You deserve to fall in love again. To be happy. You loved my sister with everything in you, but she's not here. It's okay to still love her and move on. It's okay to love someone else."

"But...I promised," I say, choked up with tears. "I promised to love her for my entire life." I stand, not sure how to deal with the emotions squeezing in my chest.

With a hand on my shoulder, Margarita turns me around and wraps me into a motherly embrace. "But your life isn't over, Kaden, and you're still so young. Please, don't you ever push love away. My daughter would never want you to live alone."

"Do you love her, Kaden?" Juan asks. "Do you love Ashley?"

I don't even have to think about it for a second. "Yes, I do. I love her so damn much. It's just..."

"No," he cuts me off. "Don't make up reasons why not to be with her, especially if you're going to place the blame on my daughter. It's okay to love, and I know my daughter would never want you to live alone and miserable."

Danielle and Margarita both pull me into a hug. "You will always be family," Danielle murmurs.

"We hope you will invite us to the wedding, Kaden. We would love to be there," Margarita says.

"Thank you, guys. Thank you for everything."

Once I'm in my car I remember I was supposed to meet Ashely and Tristan at the pool. Fuck! I call Ashley and thankfully she answers on the first ring. "Everything okay?"

I take a calming breath, finally feeling free from the guilt I've carried over these last several years.

"Yeah, it is. I'm so sorry. Are you and Tristan still at the pool?"

"We're about to head back to your parents' house now."

"Okay, please tell him I'm sorry. Can you get dressed when you get back? I need to take you somewhere. I'll have my parents watch Tristan."

THE CAR RIDE IS QUIET. ASHLEY DOESN'T TRY TO INITIATE A conversation and neither do I. I pull up to Fairmont Cemetery and can feel Ashley's eyes on mine while I drive down the dirt road. I've only been here once, eleven years ago, but I could never forget my way to where we need to go.

I park on the side, then taking Ashley's hand, we walk to our destination. When we stop in front of the two headstones, Ashley reads aloud, "Gabrielle Scott." She gasps, her hand going to her mouth.

"Your tattoo. This is Gabby." She looks at the headstone to the left. "Gabriel Scott," she reads aloud. When she doesn't say anything,

I know she's trying to put it all together. The birth and death date on Gabriel's plot are both the same. I can feel my heart squeezing in my chest. It hurts so fucking bad. I thought I could keep it all together, but being here for the first time in years is harder than I thought it would be.

Ashley's hand squeezes mine when she finally puts it altogether. Then she releases my hand to hug me. "I'm so sorry for your loss." When she pulls back, she has tears in her eyes, but they aren't the pity look I always pictured. They are full of sadness and love. My eyes burn with unshed tears, and my throat feels like I've swallowed a baseball. I pull Ashley back into a tight hug and hold her for a few minutes while I try to get myself together.

"Let's have a seat. I need to tell you what happened. Why I am the way I am."

We sit in the grass in front of the two most important people of my past.

KADEN

Eleven Years Ago

"LEFT JAB...RIGHT JAB...BLOCK...BLOCK...BLOCK!"

"I am blocking!"

"You aren't blocking and if you keep blocking like that you're going to get your ribs smashed in at the tournament this weekend."

I hear my phone ring and run over to it. I don't normally keep my phone on me while I'm teaching an MMA class but these days I have a good reason to keep it on me and everyone understands. I look at the screen and grin at the picture staring back at me of the most beautiful woman in the world.

"Hey Gabby, is everything okay?"

"Yes, but it's time."

"It's time for…?"

"Kaden! It's time to have this baby!" She giggles into the phone, making me grin harder. I know what she means, but I like to mess with her.

"I'm on my way home to get you."

"Maybe we should meet at the hospital…"

"No way, Gabs, you're not driving while in labor. I'll be right there."

"Okay, *mi amor*. I'll see you soon."

I hang up and grab my gym bag from the side of mat.

"Gotta go! Gabby is in labor."

Everybody cheers, wishing us luck, as I run to the car to go get my wife. I get to the house in less than ten minutes and she's sitting on our porch swing staring down at her belly, probably talking to the baby. She's always talking to him.

"You ready?"

She looks up and smiles. "I am! I can't wait to meet this little guy."

Grabbing her bag from next to her, I hold her arm while she adorably waddles to the car and gets into the passenger seat. I reach over her and buckle her in.

"I can buckle myself in, silly!" She giggles.

I give her a kiss on her cheek and laugh. "I know you can, but you're in labor. I'm going to make sure you don't have to do anything but bring this little guy into the world."

"You spoil me, Kaden. *Te amo*, baby."

"I don't spoil you enough. I love you too, Gabby."

I back out of the driveway and begin heading to Foothills Hospital. It's only about fifteen minutes from our house and the hospital her obstetrician delivers at.

"Ohh...Wow!" Gabby holds her stomach.

"Are you okay?" I glance over at her, concerned.

"Yeah, the contractions are just getting stronger. Distract me."

"Are you rethinking the no-drugs decision yet?"

"Very funny. I'll let you know once we get there."

"Okay." I chuckle, wondering how long it will take for her to start begging for the drugs. Her pain tolerance is probably a three.

"Do you think he will look like me or you?" Gabby asks.

"I hope he looks like you. I hope he has your dark curly hair and your black chocolate chip eyes."

"No way! My hair is a mess! I hope he has your green eyes with my tanned skin."

"What are you saying? I'm pale?" I joke.

"No!" She laughs out loud. "Well, yeah...but you know you're pale!"

"Yeah, but only against your beautiful Venezuelan skin."

The light turns red and I take a moment to glance over at my wife. She's smiling at me, excited to finally get to meet our son.

"I bet he's a beautiful mixture of the both of us," she says, looking down at her belly once again.

The light switches to green and I press the gas, moving forward slowly into the intersection. There must be some sort of accident because the road in front of us appears to be backed up.

It happens in slow motion yet so fast. In the corner of my eye, I see the tractor-trailer, and he's coming right at us. He must have run the red light. He's already too close, and I know it's too late.

Instinctively, my hand goes over Gabby's chest to protect her as the tractor-trailer hits the passenger side of the vehicle taking us with him. And then our vehicle starts rolling.

There are screams.

A crushing sound.

More screams.

And then silence.

The vehicle has stopped rolling and we're back to being in an upright position. I frantically start shouting to call nine-one-one. With shaky hands, I unbuckle my seatbelt and reach over to Gabby.

"Gabs, are you okay?" I'm shaking her shoulder, trying to wake her up.

She doesn't say anything. I search her face, but her eyes don't open. I jump out of the car and run to her side of the vehicle.

"Sir, don't move her. The ambulance is on its way."

"She's in labor!" I yell.

I open her door and reach over to unbuckle her seatbelt. There's blood everywhere: a huge gash on her forehead, cuts from glass all over her arms and legs, and then I look down and see blood all over the seat.

"Gabby, baby. Hang in there. Help is on the way." I rub her belly just like she always does and tell our little guy everything will be okay.

The EMTs arrive and within minutes they have Gabby in the ambulance. They ask to check me out, but I refuse treatment. My wife and unborn son are the only things on my mind.

We get to the hospital and they take her back, not allowing me to follow. I take the time to use the nurse's station's phone to call our families to let them know what's happened. They all let me know they're on their way.

After about an hour of waiting and pacing back and forth, a doctor walks out. "Family of Gabrielle Scott."

"Yes, I am her husband."

"I am so sorry but Gabrielle and the baby didn't make it. The internal bleeding was too severe and she lost too much blood. Her heart stopped and we couldn't save her."

"What about our son? Couldn't you take him out?"

"We attempted to deliver him via cesarean but the impact from the crash was too much. He didn't survive. I am so sorry."

I hear our family around me crying. My mom tries to hug me and I let her. I feel numb. This all feels so surreal. Like it's a bad fucking nightmare. One I will wake up from. Only it's not. It's reality, and in this moment, I wish I could go to sleep and never wake up.

"Can I see her?" I ask.

"Yes, you can see her, if you wish to."

I follow him back to the hospital room, but before the doctor opens the door, he says, "I must warn you. The accident left her banged up. She might not look like the same woman. She's covered with a sheet.

Many don't wish to remove it, they would rather have the memory of them alive than of them after they have passed away."

I simply nod then open the door. Gabrielle is lying on the bed with a white sheet covering her body.

I grab a chair from the corner and sit down next to the bed. I don't know what to say so I do the only thing I can think of. I beg her to come back to me.

"Please Gabs, I'm begging you with everything in me not to leave me. Please! I'm so sorry for not protecting you."

I push the chair away, so I'm kneeling in front of my wife.

Begging her not to leave me.

Begging God not to let her leave me.

Knowing my begging will do no good.

But still begging.

"We promised each other forever. Dammit, Gabs! Remember our vows. I love you. Please, baby!"

Lifting the side of the sheet up, I place my hand into hers, entwining our fingers and squeeze gently, but she doesn't squeeze my hand back. I know, no matter how much I beg and plead, she will not squeeze back. She's leaving me and there's not a goddamn thing I can do to change it. The truth is, even though she's right here in front of me, she's already left.

I promised to protect her and I broke that promise.

Twenty

ASHLEY

"YOU DIDN'T BREAK YOUR PROMISE. YOU COULDN'T HAVE possibly done anything different, Kaden. You are not to blame."

Kaden looks at me with sadness in his eyes, hot tears flowing down his cheeks. All these years, he's been blaming himself for his wife and son's death. I want to grab ahold of him and shake him until he realizes there was nothing he could have done.

"I know that on some level. I know it was the truck's fault for running the red light. I know it was bad circumstance, the accident in front of us leaving us in the middle of the intersection. I know all of this, but it doesn't ease my guilt. I was the one driving. I promised to protect her, and in the car with me driving, she and our son died. The most fucked up part is that the day my son was supposed to be born, he died. He never even got a chance to live."

"Tell me about her. How you two met, how you fell in love."

Kaden gives me a small smile. "We met when we were sixteen. We were sophomores. I was at the gym working out, and she decided to try out the gym. I recommended the boxing class to her while she was checking out the calendar. She showed up to the class the next day and asked if I wanted to be her partner.

"We found out we both lived in the same community and went to the same school. I couldn't believe I never noticed her before. We didn't really hang out in the same crowds, though. She was a cheerleader and I spent my time at the gym. School wasn't really my thing. I went there, did what I was supposed to do, then spent my afternoons and weekends at the gym.

"We started dating and became inseparable. After graduation, we got engaged. Gabby went to college here in Denver to get her business degree. She wanted to work with her dad. I got a job training and teaching classes locally. A couple years later, we got married, and then she got pregnant...

"After she died, I tried to live here, but it was hard. I ended up taking a job with Cooper's dad's gym. We owned a home in the same neighborhood as our families, but I couldn't live there anymore. I sold the house and moved in with Coop and Bentley for about four years.

"But even working somewhere else and living somewhere else wasn't enough. Friends of ours would see me and look at me with pity. I just couldn't take it anymore. When they decided to move to Las Vegas, I made the choice to move with them. I decided to get my own place, though. I needed to somehow move forward, so I purchased the home I live in now. Caleb was going through his own shit, so Coop asked him to join so he could room with Bentley since Cooper was buying his own place as well. This is my first time coming back to their graves since we buried them."

"So, this is why you've been single and only do one-night stands." Knowing this is the reason why my best friend doesn't want to settle down, breaks my heart.

"What if the love I have left to give isn't enough? What if I go to give my heart to someone and the pieces that are left aren't enough. If you're putting together a puzzle and only have half the pieces, can someone really feel satisfied only seeing half the picture?"

"When you find someone who loves you without limitations, she will accept any pieces you give, and her pieces will fit into that same puzzle creating a picture, it may not be perfect, but it will be beautiful nonetheless because it will be your picture. Who needs a corner piece anyway? Tristan always loses them," I say, rolling my eyes, trying to lighten the mood.

Kaden cracks the smallest, saddest smile, and my heart shatters all over for him. He's been through the worst thing anybody could ever go through, losing not only his wife, but his unborn son. He's the most beautiful man on the inside and out, and he deserves the world. Which is why I only have one choice...

"I can't marry you."

Kaden turns his head to look at me, his eyes widening. Before he can ask why, I explain.

"I want what you two had. I want a love like that. I met Tyler when I was in college and knew he wasn't good for me, but I was too young to fully get it. Listening to you tell me about Gabrielle and you, what you had was real love. I want real love. And you deserve real love. You're an amazing man, Kaden. The fact that you thought you had to stay single for the rest of your life to stay true to your deceased wife speaks volumes about the person you are. One day you're going to meet a woman who will knock you off your feet, and she is going to come with all the pieces to the puzzle you're missing. You'll fall in love, and while it won't be the same as what you and Gabby had, it won't be any less. It'll just be different. You're older and wiser, and you're capable of love."

I wipe the tears that are falling down my face. I would give anything to experience, even for a short time, the love Kaden and Gabrielle experienced.

"I can't fake marry you. I can't let you stand in front of your family and say fake vows. I'm sorry. I have never been married before, and I hope one day, when I get married, I'll have a love like the one you and your wife had. It sounds like a truly amazing kind of love."

I get up and head back to the car, not being able to sit here any longer. Kaden never says a word. He drives us back to the house in silence. While he's driving, I think about everything he told me and everything I said in return. I love Kaden. I love him with all my heart, but I know that if I married him for fake, it would leave me heartbroken in the end. And knowing he's capable of loving a woman so strongly, I can't accept just a piece of him. He deserves to meet a woman he can fully give his heart to. I know with all my heart, he would fill all the pieces to my puzzle, but it can't be one-sided. I can't put the puzzle together myself. I need his pieces to intertwine with mine.

The rest of the day flies by. Kaden tries to get me alone to speak with me, but I don't allow it. I'm already too emotional as it is and I don't want to talk with him under his parents' roof. I excuse myself to bed early after Tristan is asleep, and Kaden tells me he'll be in later. He wants to hang out with his parents since it's our last night here. Tomorrow, after his grandmother's birthday party, we'll be taking a late flight home.

THE BIRTHDAY PARTY IS BEING HELD IN A PRIVATE ROOM AT the country club. The tables are filled with various beautiful flowers, and there must be over a hundred people in attendance. Rose sits in her seat at the head of one of the tables like a queen at her throne while everybody comes over to wish her a happy birthday. She seems more tired today, reminding me why she wants Kaden to marry soon. She wants to be present. I feel bad that I can't go through with marrying him, but I don't think deceiving her with a fake marriage would be what she would want for her grandson.

"Having a good time?" Sandra asks, sitting next to me.

"I am. Tristan has made some new friends." I point to my son in the corner, playing a board game with a couple other kids.

"He's a sweet little boy. You are a wonderful mother."

"Thank you."

"So, Kaden told me he went by Gabrielle's and Gabe's graves yesterday. I take it he finally told you about them?"

"He did."

"And how do you feel about all that?" I'm not sure what she's asking me. Am I able to love a man who already gave his heart to another woman? How do I feel about the fact that he already had a child with another woman? Some women might feel threatened by the ghost of a wife and son, but if Kaden was really mine, I wouldn't be. I have learned from experience, there's different kinds of love. One isn't better or more than another.

"I hate what he went through, but I'm glad I met Kaden. He came into my life at a time when I needed a friend, and while I hate he moved to Las Vegas because of what he went through, I feel blessed to have met him. He's a strong man. He's held me up so many times when I wasn't able to stand on my own two feet, and I know one day he'll make an amazing husband." I make sure to leave anything out about being friends and not really a couple. I'm not sure if Kaden has told his family we won't be getting married after all.

"I'm so glad my son met you as well, Ashley." Sandra gives me a soft kiss on my forehead before heading to sit next to her mother-in-law.

Twenty-One

KADEN

BRINGING ASHLEY TO THE GRAVES WHERE MY WIFE AND son were buried was probably the hardest thing I've ever had to do, aside from actually burying them. I feared what she would think or say, but she handled it with such grace. I shouldn't have expected anything less from Ashley. What I didn't expect was that she would fully understand the young love Gabby and I shared. And not only did she understand it, but she accepted it.

When she told me she couldn't marry me because she wanted to find that kind of love and that she wanted me to find it again, the image of me and Ashley popped into my head because I've already found that love again. And she's right, it's not the same kind of love, but it's just as meaningful. The only difference is, with Gabby, I went in head first, but with Ashley, I've kept her at arm's length.

I felt the ring burning a hole in my pocket, but knew no matter how understanding Ashley is, asking her to marry me for real at a cemetery is a no-no. I tried several times to tell her how I felt once we left, but she avoided me the rest of our time at my parents' house. She put Tristan between us on the plane and slept the entire drive back home.

She left early Sunday morning with Tristan, leaving me a note that said she needed to buy him school supplies. I used the quiet time to get myself together. I need to make it clear to Ashley that I want more with her. I have lived so long with the guilt, blaming myself for my wife's death, that I don't even know what it feels like anymore to just focus on my own happiness. Speaking with Gabby's family was a huge turning point. When they told me they wanted me to be happy, I felt like I was finally set free. Danielle is Gabby's identical twin sister, part of why I had to move. I couldn't handle seeing her around, the same face as my wife, but still living and breathing. Her telling me it's okay to love again meant a lot to me.

"Kaden! Look what Auntie Hayley got me." Tristan comes running into the house holding a backpack with the letters UFC sewn onto the back.

"That's awesome!" Tristan runs back outside, so I follow him to see where he's going. I walk outside to see Ashley's hood popped open and the sweetest ass bent over the front of the car. She's in tiny white jean shorts, and as she reaches onto her tippy toes to look farther inside, a bit of her ass cheeks peak out, causing my dick to twitch.

"Ahem." I make a noise in my throat, and she pops up, turning around to look at me. I'm not sure what happened, but Ashley is covered in what looks like grease. She puts her hands on her hips, letting out a loud huff as she frowns.

"What happened?" I attempt to wipe some of the grease off her nose, but it's pointless. It just spreads worse, leaving her looking cute as hell.

"I don't know. The oil light came on, so I thought I would check the oil, but I can't find where it's located."

I chuckle at her obvious frustration. "Let me have a look." I open the cap to the oil, pulling the dipstick out to check how much is in there, and see it's extremely low, which makes sense since it all seems to be on my driveway.

"You definitely need more oil. When was the last time you got an oil change?"

Her nose scrunches up in confusion. "I'm not sure. One time I needed a new tire and they were running some special on oil changes, so I got it done...Maybe like a year ago?"

I break out in laughter at that. I mean, it's not funny, but it really is. "Ash, you're supposed to get your oil changed like every three to six thousand miles."

Her face grows even more confused. "Really? I read once it said recommended, but I didn't know it was actually required."

I laugh even harder, shaking my head at how clueless she is. "Why don't you bring it by my mechanic this week? I'll let him know you're coming by. He can do a tune-up, oil change, and make sure everything is running okay. There might be a leak in your oil pan."

She shrugs her shoulders. "Okay, but I'm paying for it myself."

"Whatever you say." I'll be calling him ahead of time to make sure he charges the services she gets done to my card.

When we get inside, Tristan is in the living room with school materials, spread out all around him. Pens, pencils, notebooks, crayons, markers, it looks like my living room shit out the Target back-to-school section.

"Damn, kid. You got enough stuff there? I hope you plan to get straight A's with all those school supplies."

He just laughs while filling his backpack.

"I guess I went a little overboard," Ashley says, sounding nervous. "I've never been able to buy him everything he needed. I promise I'm going to pay you back the money you gave to Giovanni. I've already figured out a budget and payment plan. Now that I bought him his school supplies, I'm going to focus on saving for a place for us and the money to pay you back."

"Hey, stop. I don't give a shit about what you bought him or about you paying me back. Did you get everything he needs?"

"Yeah, he's fine," she says quickly.

"Mom, you said you would buy me clothes and shoes once you get paid. Don't forget!"

"So, you didn't get him everything he needs?"

"He has his clothes from last year. They'll be fine until I get paid."

I remember when I was in school and every kid would show up to school on the first day sporting new threads. There's no way I'm letting Tristan go to school in last year's clothes when I can help.

"Let's go."

"Go where?" Ashley asks.

"To the mall. We need to get Tristan clothes and shoes. Let's go."

"Kaden, I'll handle it. He's fine."

"I know he's fine, but I want to do this. So, stop arguing and get your ass in the car, please. Tristan! Let's go, bud."

The mall is fucking crazy! Everybody is doing last minute school shopping. Moms are yelling at their kids to try on clothes, kids are arguing they hate collared shirts. A dad is arguing with his daughter that the skirt is too short, while the daughter pouts. A little boy, no older than Tristan, is begging for two hundred dollar shoes because they're made by his favorite basketball player. It's great!

After we pick up all the clothing necessities and Tristan picks out the shoes he wants (and no, they aren't the two-hundred-dollar basketball shoes), we head to the food court to eat dinner, where we run into Hayley and Liz.

"Oh, my God, is Kaden shopping at the mall willingly?" Liz and Hayley both laugh at Liz's dumb joke.

"Don't hate because I'm here while your husbands are...where exactly?" I look around dramatically.

"Very funny, but they actually are here. Thank you very much. They're getting our food with Bella and Marco. I made Caleb come to hold all the bags. I'm freaking exhausted. I can't believe I still have like two months to go." Hayley rubs her round stomach.

"Bella showed him the new dress she wanted out of the Victoria Secret catalogue I left on the counter and he nearly blew a gasket, insisting he join us to ensure she doesn't buy the dress." Liz rolls her eyes. I laugh at the image of Bella showing him a piece of lingerie and him almost having a heart attack.

"Why did you get dragged here?" Hayley asks.

"He didn't." Ashley huffs. "He made us come here."

I smile wide, knowing I got my way. The looks on Tristan's face when he got to pick out all the clothes he wanted was worth it. Ashley and Tristan are mine to take care of, and once we get time to ourselves to talk, Ashley will understand it's no longer her against the world. It's now me and her against the world.

"Tristan, let's go get food. Ash, pull a table over and we'll join them for lunch." I give her a quick kiss on her lips and walk away with Tristan before she can argue.

Twenty-Two

ASHLEY

"FOR A GUY WHO IS ONLY MARRYING YOU FOR PRETEND, HE seems really into you," Liz says when Kaden and Tristan walk away. When Kaden kissed me, it left me stunned. I told him I no longer wanted to marry him, so I don't know why he's still acting like we're a fake couple. We'll need to have a talk about boundaries. He keeps acting like this and I'm going to have my heart even more broken than it already will be.

"Are you guys going to Alex's fight this weekend?" I ask, ignoring Liz's comment.

"Of course," Hayley says. "I've been dying to go to New York! Caleb, Marco, and I are going to make a weekend out of it."

"We're going as well. Bella will miss school Monday, but it's fine. Cooper is going up Tuesday with Alex and Kaden, and the kids and I will meet him there on Saturday. We're flying out early Saturday morning." Liz pulls out some baby food and, after placing a bib on Nathan, starts feeding him.

"Are you going?" Hayley asks.

"Going where?" Caleb chimes in, setting their food down. Cooper and Kaden set their trays down as well, and the kids grab their happy meals from Chick-fil-A, taking them to a table next to us, apparently starting their own kids' table.

"New York," I say, then turn to Kaden, who's taking a bite of his grilled chicken sandwich. "I didn't know you were leaving to New York on Tuesday."

Kaden finishes chewing. "Yeah, we leave early as hell Tuesday morning. You and Tristan should join me. You guys can fly over with the other women for the weekend. Saturday will be crazy busy, but we can spend the day together Sunday and Monday before we all fly back."

"I'm not sure I can take off work. Caleb already let me off for the week to visit your family. It would be rude to ask for time off again. Plus, I need the money," I whisper to Kaden, hoping nobody else hears.

"You can have off." Caleb winks at me and Kaden laughs.

"And we're taking the private plane so it won't cost you a dime," Liz chimes in.

"Are you working tonight?" Kaden asks.

"Yeah."

"We need to talk."

"Okay, but it's going to have to wait. I actually need to get going soon, so I'm not late to work."

Kaden glares but doesn't say a word.

"Mom, when is the *Newbreed* tournament?" Bella asks Liz.

"Next month, sweetie."

"Can Tristan go?"

"That's up to his mommy, Bella."

The Newbreed tournament is a fighting tournament for amateur fighters and focuses on the fighter's techniques they've learned in class such as Brazilian Jujitsu. The classes Kaden and Bentley teach are mostly BJJ and grappling. Bella goes to most of the tournaments in the area and some in other states, but Tristan and Marco have never been. They're expensive to enter, and if they aren't local, you have to pay for travel and the hotel.

"Marco and I are going," Bella says. "Can Tristan go too? We're going to visit Mickey at Disney too!"

"That sounds like a lot of fun, but..."

"That does sound like fun," Kaden cuts me off. "Tristan, would you want to go? Do you feel confident enough to enter the tournament?"

Tristan's face lights up, and I want to punch Kaden in his face.

"Yes! I know I'm ready. Can I go, Mom?"

"We'll talk about it at home. I really need to get to work. Say goodbye to your friends."

I get up quickly, throwing my food away, then say bye to everyone. I start walking quickly to the car, ignoring Kaden calling my name. Once I'm at the car, I have no choice but to wait outside the passenger door for him. I obviously didn't think this through.

"What's your deal?" Kaden asks when he catches up to me.

"Can we talk about this later?" I glance Tristan's way hoping Kaden will get my hint of not wanting to discuss this in front of Tristan. I'm embarrassed enough that Kaden brought it up in front of our friends. He knows damn well I can't afford to just fly to Orlando, and there's no way I'm taking more money from him. I owe him enough as it is.

We never get a chance to talk, though. I rush off to work, and then get home late. When I get up in the morning, Kaden is already gone to the gym. Tristan and I head to visit his new teacher and new school at open house. Then we go to lunch with Hayley. I hate spending unnecessary money, but Hayley pretty much threatened our friendship if I didn't join her.

"Hey girly!" Hayley adorably waddles into the restaurant. "Did you meet your teacher, Tristan?"

"Yeah. Her name is Mrs. Luongo and she's nice."

"I can't believe Marco is starting middle school this year! I had to drop him off for his open house. They spend the day showing the sixth graders around so they aren't lost and confused tomorrow."

After the waitress comes over and takes our order, Hayley says, "Soo...Caleb said he's hoping you'll take over managing soon."

"I hope so, too."

"Why are you still..." She leaves out dancing since Tristan is sitting at the table with us. He's coloring a picture on the kid's menu, but you never know what he's listening to. "...if he offered to let you train without..."

"I'm not letting him just give me the job. I'll lose the respect of all the other employees there. I need their respect to run the club. I'm learning a lot and I plan to switch to management before the baby comes."

Hayley rolls her eyes but doesn't argue. "Okay."

"Have you thought of any names for the little girl in your belly?"

"Yes, but Caleb, Marco, and I aren't in agreement. I should get the final say. I'm the one incubating this little princess for nine months, after all. Do you think you will ever have another baby?"

"I hope so, but the next time I have a baby I'd like to be in a relationship that's more stable. I would rather not have to do it on my own again. But right now, I need to focus on finding a place to live."

"Did Kaden kick you out?" Hayley's eyes turn sinister, switching into best friend mode. We've become extremely close over the last year or so.

I want to tell her about Kaden and what I now know about him, but it's not my place to say anything.

"No! No, he would never do that. But I've told him I can't marry him for pretend anymore. I want to marry a guy that I love. A guy that loves me back, and not just as a best friend."

"Well, I know you love Kaden...as more than a best friend."

"Yeah, but he doesn't feel the same way. He doesn't want to get married for real, and even though I respect his choices, I can't be the one to do it."

"Have you told him this?"

"Yeah, and he wasn't too thrilled. He's said we need to talk, but we haven't had time. We've both been crazy busy since we got home."

My cell phone dings.

Kaden: We had to leave for New York today instead of tomorrow. The photoshoot needed a couple more shots before the fight. Can Britni babysit

tonight? Or you just quit?

"Oh, shoot. Kaden let me know they had to leave earlier than planned. He was supposed to babysit tonight. I forgot to tell him Britni left for college. He's been home with Tristan lately, so I forgot to mention it."

Ignoring his comment about me quitting, I type back: **I'll handle it. Have a safe flight!**

"Why don't you just have him spend the night with me?"

"Okay, thanks. Damn, it's his first day of school. I wanted him to get a full night of sleep at home."

"It will be fine."

After lunch, Hayley takes Tristan with her, so I can head to work. The night isn't too busy, and I'm able to close the club down on time right at two with the help of Scarlett. After I started working at *Assets*, Scarlett applied for a job and was hired as well. I love getting to work with her again. Thursday through Saturday the upstairs is open, but Sunday through Wednesday only the first floor with the restaurant are open.

"How's the training going?" she asks as the bouncer on duty escorts us to our vehicles.

"It's going good. I just always thought my career would be geared toward children, not managing a club. You know, with your business degree and experience, I bet he would train you as well. He is going to need someone else once he's back to fighting full time."

"That would be awesome. I'd love to learn more about the club business. I'm getting my master's in business management. I'd love to manage a club. I'm actually hoping to open one myself one day."

"I'll talk to him and see what he says."

"Thanks, Ashley. Have a good night."

After I get home from work, I'm shocked to find Hayley and Caleb both sleeping in the guest bed and Marco and Tristan asleep in Tristan's bed. I'm so thankful to have the friends that I have.

Twenty-Three

KADEN

I NEVER GOT A CHANCE TO SPEAK WITH ASHLEY BEFORE I had to leave for New York, but I'm going to speak to her once she and Tristan arrive Saturday. I just need to make arrangements for Tristan so we can speak alone.

Me: How would you like to do me a favor?

Hayley: What kind of favor?

Me: Watch Tristan for Ashley and me Saturday night. I need to talk to her alone.

Hayley: Does it involve you breaking her heart?

Me: I'm hoping the opposite.

Hayley: Don't fuck it up or I'll beat your ass!

Damn! When did Hayley get so violent?

Hayley: That wasn't me! That was Caleb! But I agree with him! <insert red

faced mad emoji>

Every day I've been gone, Ashley and I have texted but it's been very formal.

How are you?

What are you up to?

How was Tristan's first day at school?

Now it's Saturday and I'm excited to finally see her and Tristan. It's crazy how much I've missed them.

I wanted to be there at the airport to pick them up, but I need to focus on Alex and his fight. Caleb flew in with all the girls, so he's driving them to the hotel to get situated before they meet us here at Madison Square Garden for the fight. I insisted Ashley and Tristan stay with me in my room so she can't say anything about spending money on a hotel room.

THE NIGHT IS LONG BUT FUCKING AMAZING. ALEX IS THE main event and kicks ass. He wins with a knockout in the third round and the crowd goes crazy for him. I'm damn proud of the kid. We all decide to meet up at the local club to have a drink to celebrate. Hayley didn't want to go to the club in her pregnant state so she and Caleb brought Tristan and Marco back to the hotel with them. I'm planning to have one celebratory drink then taking off with Ashley so we can finally talk.

Since the arena was crazy, and Ashley was sitting with Cooper, we agreed to meet up at the club. Somehow, I got here first, right after

Alex and his wife. We order a round of double shots of Johnny Walker Black, toasting to his win. Because of the fight being on pay-per-view, Alex is VIP and we have an entire area to ourselves.

I feel small hands come around my waist, but when I look down they're fake and painted red. Ashley's nails are real and she paints hers herself. Grabbing the woman's hand, I remove them from my body and turn around to move her away as well. When I turn, she quickly moves her body up against mine, attempting to grind up against me.

"Hey there, handsome, want to buy me a drink?" She reaches past me to grab one of the shots, and downs it.

"Umm, no, I don't. So, take that shot as a parting gift and walk your ass away now." Unfortunately, she isn't taking no for an answer and tries again by running her hand down my chest. This time, I take her hands in mine and, holding them tight, push them off my body, forcing her body away from mine. She pouts but gets the message.

I grab another shot and sit in one of the booths to look for Ashley. Through the crowd, I spot a glaring Liz, but don't see Ashley or Cooper. She walks toward me, her eyes shooting daggers.

"Where's Ashley and Cooper?"

"I'm pretty sure she went back to the hotel room."

"What? We said we were meeting here."

"She saw that skanky woman all over you and took off. Cooper chased her outside."

"Fuck! I need to go find her."

I run out of the club to see if I can find Cooper and Ashley, hoping she hasn't left yet. I spot Cooper walking back with no Ashley in sight.

"She took off. I made sure she got safely into a cab."

"Damn it! All right, I'm going to go find her."

A cab pulls up and I jump in. "Four Seasons."

"Sure thing."

After swiping my card to pay, and adding a tip, I head through the lobby to the elevator to the room Ashley and I are sharing, praying she's in the room. She's never traveled anywhere and New York is not the place to go exploring on your own.

"Ash? You here?" I call out.

She's sitting on the couch, crying. "Go away."

"I'm not going anywhere until we talk about us."

"I have nothing to say to you."

"There's plenty to say."

"What? Like you are a manwhore, who would rather be with random women than with one who actually cares about you." She sniffles, refusing to make eye contact with me. The manwhore comment rubs me the wrong way, and before I can think about what I'm doing, I lash out at her.

"Seriously? I'm a manwhore? That's rich coming from a stripper." I regret the words the minute they leave my mouth.

"Wow, Kaden...real nice. I'm stripping to make a living. You're whoring around by choice."

"I'm sorry, but I'm not whoring around, Ash. The only woman I want is you." I raise my voice, getting pissed off. This is not how I wanted this conversation to go.

"Yeah, for fake."

"No, for real. I want you for real, Ash."

"What about all the women?" she spits out.

My arms open wide to make my point. I'm so fucking annoyed right now. "What fucking women, Ashley? What. Fucking. Women?"

"What about the woman at the bar tonight? Huh?"

"Oh, give me a damn break! You saw some skank come on to me and didn't even stay long enough to see the outcome. You saw what you wanted to see. You have it in your head I'm off sleeping around with all these women, when the truth is, I haven't had sex with anyone but you in the last nine fucking months! And sadly, I don't even remember us having sex."

"You haven't?" Her eyes finally meet mine, and I take a deep breath.

"No one, baby. You're all I want." I bend in front of her, taking her hands in mine. "The day we talked at the cemetery, I knew you were it for me. No, that's a lie. I've always known it was you. I just chose to be in denial out of guilt. The day in the cemetery, when I told you about Gabby, and you didn't get jealous, but instead said you wanted what we had, I finally accepted it. I love you, Ashley, and I don't want to live in guilt anymore. I want to love you and Tristan. I want to marry you for real."

Ashley gives me a watery smile, wiping her eyes. "I love you too, Kaden."

That's all I need to hear. I grab Ashley's ass, pick her up and carry her to the bedroom, tossing her onto the bed. "The last time we had sex doesn't count. I was drunk and didn't remember it, and I'm sure I fucking sucked. But I promise you, tonight, when I make love to you, not only will I remember it, but I will make up for the first time, and you will never forget it."

Ashley laughs loudly. "We didn't have sex, Kaden. Yeah, we made out some, but then you felt sick and ran to the bathroom to throw up. I brought you some water and you threw up on me as well. We both got naked and showered, and when I tried to get dressed, you grabbed my clothes and hid them. You were so adamant we sleep naked, I didn't want to argue with your drunk ass."

"Oh, thank God." I remove my shirt and shorts, leaving only my boxers on. She sits up, lifts her shirt over her head, then lifts her ass up, pushing her pants down. Getting onto the bed, I go to hover above her, but instead she pushes me down so I'm lying on my back. Then she crawls onto my lap, placing one leg on either side of me. Her ass is grinding against my stomach as she leans down to kiss me. Her lips are soft, and her tongue moves in perfect sync with mine.

Grabbing her ass, I sit up, moving her body down, so it's rubbing against my cock. We continue to kiss, our tongues moving frantically against each other as she grinds against me, creating perfect friction with our bodies through our clothes. Reaching behind her, I unclasp her bra then bring the straps down her arms, exposing her perfect, luscious tits. Just as I'm about to take one of her perky pink nipples into my mouth, she pushes me back down again.

Starting at my chest, she trails wet kisses down my torso slowly, too damn slowly, until she gets to my cock. My fingers are entwined in her hair, letting her know it feels good, but not forcing her to do anything she doesn't want to do. She clearly wants to be in control and

I'm man enough to give that to her.

She gives my cock an open-mouthed kiss over my boxers, then looks up at me smiling shyly. Her smile is infectious. She moves my boxers down just enough, that my hard cock springs out ready for her. She wastes no time grabbing the shaft, jerking it slowly as she swirls her tongue over the head. She brings her mouth down the entire length until I feel the head of my cock hit the back of her throat. "Holy fuck, Ashley."

She moans around my dick, then continues to suck and pump my shaft. For several minutes, she fucks my me with her mouth and tongue...fucking her mouth isn't even the right word, though. It's like she's making love to it, worshiping it. The slurping and sucking sounds cause my dick to grow even harder, to the point I feel like I'm going to come. I refuse for this to come to an end this soon, though.

As I gently pull her head up by her hair, her mouth comes off my dick, making a popping sound. She looks up at me frowning like I just took away her favorite toy. "Baby, I need your pussy."

Grabbing her ass, I flip us over so I'm once again on top. Her lips are plump and swollen from being wrapped around my dick, begging to be kissed. Leaning down, my mouth connects with hers. Our tongues move frantically against each other. I can't get enough of her.

She grips my dick cock and strokes it. "I need you," she murmurs against my mouth.

Needing to feel her lips once again, I give her a chaste kiss then nibble on her bottom lip. Then I lick it once, needing to taste her before I move to her tits, sucking on each one until her nipples harden into perfect rosy peaks.

"Kaden..." She moans out my name with need.

"I got you, baby."

Grabbing her hands, I place them on her tits so she can continue to play with her nipples herself, as I lick a trail down her middle.

My eyes never leave her hands as they twist and pull at her nipples, causing her to moan softly. Once I'm at her pussy, I pull her panties down, then give her bare pussy lips a soft kiss. Spreading them open, I run my tongue over her clit then bite down softly.

"Kaden, please..." Ashley's moans get louder, needier, more desperate.

Placing two fingers into her, I fingerfuck her while I suck on her clit. I look up and see she's still massaging her tits, her eyes are closed and her head is tilted back in pure ecstasy. I stick another digit in, pushing in deep to hit her G-spot. Her back arches, telling me she's close. I could make her come like this, but something in me needs to be in her when she comes.

I pull my fingers out, then crawl up her body until my dick is lined up with her warm center. I move her hands from her tits, replacing them with my own as guide myself into her tight pussy. Slowly thrusting in and out, I tease her pussy while tweaking her nipples.

"Kaden! Harder! Please..."

Grabbing her hands and placing them in mine, I pin them over her head then start to pump my cock in and out of her, faster and deeper.

"Yes, fuck yes," she groans.

Grabbing her leg, I lift it up and over my shoulder so I can go deeper. Ashley's groans turn to screams, her voice now hoarse. A few deep thrusts more and she's coming all over my cock. When she comes down from the orgasm, she sits up and, pushing me back, grabs my shaft in her hand, guiding my hard length back into her warmth. Up and down, she rides me as I watch, entranced by her perky fucking tits bouncing up and down. I grab one in my hand and pull it to me to suck on it hard, causing Ashley to pick up the pace. Her inner walls grip my cock like a vice, letting me know she's ready to come again.

To help her along, I push my thumb into her wetness. I can feel her pussy wrapped around my dick, gliding up and down. Using her juices, I massage her clit. "Fuuuck...Kaden! I'm going to come again," she screams. Her pussy contracts as she finds her orgasm, only this time I'm right there with her, spilling my seed into her as she milks my dick of every last drop.

Twenty-Four

ASHLEY

AFTER WE BOTH FIND OUR RELEASE, I ATTEMPT TO MOVE off Kaden, but he isn't having it. "Not yet. I just need to hold you for a minute." Leaning down, I put my head on his chest, feeling his flaccid cock still in me, our mixed juices running down the insides of my thighs.

"I'm on birth control," I whisper. I don't want him to think I'm going to trap him into anything.

"Well, you need to get off that shit immediately. What are you on? The pill?"

"Yeah..."

"Throw that shit away. I don't want to waste any more time with you. I'm thirty-five years old and I'm sure as shit not getting any younger. I was a fucking idiot, Ash. I want to marry you and I want us to have mini versions of us running around." He gives me a kiss on my forehead as I turn my head to look at him. I'm shocked at what I'm hearing. Not even a week ago he was sharing with me stories about his deceased wife and baby, and now he's telling me he wants me to mother his future children. I sit up and try to get off him again, needing some space. This time, he lets me.

Taking the blanket from the bed, I wrap myself up and go straight to the bathroom to get cleaned up. I turn the shower on and wait for it to heat up.

"What's wrong?" Kaden asks. coming up behind me. I didn't realize he followed me into the bathroom.

"It just seems too good to be true. I've learned the hard way that if it seems good, there's probably a catch." I'm still facing the shower, my back to his front, not wanting to look him in the eyes, not wanting him to see the insecurity I feel.

Kaden bridges the gap between us, dropping the blanket to the floor and wrapping his arms around me. He places soft kisses along my neck. "What we have is real, baby. We've always had this. I was just too consumed with guilt to open my eyes and see what I have right in front of me. I love you and Tristan." Kaden turns me around, then drops to one knee, and right there in the bathroom, with both of us naked and vulnerable, he opens a small black box showing me the most beautiful diamond engagement ring. "Marry me, Ashley. Not for pretend or for an inheritance. Marry me because you love me and I love you, and we belong together. I can't change the past, baby, but I can create a future, and I want to create one with you and Tristan as a family."

His words choke me up. My throat feels like it is clogged with a large lump in it, not allowing me to speak. So, I nod. I nod repeatedly as tears spill down my cheeks. Then I wrap my arms around Kaden and kiss him like he is everything to me. Because he is.

He throws the ring box onto the counter and picks me up, my legs wrapping around him, and opens the shower door, taking us both inside without breaking our kiss. The hot water rains down on us as he pushes me against the wall devouring me. His hard length pushes against my ass, so I wiggle a little to let him know what I want. Kaden chuckles softly, stopping our kiss.

"You want me in you, baby?"

"Yes."

"Oh? So, you will say yes to my dick, but not to my marriage proposal?" He moves my wet hair from my face, then starts to suck on my neck until it tingles.

"Yes! Yes to marrying you. Yes to having babies with you. Please, just fuck me."

"No."

"No?" I snap my head up, rejecting him access to my neck.

"What do you mean no?"

"I'm not fucking you, Ash. I'm making love to you. It might be dirty as fuck, but I'm making love to you."

Tightening his grip on my ass, he pushes me farther against the wall, then with one hand, guides his dick into me. He starts off slow, thrusting in and out of me, but once his dick is completely hard and deep inside me, he grips my ass and begins pounding into me, the sound of wet flesh slapping echoing in the bathroom. The angle at which he hits, ignites a spark deep within me, and a few thrusts later, my pussy spasms around his dick as Kaden grunts out his orgasm.

"Jesus, I can't get enough of you." Kaden sets me down on shaky legs and I use the wall to hold myself up. Three orgasms in one night is a record for me. Tyler was the only guy I slept with, and he was way too selfish in bed to try to make me come once let alone three times.

Kaden and I wash up in silence, then he turns the water off, grabbing us both towels. Once we're both dried off, we grab clothes from our luggage. He looks sexy as hell in his basketball shorts and white shirt, while I'm in my long cotton pajamas. I probably should have packed something sexier.

"My relationship status is Netflix, pajamas, and wine," Kaden says, reading the front of my shirt. "I will gladly Netflix and chill with you, baby, but your relationship status is taken." Kaden laughs at his own joke, giving me a wink.

"You're such a cheeseball!" I slap his chest, laughing at his cheesiness. I grab a bottle of water from the mini fridge then climb into bed, pulling the covers over me. Kaden runs back into the bathroom then joins me, lying on his side and pulling me close to him. He grabs my leg and hooks it over his own, cuddling close to me, then holds out the black box from earlier.

"We didn't make it to the part where you put the ring on. This is my grandmother's ring. She gave it to me while we were in Colorado to give to you. She knew I was too in denial to admit how much I love you. Will you wear this ring and become my wife?"

This time, I voice the words I couldn't earlier. "Yes, Kaden. I will marry you."

He plucks the ring out of the cushion and places it onto my finger.

It fits perfectly.

"It's beautiful."

"You're beautiful. The ring simply complements your beauty." He brings his lips to mine, making love to my mouth before he makes love to me for the third time tonight.

Twenty-Five

ASHLEY

"I WANT TO GO TO SEE LADY LIBERTY!" BELLA SQUEALS.

"Yeah! Me, too!" Tristan agrees.

"Oh! And I want to go to American Girl!"

"No! I don't want to go there. I want to go to the big Toys 'R' Us." Tristan shakes his head in disagreement.

When we told Cooper and Liz we were going to spend the day checking out New York, they decided to join us. Hayley, Caleb, and Marco flew back this morning with Alex and his wife, Jessica. We're all going to fly back tomorrow afternoon.

"How about we take the ferry around the statue of liberty, then while Bella goes to American girl, we can take you to the toy store?"

"Yes!" Tristan and Bella both yell in unison, jumping up and down.

"You and I are going to come back here, just the two of us, one day," Kaden says into my ear. "I want to show you central park, take you shopping, and spoil you with fancy eating."

"You already spoil me. I don't need any of that. I just need you." I give him a quick peck on the lips. He pouts when I pull away, pulling me toward him and deepening our kiss.

"Eww! Mom! Kaden! I thought you were just playing pretend for Grannie. That's not pretend!" We both stop kissing, and see Tristan's cute little face all scrunched up in disgust.

"Yeah, guys. Thought it was pretend..." Cooper adds with a laugh.

"Oh. My. God!" Liz shrieks, grabbing my left hand and narrowing in on my engagement ring. "This ring is most definitely not pretend!"

"Yeah, about that..." I begin to think of a way to explain to my almost seven-year-old about our engagement, but Kaden beats me to it.

"Remember you said it would be okay if I married your mom for real?"

"Yeah."

"You still cool with that, bud?"

"Yes!" Tristan runs to Kaden and throws his arms around him. Kaden picks him up and hugs him back, before setting him back down.

"So, when's the wedding?" Liz asks.

"We haven't picked a day..." I say, but Kaden cuts me off. "As soon as possible."

"I guess as soon as possible," I repeat, laughing.

We spend the entire day experiencing New York. After we take the ferry around the statue of liberty, we go to the nine-eleven memorial site. Then, while Bella goes with her parents to American Girl, we take Tristan to the toy store. Kaden buys him tons of toys that Tristan swears are only available in New York. Afterward, we all meet up to eat dinner before heading back to the hotel for the night. It was a great day, one I won't ever forget.

IT'S MONDAY NIGHT AND WE'RE BACK HOME AND JETLAGGED, lying on the couch watching TV. Tristan passed out the minute we walked through the door. Kaden's phone rings alerting him of a Facetime call. "It's my grandmother." He swipes accept, then her face comes onto the screen. "Hello, Grandmother. How are you?"

"I'm good, sweetie. I just wanted to check in...any news?"

Kaden chuckles. "Real subtle, Grandmother." Taking my hand, he puts it up to the camera for her to see. "Oh! Yay! I am so glad you are wearing my ring."

"It is gorgeous, Rose. Thank you for passing it down to us. I will always cherish it."

"And when is the wedding?"

"We haven't picked a date yet."

"How about a spring wedding?" she suggests.

Kaden looks to me for my approval. A spring wedding in his hometown sounds beautiful.

"I think that would be wonderful."

"Victor! Did you hear that?" Rose calls out, moving out of the line of the camera.

"Yes, Rose, honey. I heard. A spring wedding. Congratulations, you two."

"Thank you, Victor."

"Thank you, Grandfather."

"I'm going to call Sandra and let her know we need to start planning a wedding. Ashley, dear, would it be possible for you to visit soon so we can go dress shopping?"

"I'll have to look at my work schedule, but I should be able to make it work." Kaden glares at me, and then it hits me, my work schedule. I'm engaged to be married to Kaden and I'm still a stripper.

After we say goodbye, I address the elephant in the room. "I'll speak to Caleb about only managing the club. I'm still going to pay you back, though."

"No, you aren't. You're my fiancée, soon to be my wife, and hopefully soon to be the mother of my children. You aren't paying me back a damn dime. Part of being in a relationship means everything separate comes together as one."

"Kaden, I can't just take thousands from you and not pay you back."

"It's *ours*, everything is ours. And once we're married, you will be an extremely wealthy woman so you better get used to it. I'm not going to stop you from managing the club, but once you're pregnant, I hope you'll consider taking some time off. You said before you had to work while Tristan was little. You don't have to work, baby." Kaden takes my hand in his, squeezing it lightly. "Just think about it, okay?"

"Okay, I will. Do you think we should wait until after we're married for me to get off birth control?"

"Hell no. I researched it on the plane and it can take months for the hormones to leave your body. Tristan is already almost seven years old. No more pills, and if you get pregnant, great. We'll be married soon anyway." Kaden leans toward me, our lips meeting for a moment before he pulls back. "Let's go to bed. I think we need to practice making a baby. Practice makes perfect, you know." He shoots me a flirty wink before he stands up and, taking my hand in his, guides us to the bedroom where we practice making a baby...three times.

"NO. NO. NO. NO!" MY FOOT PRESSES THE BRAKE WHILE MY hands hold tightly onto the steering wheel. Cars are honking and flying around me as I try to steer my car to the side of the road. I finally get it out of traffic and turn it off. Stepping out of the car, I smell something burning, and before I can pop the hood, a loud booming sound goes off and my hood is in flames.

My phone, purse, and keys are all in the car, so calling nine-one-one is out of the question. It's a busy street and luckily someone pulls over. A gentleman who looks to be in his mid-thirties gets out of his sports car and comes jogging over to me. I recognize him from somewhere, but I can't put my finger on it.

"Your car is going to explode, you need to get back," the gentleman screams at me. Grabbing my body, he drags me away from the car and, a few seconds later, my car does indeed explode. The entire car is in flames. Black smoke is rising from the hood, and the windows are shattering from the force of the heat.

The man who saved my life calls the fire department and gives them our location, then after he hangs up, hands me the phone. "I'm thinking you might need to call someone to let them know."

"Thank you. How did you know my car was going to blow up like that?"

"My name is Benjamin Fields. Racing is a hobby of mine. Cars are my life. I saw the color of the smoke coming out of your hood and knew immediately it would blow. I'm just glad I got to you in time."

"Thank you for saving me. My name is Ashley Myers. Do I know you from somewhere? You look so familiar."

He gives me a sheepish smile before he says, "Yeah, I'm friends with Caleb, your boss. I've been to *Assets* a few times. I bought the one from him in Colorado and I'm interested in buying this one as well. I've seen you dance."

Okay...and now it's officially awkward.

We both stand at a distance from the car in silence, watching the fire engines and police pull up and work together to put the fire out.

"I'm going to call my fiancé." I hold up the phone he handed me a few minutes ago. He's probably at the gym and doesn't have his phone on him, but I try anyway.

After the third ring, Kaden answers. "Kaden Scott."

"Hey...Kaden, it's Ashley."

"Ashley? What number are you calling from?"

"Umm...Well, it's a long story, but I'm using Benjamin Fields's phone..."

"Who the hell is Benjamin Fields?"

"A man." I mean, really, how the heck else do I answer that?

"Ashley, why the *fuck* are you using another man's phone to call me?"

"Kaden! If you would stop cutting me off, I can explain," I whisper-yell, not wanting Benjamin to think Kaden is crazy.

When Kaden doesn't say anything, I continue. "My car kind of had an issue, and I need you to come get me." Benjamin chuckles next to me at my downplaying of the vehicle blowing up.

"What kind of issue, Ash? You were supposed to bring it to my mechanic."

"I know, but we got busy with going to New York. I might have forgot...and umm...well...it may have caughtonfireandblewup."

"It what?"

"It caught on fire and blew up."

"What. The. Fuck. Woman! Where are you?"

I give Kaden the location of where I am, and he tells me he's on his way before hanging up.

"Thank you," I say softly, handing him back his phone. "You don't have to stay. My fiancé will be here shortly."

"That's okay. I think I'll wait here with you. He sounded kind of pissed on the phone," Benjamin says worriedly.

"Okay, if you want."

We both have a seat in the grass and watch the firemen continue to work on containing the flames that are still rising from my burnt hunk-of-junk.

"So, you want to buy Assets?" I ask, trying to make conversation.

"Yeah. I own several clubs. At the time when I bought Assets in Colorado, he told me he wasn't interested in selling the one here, but he's apparently changed his mind. I love the concept he's created and would love to buy this one from him so I can trademark the name."

Before I can respond, Kaden pulls up. "Oh, my fiancé is here." I point to his car stopping right in front of Benjamin's car.

"Your fiancé drives a fucking Aston Martin while you drive that piece of shit?" Benjamin looks from me to Kaden's car incredulously.

"Yeah, well, I am a stripper, remember?" My hand goes to my mouth to stop the word vomit.

Benjamin shoots daggers at Kaden as he comes running over to us.

"Baby, are you okay?" Kaden pulls me into his arms, planting kisses all over my face and neck.

"She would've been killed by fire in that death trap if I hadn't pulled up and gotten her away from the vehicle," Benjamin barks.

Kaden stops kissing me and turns to Benjamin. "Thank you for saving my girl's life. I owe you one for sure." Kaden assesses Benjamin for a moment before extending his hand to offer a shake.

Benjamin glares at his hand. "Why the fuck is *your girl* driving around in that death trap while you're driving that." He points from the scraps of my burnt-to-crisp car to Kaden's vehicle that I'm sure is worth more than most people's homes.

"Trust me when I tell you she won't be driving around in a piece of shit like that again."

"She shouldn't have been driving around in it in the first place, let alone working at a strip club."

"I thanked you for saving my girl, but now I'm going to ask that you mind your own damn business."

The guys stare each other down and I swear I can smell the

metaphorical piss running down my leg as Kaden takes me into his arms.

"Okay, well, Benjamin, I appreciate you caring about my well-being, but since you don't know us, you wouldn't know that I chose to drive this car. I don't accept help very well. So, let's all calm down."

"It looks like the fire is close to being put out. I'll let them know I was here when it happened in case they have any questions. I'm sure I'll see you around, Ashley."

Benjamin gives Kaden a curt nod before walking toward the police officer.

"How the fuck does he know you work at a strip club?"

"He's been in there before. He owns the club in Colorado and is looking to buy the one here from Caleb as well."

"First, we're going to go get Tristan from school, then we're going to buy you a new car, and I don't want to hear a single complaint out of your mouth." Kaden grabs my hips and gives me a kiss that makes me want more.

"Okay."

"And Ashley..."

"Yes?"

Kaden looks me in the eyes. "Please, baby. No. more. Stripping."

"Okay."

Twenty-Six

KADEN

WHEN ASHLEY TOLD ME HER CAR HAD ISSUES, I WAS PISSED. At myself, for not forcing her to get a new car sooner. At her, for being so damn stubborn. Then, once I got there and saw her piece-of-shit car looked like a marshmallow placed over the bonfire for about ten hours too long, I just about flipped my lid. Ashley could have been killed. The car could have exploded with her in it.

The visual of the car on fire caused my anger to dissipate, fear taking its place. Visions of Gabrielle dying in my car all those years ago invaded my thoughts. Then to have that motherfucker insinuate I'm letting Ashley strip while putting her in danger by making her drive that shitty car while I'm driving a two hundred thousand dollar car made my blood boil. I don't give a fuck what Ashley wants, she's getting a new, expensive, top of the line, safe vehicle and she better not argue with me. I've let her run this show every step of the way, but I'm done.

After we pick Tristan up from school and go by the wireless store to get Ashley a new cell phone, we head to the Land Rover dealership.

"Oh, c'mon, Kaden. A Range Rover? Everybody always gets one of those. Don't make me be a cliché, please."

"Okay, so what do you want?"

"I don't know...like a Toyota, maybe."

"Ashley, you can be reasonable or I will get you whatever I want."

She huffs loudly, annoyed with me. I don't give a shit. She's my queen. She should be driving something equivalent to me. I know it's fucking petty, but that Benjamin guy pissed me off.

Using her phone, she searches through images of vehicles until she stops at one, showing it to me. "This one is cute."

"A Maserati Levante? It's more than cute, babe. That car is badass." She has no idea she just picked out a car almost worth half of mine.

I pull up the directions to the Maserati dealership in our area and see it's not too far from us.

With Tristan in tow, we park and enter the dealership. Without letting her see any prices, I ask the salesman if Ashley can test drive the car she wants. After giving them her proof of insurance and driver's license, we all get into the SUV to check it out.

"I love this car!" Ashley is bouncing around in her seat like a little kid on a sugar high as she runs her fingers across the leather and messes with all the knobs. When she puts the vehicle into reverse, the view behind her pops up. "Oh, my God! It has a camera! Like Liz's car!"

We pull out onto the main road and go for a quick test drive. The car drives smoothly and Ashley is in car heaven. Once we get back, we park and head back inside so we can purchase the car.

While I'm talking to the salesman, I hear Ashley screech. "Kaden! That SUV is like a hundred grand! I can't get that!"

I laugh at her freak out. She test-drove the SUV and fell in love immediately. She's getting the vehicle. I figured she had no idea of the kind of vehicle she showed me and her freak out right now confirms it, but it's neither here nor there.

"What color?"

"Kaden! How can you afford this car?"

"It's just a payment, babe. It's fine."

"Yeah, a goddamned mortgage payment."

"What color, Ash?"

Tristan is running around the dealership checking out all the cars, picking out his future car based on how many televisions are in the seats. Priorities.

"White, I guess."

"White, really?"

"Well, I heard once white is cheaper than other colors."

I laugh at that. "I'm pretty sure that's not true. Paint is paint. They just usually have white in stock. Now, what color do you want?"

"Umm...well...I like the blue your car is."

"Aww, babe, you want to have matching colored cars?" I throw my arm over her shoulder and give her cheek a kiss. "That's such a couple thing to do." I shoot her a wink.

After we have her car ordered and paid for, they send us off in a loaner so Ashley will have a car to drive until her new one comes in. The color and style she wants needs to be shipped from another location.

"I have to work tonight. Can you take Tristan, so I can go straight to work?"

"Sure," I say, giving her a kiss tenderly. I'm so thankful today didn't end up with her hurt or worse...dead.

"No stripping, Ash," I whisper into her ear.

"I didn't think about it, but I'm already on the schedule tonight."

"I already texted with Caleb and he said it's fine."

"Kaden!"

"Love you, babe." I smack her ass and walk to my car where Tristan is already in the back seat, Facetiming with my mother. They've grown close since our trip to visit them almost a month ago and she likes to Facetime him a few days a week.

"Hey, Kaden," Ashley calls my name.

"Yeah?"

"Thank you. I love you." She runs over to me and, throwing her arms around my neck, jumps up knowing I'll catch her. I kiss her hard for a good minute before we need to break for air.

"You're welcome."

I watch her walk away, swaying her hips without even meaning to, and smile to myself. This woman and her son have fast become my entire world.

Tristan and I get home and take showers. I cook us dinner, and we watch some television until it's nine o'clock, which his bedtime.

When I walk into his room to tuck him in, I notice his room is plain. It doesn't look like a kid's room. It still looks like a guest room.

"Hey, bud. What do you say after we get back from the tournament we have your room decorated how you want?"

"Really? Can I have UFC stuff?"

"Sure."

"Wait! Does that mean I can go to the tournament with everyone?"

"I signed you up today. You're good to go!"

"And we can go to Disney with everyone, too?"

"Of course." I ruffle his hair, then kiss his forehead. "Night, buddy."

After doing the dishes and rotating a load of laundry, I sit down to go over some bills, when I see a recent transfer of fifteen million into my account. I immediately call my grandfather.

"Kaden, how are you, my boy?"

"I'm good, Grandfather. Really good."

"And how is Ashley?"

"She's good. She's the reason for my call."

"Okay, talk to me."

"I saw the money you transferred to me. I don't want the money you offered me to marry someone. I'm marrying Ashley because I love her and I don't want it tainted with a bribe from you."

"There's my grandson. Welcome back, son. We missed you."

I chuckle softly. "I must admit, your bribe did give me a reason to pursue her and get her to come with me to Colorado. I have a feeling if it wasn't for you twisting my arm, we'd still be here, dancing around our feelings for each other."

"I am very happy for you, Kaden. The truth is, we always planned to give you your trust fund. I was just hoping it would push you to find love again. The money was wired a few days ago, and if you recall, I originally said once you're married. You aren't married yet."

"Why didn't you ever tell me? I always assumed I would just get some money in your will."

"We wanted to make sure you earned your way in this world first. We always planned to give it to you once you turned thirty-five but held off when you appeared to still be lost."

"Damn, Grandfather, that's a lot of money. Are you sure?"

"Your grandmother and I have had that set aside for you for many years. You're our only grandson. We love the man you've become. Now continue to be that man for Ashley and Tristan."

"I will. I love you."

"I love you, too, my boy. Goodnight."

"Night. Tell Grandmother I said hello and I love her."

"Will do. You've made her very happy finding Ashley and bringing her to Colorado with you. She loves Facetiming with Tristan. Goodbye."

"Bye."

I make note to call my accountant in the morning. While I plan to spend my life with Ashley, I know first-hand anything can happen, and I need to make sure she and Tristan are taken care of. I also need to get ahold of her account info so I can transfer some money over to her. I hate the idea of her only having the money she makes at *Assets* to spend.

Twenty-Seven

ASHLEY

IT'S BEEN FOUR MONTHS SINCE KADEN AND I OFFICIALLY became engaged for real, and everything has been going great. I've been managing the club full time, which makes Kaden happy, even though he's let me know several times I'm welcome to stay home. I know the money I make is nothing compared to the money he makes and has, but it's important to me to work and be independent in some way. I look at the employment ads daily, hoping maybe I can find something else I might enjoy, but nothing jumps out at me.

Hayley gave birth to a beautiful little girl the day before Thanksgiving. 7lbs 4 oz., 21 inches. They named her Mackenzie Colette Michaels. Mackenzie was Caleb's mom's name, who died years ago from cancer. Colette was his sister's name, who was tragically killed. Caleb and Hayley wanted their names to live on through love. She is a perfect mix of the two of them.

For Christmas, everyone decided to go to Bentley's cabin in Breckenridge. Since his parents' place only has four bedrooms, when the home next to theirs went on the market, he snagged it up. Six bedrooms and four bathrooms, the place is stunning. Kaden and I spent the week skiing with Tristan. Kaden insisted on him taking lessons, and after a couple days, he was skiing like a pro. Kaden also had us check out a couple places in the area. We would love to make coming here for Christmas a yearly tradition.

For New Year's, we visited my parents. They have an annual New Year's party and we missed it last year for Kayla and Bentley's wedding. At the end of the night, Tristan ended up staying with my parents and Kaden surprised me with a romantic night at a resort. I smile at the memory of us on the balcony...

"Close your eyes."

"Why?"

"Just do it, woman."

Squeezing my eyes shut, I rely on Kaden to walk me to wherever we're going. I already know we're at the Palms, a luxurious resort in the area.

I hear a door click open and we walk a little farther. Another door opens...or maybe a slider?

"Okay, open."

"Oh, my God! Kaden! This is amazing." We're standing out on a balcony on the top floor. It must be the penthouse of some sort. There's a beautiful mini-pool that's just ours to use. The balcony railing is see-through glass, creating an illusion of the pool water flowing down over the balcony. There are candles spread out around the perimeter of the pool, and in the corner is a bottle of champagne in a bucket of ice with two glasses.

"It's beautiful. What is this all for?"

"Well, aside from it being New Year's, it's also our four-month anniversary. You agreed to marry me four months ago, today."

Reaching up onto my tippy toes, I give Kaden a kiss. "Thank you."

"There are bathing suits in the bathroom. I had our stuff sent up while I was checking in."

"Can anybody see us in the pool?" I look to both sides and there's a concrete wall. I glance down and see the beautiful city of Las Vegas.

"No."

"Then I'm pretty sure we don't need bathing suits." Giving Kaden a flirty wink, I remove my dress, bra, and panties, then walk into the heated pool. "Are you joining me?"

"Hell, yes." He throws his shirt over his head, then pushes his jeans and briefs down. He saunters toward me with a mischievous smirk, and before I can consider why, he walks right into the pool and picks me up, wrapping my legs around his body.

"I love you, Ash," he murmurs, pressing his lips to mine. Suddenly, his soft kisses aren't enough. What was tender between us becomes more ravenous and soon we're both all hands and mouths and tongues and teeth. Kaden sits me on the edge of the pool, then leaves me to grab the champagne from the bucket. After popping the cork, he spreads my thighs.

"You know what would taste even better than your pussy?"

"Hmmm?" I ask, distracted by the fact that he's about to eat me out.

"Ashley with a side of champagne. Lie back."

I do as he says and a few seconds later, cold champagne is running down my breasts. Kaden is hovering above me, sucking the champagne off my nipples. Then he pours some into my belly button, eliciting a shiver out of me from the coldness.

"Damn...This is some good champagne. Want some?" he taunts.

"Yes," I moan. He's sucks the champagne out of my belly button and the feeling of his tongue on my body sends sparks straight to my core.

"Sorry, you'll have to wait. I'm not done drinking yet."

I lift my body up a little bit so I can see him. He's back on the steps of the pool and his face is parallel to my pussy. He spreads my lips, then lifts the champagne above my mound, pouring the cold liquid over me. Keeping the bottle in one hand, while holding my lips open with the other hand, his face disappears between my thighs, slurping the champagne off my clit.

My body ignites from the pleasure.

"So. Fucking. Delicious, baby." He pours some more over my clit. He sets the bottle down then disappears again, eating my pussy like he's a starved man.

Just as I'm about to come, Kaden lifts my ass up slightly and pushes a finger into my tight hole, causing my body to detonate. My eyes close as my climax hits and fireworks go off in the back of my eyelids, my body shaking from the intense orgasm.

When I no longer feel Kaden's mouth and hands on me, I open my eyes and see him smiling at me.

"What?"

"It's a beautiful sight watching you come."

Taking my hand, he guides us over to the lounge chair. "Come ride me, baby."

I admire him for a few seconds. His cocky smile. The couple days of scruff on his face that, without a doubt, left red marks between my thighs. His toned pectoral muscles and tight six pack of abs that I love to run my tongue down. His throbbing dick that's standing at attention waiting for me.

"It's my turn," I say.

Kaden looks at me quizzically, lifting one eyebrow.

I grab the champagne from the ground where he left it. Then, sitting on top of his legs, I pour a small amount of champagne over his dick and watch it trickle down his thick shaft and balls. Leaning down to take his balls into my mouth, my hard nipples brush up against his thighs causing me to shutter.

I suck the champagne off each of his balls, then lick my way up his shaft to the head. Pouring a little more champagne over the top of his dick, I swirl my tongue around the hole before taking him all the way into my mouth.

"Fuck, Ash. I need to be inside you."

I continue to fuck him with my mouth, until he pulls my head up by my hair, his tell-tale sign he's about to come. Lifting onto my knees, I hover above his dick then impale myself right onto him.

"Fuck, baby!" Kaden growls, throwing his head back. I rise up until only the tip of his dick is touching me, then sit back down again, his dick hitting my cervix.

I lift up once more, but this time when I come down I keep moving up and down riding Kaden. His dick hits that spot deep within me over and over and over again, and it feels so good. Kaden's hands hold my hips tightly as his lips close on one of my nipples. My eyes shut and seconds later I'm climaxing.

Before I can open my eyes, Kaden has me flipped over so I'm underneath him, my back flat on the lounger. His hands are on either side of my face and he's gazing into my eyes as he enters me. Slowly but deeply he thrusts inside me, his eyes never leaving mine.

His dick is rubbing my clit just right and I can feel an orgasm already starting again. "C'mon, baby. Give me one more." His thrusts are done with purpose, rubbing my sensitive clit repeatedly. His mouth comes down, sucking on my bottom lip. Then he moves to my neck, sucking on my sensitive flesh right below my ear. The friction between his dick and my clit is too much and my body spasms around him once more, this time bringing Kaden over the edge with me.

He thrusts still and presses his lips to mine, giving me a soft kiss. "Maybe this is the time we created a mini us." He smiles wide and I laugh.

"And if it's this time, which sex will it be, oh wise one?"

"A girl, of course. Missionary is a girl."

Bringing my thoughts to the present, I shake my head with a laugh. It's been four months since I stopped taking birth control and I haven't gotten pregnant yet. The doctor said it can take several months so we aren't worried, but Kaden always jokes, wondering which time it'll be when we create a baby.

His silly behind researched baby-making and found some ridiculous site that showed statistics on which positions will create which gender. He swears he's keeping track to see if they're correct, but I don't see how. As often as we have sex, I don't think he'll know which position was the one that made the baby.

"What are you smiling about?" Kaden asks. I didn't hear him come into the room.

"I was remembering New Year's Eve. The champagne."

"Oh, you were, huh? Does my dirty girl want a repeat of that night?" Kaden wraps his arms around me and suckles my neck.

"Mmhmm."

"We can definitely make that happen, but not right now." He smacks my ass and laughs, walking over to the luggage.

"Not cool." I pout.

"If we don't leave here in the next fifteen minutes, we're going to miss our flight to Orlando."

"I seriously doubt Bentley is going to let the plane leave without us."

The Newbreed tournament is this weekend, so we're all flying to Orlando. The tournament will be all day Saturday, then Sunday and Monday will be spent at the Disney parks. Kaden and Tristan will be flying home Tuesday, but I'll be flying to Colorado to go dress shopping with Sandra and Rose.

We've decided to get married the weekend before spring break, so we're planning to stay the week in Colorado to take Tristan skiing again. The kid is obsessed!

Twenty-Eight

KADEN

THESE LAST FEW MONTHS WITH ASHLEY AND TRISTAN HAVE been nothing short of amazing. The moment I pushed the guilt of my past away and accepted what I already knew, that I'm in love with Ashley, everything seemed to just click into place. Not a day goes by that I don't think about Gabrielle and our son, but I've learned I can love and remember them and still be happy. I've also learned my girl has the biggest heart I've ever seen.

I came home one day to find Ashley cleaning out the room I use for storage. We discussed turning it into a playroom for Tristan, and using the guestroom for a future nursery. She was staring down at something in her hands and crying softly...

"Ash, you okay?"

She swivels around, her eyes growing wide.

"Yes, I'm sorry."

"What are you sorry for? What's wrong?"

She holds out a picture frame for me to take. I take it from her and study it for a minute, the memory of the day it was taken. It was at the baby shower Gabby's sister threw for us. We were holding up a onesie that read, "Daddy's little fighter." We're both smiling happily in the picture. I place the photo back into the box Ashley took it out of.

"I feel so guilty," Ashley says. She blinks a couple times to let the tears spill out. Reaching over to her cheeks, I wipe them away. She swallows thickly and continues.

"I feel like I was meant to meet you, like you were supposed to be in my life, be my husband. But then I see these pictures and remember that in order for you to have met me, you had to lose your wife and son, and I hate that. I hate that you had to go through that.

"Thinking that if she and your son were alive, we would never have met and fallen in love makes me so sad, but if I could snap my fingers and bring them back to life for you, I would." Tears stream down her face and I just want to kiss them all away. So, I do.

Taking her by her waist, I kiss each of her cheeks, tasting the saltiness of her tears. "And I love you for that, baby. I love your heart. But we can't think like that. You're the one that reminded me that we can't live in the past."

Taking a different photo out, one of a 4D sonogram of Gabe, she says, "I think we should frame it and put it in your office. You shouldn't keep it hidden. You may not have gotten to raise him, but he was your son, Kaden."

I get choked up by her words, so I just nod. Then after swallowing the lump in my throat, I say, "That would be nice."

The next day when I got home from work, when I sat at my desk in my office to go over my schedule for the following week, right there on my desk was a simple silver picture frame and inside it was the 4D ultrasound picture. Ashley will never understand what that simple gesture means to me, or maybe she does, and that's why she did it. I'm definitely one lucky man to have her in my life.

"Hello...Kaden are you spacing out?" I look at Ashley waving her hands in front of my face. She's the most captivating woman in the world, and I can't wait to make her my wife.

"Sorry, just thinking about how much I love you." I give her a chaste kiss before getting up to grab the bags we brought on board.

"You ready for this tournament, bud?" I ask Tristan.

"Yeah, but do you think we could go to the gym at the hotel and practice? I'm kind of nervous."

"Can I go, too?" Bella chimes in.

"Yeah, I want to practice, too," Marco adds.

"Absolutely. And tomorrow we can get there early so you can warm up and practice."

After we all file out of the plane, we pick up our rental cars and head to the hotel.

"Kaden," Tristan says on our way to find the hotel gym.

"Yeah, buddy?"

"Tomorrow, at the tournament, will you stand ringside when I'm fighting."

"Of course! Just call me your personal trainer." I give him a wink.

"Umm...do you think when you and my mom get married you could be my dad *and* my trainer?"

My breath feels like it's been knocked out of me. "You want me to be your dad?"

"Yeah."

"I would be honored to be your dad, Tristan."

He runs the short distance to me and gives me a hug around my waist. Bending down, I give him a kiss on top of his head. I would never wish Gabrielle or Gabe harm, and I know without a doubt if they were alive, I never would've met Ashley or Tristan, but in this moment, I feel like the tragedy that was out of my control brought the blessing in front of me. Tristan may have a shitty father, but I vow to do everything in my power to make sure he never lacks the dad he deserves.

IT'S SATURDAY MORNING AND WE'RE AT THE NEWBREED tournament. The place is filled with hundreds of people. The competitors ages range from six years old to adult, and there are gi and no-gi competitions. Boys and girls under twelve fight each other. Because of the age range, even though Tristan recently celebrated his seventh birthday, there's a good chance he and Bella will still be fighting each other. Marco will be competing in the teen competition with the twelve and thirteen-year-olds. All three of them are signed up for the gi and no-gi tournaments, so it will be a long day if any of them win their fights.

"Check out the schedule." Cooper hands me the lineup. Sure enough, if Tristan and Bella both win their first fight, they'll be fighting each other in the following round.

"You know Bella is going to kick Tristan's ass, right?"

"Hey, now. Tristan and I were sparring last night and he's gotten good."

"No, not because he isn't good. Because there's no way he'll hurt Bella."

I chuckle at that. Cooper has a point. While Tristan loves fighting, if it's possible for a seven-year-old to be in love, then Tristan is most definitely in love with Bella. They might be young but their friendship goes deep.

"You never know. He takes fighting seriously."

"We'll see."

I find Tristan waiting outside the makeshift ring he's going to be fighting in. He's watching the two kids go at it with complete rapture, pointing out the strengths and weaknesses he observes in each fighter knowing whoever wins could eventually be his opponent. The kid in the red shorts grapples the other kid to the ground and quickly moves him into a position, forcing him to submit. The kid taps out.

"You ready?" I ask him. Unlike in class, where we focus on all types of MMA skills, Newbreed Tournaments focus on skills and submission. It's a grappling only competition, which means there's no striking of any kind allowed.

Tristan puts his mouth guard in and nods.

"You got this, buddy."

He walks to the middle of the mat, and after the referee quickly reminds them of the rules, Tristan and his opponent shake hands to begin the fight. I see Ashley on the other side, gnawing on her bottom lip and clapping nervously.

Immediately, the other kid dives down and grabs Tristan's legs, bringing them both to the mat. Tristan uses this opportunity to wrap his legs around his opponent's waist, and his arms go into a head lock. His opponent pushes up several times and breaks free.

Before he can get on top, though, Tristan moves back on top of him and forces him into an arm bar triangle. The kid taps out. The entire fight couldn't have lasted more than a minute.

"Yeah, Tristan!" I yell, clapping. He smiles at me, then at his mom. The referee holds both their hands, then raises Tristan's hand up in the air, announcing him the winner.

"Good job, Tristan!"

"Way to go!"

Everyone in our group mauls him, quickly congratulating him. Tristan thanks everyone then goes in search for someone. "Where's Bella?" Tristan asks. "Did she see?"

"I saw you, Tristan! You did so good!" Bella gives him a hug. "I won, too! My dad said that means we'll be fighting each other!" Bella looks ecstatic while Tristan looks like someone just broke his PlayStation.

"I'm fighting you?"

"Yep! After Marco's fight!"

"Great." Tristan sounds like it's anything other than great, though. Cooper catches my gaze, and smirking, gives me a knowing wink.

"Tristan, come here, bud. We need to talk." Cooper hears me and starts laughing.

"Yeah?"

"Let's talk while we walk over to where Marco is about to compete." Ashley eyes me warily so I give her a quick wink. She walks over to Hayley, taking Mackenzie out of her arms to hold her. The baby looks like she belongs in Ashley's arms. I can't wait until my fiancée is knocked up.

Slinging my arm around Tristan's shoulder, I ask him how he feels about fighting Bella.

"I want to win, but…"

"But?"

"I hate hurting her. Whenever we're in class, I always let her win. I don't want her to be sad if I beat her."

"Tristan, I can't tell you what to do, but if I were Bella, I would want to win fair, not because you let me win."

"But what if she stops talking to me?"

"If Bella is your friend, she won't stop talking to you for winning."

"What if I hurt her?"

"Did you hurt the kid you just fought?"

"No, but Bella is a girl."

"Tristan, my man, don't let a woman hear you say that…especially Bella. When you're fighting here and in class, there are no boys and girls. It's just fighters, and you and Bella are both the same color belt. You're both equal."

"Okay."

We stop in front of the ring just in time to see Marco's fight begin. This past year the kid has grown a few inches and is starting to gain a little bit of muscle. After about three minutes and a close fight, Marco's opponent forces him into submission. After the referee announces the winner, Marco stalks off pissed.

"I'll go talk to him," Caleb says, running after Marco.

The rest of us stay here waiting for the next fight to be announced, which will be Bella and Tristan. I see Cooper talking to Bella but can't hear what he's saying. Her hands are on her hips and her head is tilted in defiance. Whatever he's saying, little Bella isn't liking.

The referee stands in the middle of the ring and Bella and Tristan's numbers are called. They both go to the center and wait for the ref to finish replaying the rules before they shake hands. Cooper is standing on one side and I'm standing on the other, both watching to see what will happen.

After a couple minutes of grappling, it's clear Tristan is giving it his all. He's on top until Bella pushes him off. Bella then gets the upper hand, her legs locking around Tristan's upper body with his arm locked above her legs. Tristan tries to buck her off and successfully gets her on her back, but she twists her body so his arm gets pulled back farther and he has no choice but to tap out.

The referee announces Bella the winner, raising her hand into the air, and once he let's go she runs to Tristan, giving him a hug. "You almost beat me!"

"You did good, Bella."

"Thank you."

The day goes by quickly. Bella fights three more rounds and wins them all, making her the no-gi champion. The gi-on tournament goes by quickly. All three of them win their first and second round, but only Bella wins the third, so she and Tristan won't be fighting each other. She wins the fourth and fifth round, and she's officially the gi and no-gi champion for the kid's six and seven-year-old division.

"How does it feel to be a two-time champion?" I ask Bella at dinner. We're all eating out at a local Hibachi restaurant. I hold the spring roll I'm about to eat up to her mouth, making it a fake microphone.

"It feels good! I think I'm going to one day become a UFC women's division champion, and then I will start a petition to change the rules so I can beat all the boys too." Everyone laughs.

"How do you know what a petition is?"

"Mommy told me what it is."

"So, I have to ask. Before your fight with Tristan, your dad was talking to you, and you looked mad. What did he say?"

"He told me not to be mad at Tristan if he beat me. I told him he's crazy! Tristan is my best friend. I could never be mad at him. That's just stupid."

Cooper looks over at me and smiles, knowingly nodding. We have some damn good kids.

"Hey, Dad!" Tristan calls across the table. "Tomorrow at Disney, can we go on all the rides?"

Ashley gasps. "He called you Dad?"

"He asked me last night if I would be his dad. You were in the bath when we got back to the room and then it completely slipped my mind."

She looks at me with unshed tears in her eyes, then rubs her nose trying to stop herself from crying. "I love you."

"I love you, too, babe." I give her a kiss on her cheek.

"We can go on all the rides," I tell him. "We may have to stand in line for hours at a time, but we can go on anything you want."

"Yes!" Tristan fist pumps. "You hear that, Bella? All the rides!"

Twenty-Nine

ASHLEY

"OH, DEAR, THAT DRESS LOOKS GORGEOUS ON YOU. HOW do you like it?"

I glance at the price tag and almost have a heart attack. It's a beautifully simple sweetheart A-line dress with a beaded sash. It has a strapless bodice and the back is crisscross strapped like a corset holding everything up top in place. The dress is fitted up top but gently flares out at the bottom. It's floor-length with no train, which I love. It fits me perfectly, and if I'm honest, it makes me feel like a princess. However, I could live off the cost of this dress for like three years.

"Umm...well, it's beautiful, but..."

"But what? What's wrong?" Sandra gets out of the leather seat she's been sitting in and puts down the complimentary champagne the sales associate gave us when we walked in. When she walks up to me and puts her hand on my shoulder, I choke up. I don't know why but I've been so emotional over the little things lately.

"Talk to me. Why are you crying?" She wraps her arms around me in a hug.

"What's wrong?" My mom comes out from the bathroom and rushes to me. I didn't know it, but when I showed up in Colorado, my mom was getting off her flight as well. Kaden surprised me, knowing I would want my mom to be here when picking out the details for our wedding. It was one of the best surprises I could ask for.

"Sandra, give the girl some space," Rose speaks up from her chair. When I look at her, she gives me a wink.

"I'm sorry. I love the dress. It's just a lot of money. I don't feel right spending this kind of money on a dress. Kaden and I are supposed to become equals, partners in a marriage, right? Isn't that what Dad and you always said?" I direct my question toward my mom. "I just feel like I have nothing to contribute."

"Oh, sweetie, you contribute plenty," Sandra says. "You make Kaden so happy. There was a time when we thought he would never find love again, but he did, and he found it with you and your sweet son. Partnership isn't about money. It's about trust and friendship. It's about supporting and respecting one another."

Rose stands and places her hands in mine. "Don't allow money to come between you and my grandson. Whether you are rich or poor, money can destroy a relationship. Don't ever feel like you are inferior. No amount of money can buy the friendship and love you and Kaden have created. Let him love you. He wants you to have the perfect wedding. Don't look at prices. Enjoy yourself, so when you look back you remember the beautiful moments. Don't allow them to be tainted with who has more money." She pulls me into a loving embrace and kisses me on my cheek. "Welcome to our family, my sweet girl."

I turn to look in the three-way full length mirror and without thinking about the price, fall in love with the dress. "This is the one I want."

After picking out the dress and sending pictures of the bridesmaids' dresses to the girls, who let me know they appreciate me not sticking them in crazy ugly-colored dresses, we go to meet the wedding planner, Julie, for lunch.

"Is there a venue you're thinking of for the wedding?" Julie asks.

"We can just do it at the club…Wouldn't that be the easiest?"

Rose and Sandra exchange a look.

"What?"

"Well, it's just that Kaden and Gabrielle got married there."

"Oh no, I didn't even think about that. I'm so sorry." I bury my face in my hands. How could I not have thought about the fact that Kaden has already been married? What if I choose the same colors they had or the same style dresses? Will he remember her instead of thinking of me? Tears quickly form and I have no choice but to release them so everything isn't blurry.

"I'm sorry, Julie. I know you came here to discuss the wedding, but I don't think this is a good idea."

I drop my napkin onto the table and rush outside, needing some fresh air to collect myself. I'm walking down the sidewalk, not paying attention to where I'm going, when I run into a woman walking in the opposite direction.

"Excuse me." I look up and see a ghost. It's the woman in the pictures. Gasping, I look around to see if someone is playing a joke on me. "Gabrielle?"

The woman's eyes widen before smiling sadly. "No, she was my sister. You're Kaden's fiancée, right? I saw you that day in the club when we ran into Kaden, but you probably weren't thinking about that at the time."

"Oh, right. You were hugging him. I didn't see your face clearly. You're Gabrielle's twin?"

I palm my forehead at the stupid question. Why else would this woman be a spitting image of Kaden's dead wife? "I'm an idiot. Please ignore me."

The woman laughs. "That's okay. My name is Danielle. It's nice to meet you. You looked like you were in a rush, and you're crying. Are you running to or from something?"

"From...I was at a lunch with the wedding planner and I kind of got overwhelmed. But you don't need to be bored with the details of my crap." I wave my hand.

"I don't mind. Kaden and I have been friends for years. I'm happy he found you. When he came to visit my family a few months ago he seemed to be turning a corner. Congratulations on the engagement."

"Thank you. And I'm sorry for your loss."

"Thank you. So, what had you feeling overwhelmed?"

"It's going to sound stupid, but I was supposed to pick the venue, so I picked the country club, which was the same location where Kaden and your sister were married. Now I'm second guessing everything. It's my first wedding, but he's already done all this."

"Ahh...and you're afraid you'll either be repeating what they did or he won't like what you chose and compare it to their wedding."

"Yeah. Stupid, right?"

She laughs softly. She has a pretty smile just like her sister did in all the photos I looked through. "No, it's not stupid. Talk to Kaden. Tell him how you feel. Otherwise you'll drive yourself crazy with worry."

"You're right, I will. Thank you. It was very nice to meet you."

"You, too. I look forward to the wedding." Danielle gives me a quick hug, then walks off. The wedding? I never would have thought her family would want to attend our wedding...

My phone goes off.

Kaden: Ash....

Me: Yes?

Kaden: Talk to me, babe. My mom said you ran out of lunch crying.

Me: Can we just elope like Caleb and Hayley did?

Kaden: We can do whatever you want, baby.

I think about how selfless he is. I know if I really wanted to, Kaden would go to the strip, find a little church, and marry me tomorrow. But then I remember our family, especially his grandmother, who wants to see us get married. It would be selfish to deprive them from being there to witness us getting married. I feel so lost and confused. I sit on the bench and start crying again.

Kaden: You there?

Before I can reply, my phone rings.

"Hello?"

"Baby, are you still crying? What's going on?" The sound of his voice makes me cry harder.

"I-I don't know what's wrong with me." My cries turn into sobs. "We were deciding on a location and I pick the wrong one. I picked the one where you married Gabrielle." I'm now crying so hard I'm hiccupping, and I can't stop.

"Ashley, baby, please calm down."

"I-I can't. What if our wedding is horrible? What if you liked your first one better? What if I say the wrong things? Or pick the cake you already had? You didn't want to get married again because you were only supposed to get married once. You already had your perfect wedding."

"Oh, baby. I wish I were there so I could wrap my arms around you and hold you. I miss you."

"I miss you, too." I sniffle and it sounds horribly unladylike, "Ugh! I'm all snotty. I sound like a vacuum sucking up snot."

Kaden chuckles softly.

"I don't think I can do this, Kaden."

"Do what? Marry me or plan the wedding?"

"Plan the wedding. Of course I want to be your wife."

Kaden sighs into the phone.

"I'm sorry."

"You have nothing to be sorry about. How about we do something a little untraditional? How about I plan the wedding? You already picked out your dress, right?"

"Yeah."

"So, everything else is just details. I don't like you sounding like this. It's not worth the stress. Our wedding will be one-of-a-kind because it'll be ours. Everything could be the same: the colors, the venue, the food…It wouldn't matter because the only important detail, the only thing I care about, is you and me and Tristan. It will be perfect and original because I'll be marrying you."

"Everything you say is always so damn perfect." My cries that slightly subsided start back up again in full force and Kaden chuckles into the phone.

"They weren't meant to make you cry, Ash. Go back to the restaurant and eat lunch. Enjoy your time with our moms and my grandmother. Go to the spa, get a massage, and then come home. I'll handle the details. Okay?"

"Okay."

"And baby…"

"Yeah?"

"I love you and your cute snotty sniffles."

"I love you, too."

Thirty

KADEN

"WHAT THE HELL WAS THAT ABOUT?" BENTLEY ASKS. THE guys are all over my house to watch the Super bowl. With Ashley being out of town, we all figured my place would be best to drink beer, eat shitty food, and watch the game. No women are allowed. Cooper, Bentley, Alex, and Stephen are already here and Caleb is on his way over with Marco.

Just as I'm about to answer, Caleb and Marco walk through the door. "What's up!" Caleb says hi to everyone then grabs a beer from the fridge before plopping onto my couch, Marco joining Tristan to play video games in his room.

"That was Ashley. I guess there's something I should tell you guys."

Everyone looks at me waiting for me to continue. "So, you know I was married before, but you assumed she left me, and I let you believe that without correcting you. The truth is I was married before, but she didn't leave me. Her name was Gabrielle and she was killed in a car accident on our way to the hospital for her to give birth to our son."

I give the guys a minute to soak in what I just said before I continue. "Ashley's upset because she went to pick out the venue and it was the same venue where Gabrielle and I were married."

"Fuck, bro. That's why you got upset when I mentioned your wife at the wedding. I'm sorry." Cooper comes over and gives me a bro hug.

"Nah, it's all good. My mom just said Ashley is extremely emotional and feels bad. I told her I'm going to plan the wedding. I don't want her to think anything she plans won't be good enough or will upset me because I already experienced it with Gabby."

Bentley smirks. "Your ass is going to plan the wedding?"

"How difficult can it be? Pick out some colors and shit, a cake... good to go...right?"

All the guys bust out laughing. "You're fucking nuts," Alex stops laughing long enough to say.

"The gesture is sweet as fuck," Cooper adds. "But you better make sure it's the wedding of Ashley's dreams. Sure, she's upset and willing to let you take over the planning right now, but when the day gets here she'll be expecting a goddamned fairy tale."

All the guys nod repeatedly in agreement. I pull out my phone to text my mom, realizing I'm going to need back up. I have a feeling I'm in over my head, here.

"Who are you texting?" Caleb asks.

"Who else? My mom."

The guys all laugh.

"Hey, I spoke with the contractor for the Rec Room and he said they should be able to break ground next month." Even though the four of us have gone in equally to build the sports complex for kids to go to, Bentley's taken on the brunt of the work. We purchased the property next to the gym and had the old building demolished. Bentley has been dealing with the architects, the city, and now the contractors to get this place built.

"If all goes well we should have this place up and running by the end of the year," Bentley says. "We're going to have to start thinking about staff. We don't want to wait until the last minute."

"With that Benjamin fucker buying Caleb's club, maybe Ashley would be interested in running the place. She loves working with kids."

Caleb laughs. "Benjamin fucker? The guy saves your fiancée's life and you're still pissed at him for calling you out?"

"Fuck him. Anyway, what do you think?"

"I think It would be a great idea. Liz has already agreed to handle all the accounting shit," Cooper says.

"Ashley is great at managing the club, and with her experience as a teacher, I think she'll be great," Caleb adds. "Talk to her and let us know."

"Sounds good."

THE GUYS HAVE ALL LEFT, TRISTAN'S SLEEPING, AND I'M wiping down the counters after putting away all the food and drinks, when my phone rings. Pulling it out of my pocket, I see it's Ashley video calling me. I hit accept and her beautiful face appears on the screen.

"Hi," Ashley says softly. I can see a bit of the background and know she's in my old room at my parents' house. She and her mom both fly home tomorrow.

"Hey baby. I miss you."

"I miss you, too. I forgot what it's like to sleep by myself. I would take your snoring over the quiet any day." She laughs at her own joke, making me smile. Earlier, when she was sad, my heart was broken. I don't like to see her sad, ever.

"So, what are you wearing?"

"Ashley," I say admonishingly. "Are you trying to start phone sex with me while sleeping in my old bed in my parents' house?"

"Maybe." Her cheeks turn a light pink and it makes my cock stir. I go to our bedroom, pull my basketball shorts off, and lie on the bed.

"I just laid in bed and I'm in nothing but my briefs. You?"

She looks down and her cheeks turn brighter. "Can I pretend I'm in something sexier? I'm in a shirt that says, 'I'm crabby in the morning' and there's a crab on it."

I laugh. She has tons of shirts like that. They all say weird and funny shit. I wouldn't expect her in anything else.

"How about you take it off, then tell me what you're wearing?"

The phone gets put down and when she comes back I have a view of her shy face and a little bit of her tits at the bottom of the screen.

"Okay, now I'm naked." My cock swells.

"Ash, put your fingers in your pussy, baby. Is it wet for me?" She does what I tell her to, and I know when her fingers are in because her eyelids flutter in pleasure.

"That's it, baby, finger yourself good."

"Kaden..."

"Yeah, baby?"

"Will you...do it, too?"

I look down at my hard cock that's already getting stroked. "Oh, I am, baby."

"Tell me something you want to do to me. Something we've never done before."

This woman is going to be the death of me.

"If you were here right now, I'd start by fingering that perfect pussy of yours. Then after making you come, I would put you on your hands and knees, and taking that baby oil you put on your body every night, I'd squirt some right onto your ass."

"Mmm...Kaden. Are you about to fuck me in the ass?" Ashley's eyes are closed and I can hear the noise her pussy's making as she fingers herself. She's soaking fucking wet.

"Baby, I am about to *devour* your ass."

"Keep going."

"I'd rub the baby oil all over your ass cheeks, then opening your ass up, I'd apply it to your tight hole, sticking one finger, then two in there, getting it ready for my dick."

"Stick it in my ass, Kaden."

"You want me to fuck your ass, baby?"

"Yes!"

"You got it, baby. Lining my cock up, I would slowly push in until you're completely full of me. Then I would reach forward, and wrapping your hair in my hand, I would fuck your ass. I would make you rub on your clit so we would come at the same time. Are you rubbing on your clit, Ash?"

"Yes, yes, Kaden! I'm about to come."

"Me, too, babe. Where do I come? In that sweet ass of yours or all over your ass and back?"

"In my ass. Holy shit! I'm coming, Kaden." Watching her throw her head back in ecstasy, pushes me over the edge, and my hot seed spurts out all over my hand and stomach as she moans into the phone coming as well. After a few seconds of quiet, I ask, "You still there?"

Ashley's eyes open and she looks at me shyly. "Yeah, I'm here. Umm...Kaden..."

"Yeah, baby?"

"Can we do that for real when I get home?"

"Hell, yes, we can. You don't have to ask me twice."

Ashley giggles into the phone. "I'm going to get cleaned up. I'll see you tomorrow. Love you."

"I love you, too."

Thirty-One

ASHLEY

IT'S BEEN ALMOST A MONTH SINCE I GOT UPSET WHILE trying to plan the wedding. Since then I've noticed my emotions are all out of whack. My mood swings are getting worse and I'm crying over the littlest things. Physically, I have sore boobs, I'm feeling sick all the time, and I missed my period, again. I would say all signs point to my being pregnant, but I haven't picked up a test yet.

Work has been crazy busy. Caleb went through with the sale of *Assets*. Luckily, for at least right now, Benjamin's keeping things the way they are. I'm still managing the club while Benjamin assesses everything. It's Friday night and Benjamin's out of town dealing with another one of his clubs.

After confirming the schedule and lineup for the night, I meet with Bianca to discuss the private parties for the evening. I can already tell it's going to be a busy night. I check on the tables, the bar, then work my way upstairs. When I get to the dressing room to check on the girls, there is utter chaos.

"What's going on?"

Michelle, a newer dancer, is packing her stuff up while Veronica is screaming profanities at her back. I'm confused because not only are they best friends but they're roommates.

"Whoa! Calm down. Veronica, what are you upset about?"

"This bitch slept with my boyfriend."

"You said you were broken up!"

"It doesn't matter!"

They're about to start a cat fight when Steve, the bouncer on duty, breaks it up. "Both of you, let's go." They both yell and scream, but he's not having it, forcing them to leave with him.

"We're now short three dancers," Scarlett says.

"Three?"

"Yeah, Stephanie called out. She wasn't feeling well."

"Okay, let me go down and check the schedule."

I get over to the hostess stand and take a look at the reservations for the night.

"We're going to have to cancel the party. I don't have a dancer."

"These men are VIP who do dealings with Benjamin. Are you sure it's a good idea to cancel them?"

"No, but I don't know what else to do."

I've tried to reach Benjamin several times, but his phone just keeps going to voicemail. I know the logical thing to do would be for me to cancel their party, but I'm afraid Benjamin will fire me for incompetence. He leaves and one girl calls out, and two get into a fight, leaving me short staffed.

"Ashley, they're here." The gentleman all walk in and you can tell they scream of money. They're going to be pissed if I have to tell them I don't have anyone to entertain them. Without thinking, I tell her to send them to the room, and then I go to the dressing room to get changed. I'll just have to handle this one party myself. Deep down, I know Kaden is going to be pissed when he finds out, but I'll explain to him it was a one-time thing and figure out from Benjamin what he wants me to do in this situation in the future, since there's no way I'll be making this a regular occurrence.

I borrow one of Scarlett's outfits, a sexy see-through top with leather booty shorts. I won't strip down completely naked. I'll just dance and get them some drinks. Maybe they won't even want lap dances. Who am I kidding? Of course they're going to want lap dances. I will just have to figure it out.

"You're stripping tonight?" Scarlett asks, walking into the dressing room.

"I don't know what else to do. We're short several girls and the party I was going to cancel are apparently associates of Benjamin's."

"Okay, how about you do the dance, and by the time you're done, I should have my tables under control, and I can take over and do the rest?"

"Oh, my God! Thank you!"

I quickly apply some makeup, doing a quick smoky eye, then throw on a pair of my shiny black fuck-me heels.

I take the back hall to the room then slip in the back to turn on the music and start my dance. The dance goes well. It reminds me I need to find time to take my pole dancing lessons again. I really enjoy them when my clothes are *all* on...and stay on.

After the song ends, I don't see Scarlett yet, so I do one more dance, hoping to buy some time. About half way through the song, I'm about to remove my bra when I see Scarlett walk in to take drink orders. I'm so thankful she's got my back. Dancing is bad enough, at least I don't have to explain giving lap dances to Kaden.

As I'm walking to the dressing room to get changed back into my work clothes, I am pushed against the wall from behind.

"Well, well, well. What do we have here?" I recognize the voice but can't place it right away. Before I can twist back to get a view of the guy's face, he grabs my hair and pulls my head up violently. The hairs on my head feeling like they're being ripped from my skull.

"Please don't hurt me." I try to push against the man, but he's stronger than I am.

"Hurt you? I'm about to make you feel so good." His breath is hot, and I choke on the smell of the alcohol dripping off him.

"Please don't do this," I beg, still unsure who this is. Regardless, this can't end well. We're in a dark hallway and nobody but management comes back here. Taking my sharp heel, I stomp on his feet, which only pisses him off further.

"You think you can walk around here dressed like a slut and not get fucked? You're nothing more than a cock-tease. It's time you act on it."

Keeping my hair firmly in his hand, he pushes me toward Benjamin's office. I start to yell for help, but he covers my mouth with his hand. I try to open my mouth to bite his hand, but I can't get a firm grasp on his skin. We get to the door and I pray Benjamin's in there but know he won't be. Once he's closed the door behind us, he throws me onto the couch and I finally get a look at him.

"Eric?" It's the gentleman from *Double D's*, the man whose son I used to teach. The same man who turned me in and got me fired.

"We never finished what we started. I saw you a couple weeks ago when I came here and knew one day I would get my chance, and then while looking for the bathroom I stumbled down the wrong hallway only to see you once again dressed like the fucking tramp you are. I knew it was meant to be."

"Look, Eric. I'm sorry. I never tried to tease you. Please don't do this. I'm engaged to be married."

"I don't give a shit! You ruined my life. After I reported you to the board, the principal told my wife! She left me and I've lost everything. It's all your fault! And for what? I didn't even get to fuck you."

Eric undoes his belt and drops his pants. I look around to see if there's a weapon to use on him, but there's nothing more than a tissue box. Then I remember I still have my heels on. Pulling my legs back, I kick at him as hard as I can, trying to delay him from entering me as I scream at the top of my lungs for help.

Eric jumps on top of me, covering my mouth with his hand. I bite down on his palm, hard enough that I can taste blood and scream again.

"Bitch! Shut the fuck up!" Eric slaps me across my face and grabs my shorts, pulling them down. I kick my legs, trying to stop him, but it does no good.

I feel sick to my stomach, like I'm going to throw up, but I don't give up. I keep kicking and screaming until there's a punch to my face. My head feels fuzzy and everything goes black.

"ASHLEY...ASHLEY, OPEN YOUR EYES."

My eyes open at the sound of Benjamin's voice. "Everything is going to be okay, Ashley. I've called Kaden, and the police just arrived. That fucker is being detained as we speak. He didn't get a chance to rape you. I walked in, in time. Fuck! Are you okay?"

"He didn't rape me?" I feel sick as I recall Eric on top of me. I jump from the couch and make it to the trash can just in time, throwing up everything in me.

"No, he didn't. Here, put your shorts back on." He hands me the tiny leather shorts Eric pulled off me. "My schedule got all messed up and my flight was delayed. I came straight here to meet with my business associates. I walked in and Eric was hovering over you but nothing happened. I called Kaden."

After wiping my mouth with the tissues, it hits me. He called Kaden. "Why would you call Kaden?"

"Why the fuck wouldn't he call me?" Kaden storms into the office and takes me into his arms. "You were attacked! Why the hell wouldn't your boss call your fiancé?"

"I'm sorry." Hot tears spill down my cheeks, and Kaden steps back to assess me.

"Why are you in a stripper costume?" His eyes sear into mine before he jerks his vision to Benjamin. Kaden grabs him by the collar, pushing him against the desk. "Why the fuck is my girl in a stripper costume?"

"Kaden! Stop! Don't hurt him, please. He didn't know."

"Didn't know what?" Kaden still has Benjamin pinned. Benjamin could easily fight back or push him away, but he doesn't.

"Three girls called out, and I didn't know what to do. I just danced on stage. I didn't do any lap dances or take off my undergarments, I swear."

Benjamin shakes his head. "Ashley, you shouldn't have done that. I appreciate you going above and beyond, but you should have just cancelled the party."

Kaden lets go of Benjamin and comes toward me. "You promised to never strip again." He says the words slow and so low I barely hear them.

"I know. I'm sorry." I look at Benjamin. "It was some associates of yours and I didn't want to cancel on them."

"Ashley, you are a manager. If you weren't here, do you think I would've stripped down and danced?" I appreciate the humor, but Kaden isn't having it.

There's a knock on the door. It's a police officer and he asks if I can please recall what happened. I start from the beginning, replaying the events that led to the assault, and when I get to the part where Eric slapped me, Kaden growls, "That fucker is dead."

I continue to recount what happened until I blacked out from the punch to my temple. Once Kaden hears I'm okay and wasn't raped, he stands. "Let's go home."

"Who's watching Tristan?"

"Liz is with him."

The drive home is silent and once we get inside, I thank Liz for coming over last minute.

"Anytime. Is everything okay?" She looks at Kaden warily.

"I was kind of assaulted at work." I try to whisper so Kaden won't hear me and freak out, again.

"Oh no! Are you okay?"

"Yeah." My eyes shift to Kaden, who is looking at his phone. Liz, thankfully gets the message.

"I'm going to go." She gives me a hug. "If you need anything, please let me know." She closes the door behind her, and I wait a few minutes for Kaden to say something.

When it's obvious he's not going to say a word, I do. "I know you're mad, but can we talk about this?"

He looks up from his phone then walks away from me.

I follow him into our room where he packs a bag. "Where are you going?"

"I'm going to stay at a hotel."

"Are you leaving me?" My words come out broken. The last time I watched a man pack a bag, it was Tyler, and my reaction to him leaving was relief. Right now, I feel the opposite of relief. I begin to panic.

"Kaden, please talk to me. I'm sorry. I'm sorry for dancing. I'm sorry for leading that guy on."

"What the fuck did you just say?" Kaden stops packing and glares at me, and I repeat what I said.

"I don't give a fuck if you were walking around buck-naked. You didn't lead anyone on. That fucker was wrong! He had no right to put his hands on you without your permission."

"Then why are you leaving me?"

"I just need some time, Ash. I get you want independence, but you chose to take your clothes off and willingly dance for other men tonight. We have more money than we will ever need, but you insist on working, and I've accepted that. But what you did tonight, I'm not okay with. And you promised. I don't blame you for being assaulted. That guy is a piece-of-shit. But you promised not to strip anymore and you lied."

He zips up his bag and then walks out the door, causing me to jump as it slams behind him.

I listen for the revving of his car engine, then I sink down the back of the door and, with my face in my hands, I cry, until there are no tears left. Then I grab a blanket from the hall closet and fall asleep on the couch. There's no way I'm sleeping in our bed without Kaden.

I get up in the morning and feel hungover. I guess ugly crying for hours will do that to a person. I check my phone for any missed calls or texts, but there aren't any. I remember from when Tyler left all those years ago, keeping busy is the best way to live in denial, so I make Tristan pancakes and eggs for breakfast, then wake him up to come eat. It's Saturday morning so technically he could sleep in, but I need the distraction. While he's scarfing down his food, he reminds me of

Bella's upcoming birthday party.

"Next weekend is Bella's birthday party! Can we go pick out her gift today?"

"Sure, sweetie. Finish your pancakes and get dressed. Do you have anything in mind?"

"I'm not sure. I need to think about it."

"Okay, I'm going to jump in the shower."

After we're both dressed and I put on some cover up to cover the faint black and blue marks on my face, we head to the mall to pick out Bella's gift. Kaden is on my mind the entire time, though. Which hotel did he go to? Will he come back? Are we over for good? I fucked up and broke his trust in me. What should I do or say to make it better?

And that's how the entire week goes. I try to text him a few times but he only responds letting me know he's okay. I go by the gym to see if he's there but he's not. Nobody mentions anything so I don't bring it up. His mom calls me a couple times, but I'm afraid she'll ask for Kaden and then I'll have to admit he left me, so I don't answer. When Tristan asks about Kaden, I tell him he's out of town. It's technically not a lie, right?

By the end of the week I'm sick to my stomach with worry. I called in sick to the club and Benjamin was more than understanding. Not knowing where Kaden and I stand, now is not the best time to take off work and risk the chance of losing my job, but between the crying and throwing up, I can't get myself to function properly let alone go to work.

If I wasn't sure before, I'm positive now, that I'm either pregnant or have a horrible case of the flu, and the way I'm throwing up and sick to my stomach I'm considering the latter. I don't remember ever throwing up this badly with Tristan. I make a note to make an appointment with my doctor to confirm one way or the other.

I decide to go over my bills, figuring out which ones to pay first. I log into my account and notice there's way too many freaking zeros in the balance. Clicking on the account overview, I see a deposit was electronically made four months ago! How the hell did I not bother to check my account for that long? Thinking back, I haven't gotten any debt collection calls in a long time. My paycheck is direct deposit and the only money Kaden lets me spend of my own is when I go to the grocery store. I've been so busy with my new life with Kaden, I haven't bothered to deal with everything else.

Sadly, after I borrowed the money from Giovanni, I stopped paying the credit card debts and just let them all go to collections. I'm going to need to get them up to date. With the ridiculous amount of money sitting in my account, I will finally be able to pay off all my debt and have a fresh start. I sign in to the various debt collectors I owe money to, but every single one shows a zero balance. I log on to check my credit score, to see what's still outstanding and it shows everything is current! The previous delinquencies are still on there, bringing down my score, but I don't owe anything. Every single one says satisfied in green. Kaden must have taken care of everything.

After logging out, I join Tristan on the couch to watch his movie with him. My phone goes off and I check it hoping it will be Kaden.

It's a group text with Liz, Hayley, Kayla, and me.

Hayley: Let's all do something fun with the kids. Caleb is busy at the gym training.

Liz: I'm down.

Kayla: Parrrttyyyyy!

Hayley: Ashley??

I go to type I'm not feeling well but that would raise questions I'm not ready to answer yet, so instead I type back: **Okay.**

We all agree to meet at Wet and Wild, a huge waterpark. The little ones will enjoy it and so will Marco. We meet in the front, pay, and once in the park, find a shaded spot to lay our towels down on a couple of lounge chairs.

"Mom, can we go in the lazy river?" Tristan asks.

"Sure."

We spend the next several hours relaxing in the water, the kids going on almost every water ride and slide known to man. When they start complaining they're hungry, we make our way to the food pavilion to order lunch. The kids grab a table next to the adults and immediately start talking about the upcoming UFC fight.

"How's the wedding planning coming along?" Kayla asks. Not wanting to mention Kaden and I are on the outs, I keep my answers simple.

"It's going. Kaden is handling it all."

"I should have made Cooper handle it all. As much as I loved my wedding, planning it was stressful, and it was over in a few hours."

"That's why Caleb and I eloped." Hayley shakes her head, laughing.

We enjoy our lunch, gossiping about nothing of importance, and it's nice to take my mind off my problems on the home front, even if it's just for a little while.

IT'S SATURDAY AND BELLA'S BIRTHDAY PARTY IS BEING HELD at their house. There are bounce houses and water slides all over the backyard, a cotton candy machine is set up, and there are kids running around everywhere. I look around for Kaden and am shocked when I spot him sitting in a chair under a large tent they put up for shade. I'm not sure whether to go say hi to him, but the decision is made for me when the smell of the barbeque sends my stomach rolling and I have to sprint to the bathroom to upchuck my small breakfast.

I'm sitting on the floor of the bathroom with my head down, praying Liz recently cleaned this toilet, when there's a rap on the door.

"I'll be out in a minute."

"We're coming in."

The door opens and in walk Hayley, Liz, and Kayla.

"You okay?" Liz asks.

"Yeah, just not feeling well," I say, getting off the floor.

Hayley gives me a knowing look. "Or are you pregnant?"

"That could be it. Although the timing would suck..."

"Because you and Kaden are fighting?" Kayla asks.

My eyes shoot over to hers. "He told you?"

"He told Bentley when he got here. My nosy ass overheard. You should have told us when we were all at the water park."

"I messed up."

"How?" Hayley asks.

"Long story short. I promised Kaden I wouldn't strip ever again and then the club was busy and we were short girls…"

"And you stripped," Kayla says, finishing my sentence for me.

"Yeah, only that wasn't all. This douchebag, Eric, the one who turned me in for stripping when I wouldn't screw him, was there and assaulted me."

"What the fuck!" Kayla yells.

"Are you okay?" Liz asks.

Hayley wraps me up in a hug.

"Yeah, I'm okay. Luckily, Benjamin, the guy who bought the club from Caleb, walked in and stopped him. Then he called Kaden."

"Oh boy," Kayla says.

"Oh boy is right," I say.

"Let me guess. Kaden found out you stripped and that you were assaulted. He was scared and pissed. So of course, he acted on being pissed because he's a man. Easier to focus on being mad than on being scared," Liz adds.

"Yeah, well, he's been gone for a week now. And I'm pretty sure I'm pregnant."

"Does he know?"

"No, I don't even know for sure. And I'm not going to tell him. I don't want him coming back just because I'm pregnant."

"I understand that completely, but Kaden loves you. This is just a fight," Hayley says.

"Let's do a test to find out. I'm sure I have one somewhere," Liz says.

The four of us go to her bathroom and sure enough, she has a box of them. "Damn, girl. You trying to get knocked up again?"

"No way. They're from Nathan. Bella and Nathan are enough for me. If Cooper had it his way, he would keep knocking me up, but I think I'm done."

"Same here. Marco and Mackenzie are all I need," Hayley says.

"Bentley wants to adopt one more time. Chloe and Faith are definitely enough, but I wouldn't be against having another little one in the house one day."

I pee on a stick and of course the girls all stay. Apparently once you have kids you no longer care who's in the room while you're peeing.

The stick reads **PREGNANT** and the tears start falls.

The girls all gather me in a group hug.

"Don't cry, sweetie."

"I'm just sad Kaden isn't here with me right now. He's like a hundred feet from me, yet it feels like he's hundreds of miles away. I don't know how to fix this."

"You can start by putting on a super skimpy bikini and we all go play on the water slides!" Kayla laughs.

"And how will that help?"

"Umm...duh! He's a man...One look at your sexy ass in a bikini and he'll be salivating for you."

"I didn't bring one. Liz doesn't have a pool."

"Which will be changing soon. Cooper agreed to build one! But I have a couple extra suits I bought on sale and haven't used yet. We're almost the same size."

After we all change into our swimsuits, Kayla says, "Don't take this the wrong way, Ashley, but how far along are you?"

"Why? Do I look fat?"

"No, you look great, but your belly is definitely showing a bump."

"I'm not sure...I haven't gotten my period in two months, so maybe like six to eight weeks."

"Make an appointment to see a doctor soon."

"I will."

We all walk out to join the kids for fun and Kayla whispers to me, "Don't look at him. It'll make him want you even more."

It takes everything in me, but I don't look at Kaden. I can feel his eyes on me, though. I want nothing more than to run to him, sit on his lap and kiss him, while apologizing for messing up. But I don't. I walk by pretending the love of my life doesn't exist, praying I'm still his.

Thirty-Two

KADEN

"FUCKIN' A, I'VE GOT THE HOTTEST WOMAN HERE." BENTLEY waggles his eyebrows.

"Bullshit, my wife is the hottest." Cooper hits Bentley on the chest.

"Both of you guys are a bunch of dumbasses. Hayley's perfect ass blows them all away."

I just chuckle at the three man-children arguing over who's woman is the hottest. Then I look to the left and see the four women all walking toward the water area, and my eyes land on the sexiest fucking woman at this party. Fuck that! In this goddamned universe. Ashley is swaying her hips in a bathing suit I've never seen. It's pink and white striped and looks to be just a smidge too small on her, fitting her curves like a glove. I don't even bother arguing with the other guys. Hands down, my woman is the sexiest, most beautiful one here.

My woman? Is she still mine? She's texted me several times this week, apologizing, but I've only texted back if she asks me if I'm okay. I would never want her to think something's happened to me, but I'm not ready to talk to her about us yet.

When the call came in, saying she had been assaulted at the club, I freaked the hell out. I was beyond pissed. But when I learned the entire story, I became a mix of emotions. Sure, I was still pissed. But I was also hurt and scared. I was pissed she lied and stripped for a bunch of men. I know she didn't let them touch her, but I was still pissed, nonetheless. I was hurt she put her job above our relationship. She never should have let those men see her like that. But more than that, I was scared because she was assaulted and almost raped by some crazy fucker.

Looking at her right now, I just want to grab ahold of her and kiss the fuck out of her. I want to love her and protect her and worship her.

"You still not talking to her?" Bentley nudges me.

"Benjamin told me what happened," Caleb says. "Is she okay?"

"Yeah, I think so. I was so pissed she stripped after promising she wouldn't, I left."

"Your girl gets assaulted and you left?" Cooper exclaims.

"It wasn't like that. I was pissed she fucking stripped after she promised she wouldn't. I made sure she was okay before I left."

Cooper looks at me like I'm stupid. Fuck! He's right. I left her after she was assaulted and almost raped all because I was pissed she stripped. I'm a fucking asshole.

"Kaden! Cooper! Someone come here!" I look over to the waterslides to see Liz sitting on the ground holding Ashley in her arms. I shoot out of my chair straight for Ashley.

"What happened?" I ask, taking Ashley out of Liz's arms and

pulling her into mine. Her eyes are droopy and her skin is pale.

"We were running around chasing the kids and she said she felt lightheaded. She hasn't been feeling well. I think she's dehydrated."

Cooper brings over a bottle of water and hands it to me. I open it up and put it up to Ashley's mouth. She guzzles it too quickly before I can tell her to slow down and then bends over to throw up.

"Shit, baby. You can't drink that fast when you're dehydrated. We need to take you to the hospital. If you're throwing up over a small drink, you can be severely dehydrated."

"I'm okay," Ashley says softly before she bends over to dry heave.

"All right, up you go. I'm taking you to the hospital."

"We can watch Tristan for you," Liz says.

I pick Ashley up and carry her bridal style to my car.

"Kaden, wait!" Liz comes running out, waving something in her hand. "Clothes for Ashley."

I look over and see she's still in her bikini. "Thanks."

Once we get to the hospital, I sign her into the ER and begin filling out the forms.

"Umm...actually, I'm pregnant," Ashley says when she sees me checkmark *not pregnant*. My pen stops writing and my eyes go straight to her stomach. She's wearing a hoodie and sweatpants Liz ran and grabbed her to throw on over her swim suit.

"Why didn't you tell me?"

"I just confirmed it today with one of Liz's tests. I haven't been to the OB yet." And fuck if I don't feel like the biggest asshole for walking away. At least now her mood swings these past several weeks make sense. And now that I'm thinking about it, we haven't had to stop having sex due to her period in quite some time.

"Baby, have you been sick all week?"

"Yeah, I haven't been to work all week. I'm pretty sure Benjamin is going to fire me."

"You don't even need that job. You're pregnant with our baby. And you're sick and now possibly dehydrated. You need to take care of yourself. Please don't worry about working." Ashley's eyes fill with tears.

I finish filling out the form and give it back to the nurse. Once I'm sitting back on the bench, I pull her to me so her head is in my lap. I play with her hair until I can hear her soft snores, telling me she's asleep. My mind goes to when I found out Gabby was pregnant. We were so excited the day she missed her period, we ran to the store together and picked up the test. She took it, and when it showed two lines, we called everyone in our family and then went to dinner to celebrate.

Ashley has been sick all week, worrying over whether I was going to leave her. She took a test with her friends instead of with me, and instead of telling me, she pretended like she wasn't pregnant or hurting because she didn't know where we stood.

"Ashley Myers," the nurse calls out.

"Ashley, wake up, baby. They're calling your name." She stirs awake and stands. Her legs wobble and I catch her.

"Can we get a wheel chair, please?"

"Yes, sir." The nurse grabs one and Ashley sits in it.

Once we get to the room, the nurse asks her a bunch of questions and takes her blood. She has her give her a urine sample and tells us once the tests have been run, the doctor will be in to speak with us.

"How are you feeling?" I sit next to her and take her hand in mine.

"My stomach feels sore."

"From throwing up nothing. You were dry heaving earlier. They'll more than likely give you fluids through an IV to prevent you from throwing it up."

Ashley nods and closes her eyes. The nurse comes in a few minutes later and sets up the IV. "This is to help you hydrate. Your urine came back and shows signs of dehydration and with you saying you can't keep anything down, we want to make sure you're hydrated."

She inserts the needle into Ashley's vein, and after setting up the fluids, leaves. Ashley goes back to sleep and I continue to hold her hand praying everything is okay with her and the baby.

Thirty-Three

ASHLEY

"MY NAME IS TONI AND I'M THE ULTRASOUND TECH. I'M JUST going to wheel you down the hall to do an ultrasound and then the doctor will come in and speak to you once he reads the chart."

Toni wheels my bed to the room and once she sets up the ultrasound machine, lifts my shirt up. "I'm going to try to see from here, but since we don't know how far along you are, I might have to switch to a vaginal ultrasound."

She squirts the warm gooey gel onto my stomach and starts clicking buttons on the monitor. "Okay, I'm able to see like this." She presses hard into my stomach and I want to tell her to chill the fuck out before I puke on her, but I keep my mouth shut.

"Let's see here." She continues to click. A whooshing sound hits the speakers, and I know it's the heartbeat. The breath I didn't know I was holding releases. Kaden squeezes my hand, giving me a knowing look. I forgot that even though he doesn't have any children, he and his wife went through this so he must recognize the sound of a heartbeat.

"Okay, that's the heartbeat." She types *baby A* on the monitor and screen shots it. "And.... there's the other heartbeat." She types *baby B* and screenshots it again. It takes a second for me to put two and two together, but it takes Kaden less than a second because he blurts out, "Holy fuck! There's two...like two babies in there?"

"Yep! Two babies, and it looks like you're about ten weeks. Your due date is estimated to be September seventeenth, but it can change once you see your OB."

"Huh...Well, Kaden, which position do you think it was we created twins in?"

The ultrasound tech looks at us in confusion, but Kaden throws his head back with a laugh.

"It could have been any number of them. Maybe it was the time in the bathroom..."

"Okay!" I cut him off. "I'm pretty sure Toni here doesn't want a play-by-play of our sex positions."

"Hey now! You asked."

Thankfully, the tech speaks up. "I'm just going to take a couple more shots of the uterus for the doctor and then I can print a couple pictures of your little kumquats."

"Excuse me?" I manage to find my words. "What did you call my babies?"

Toni laughs. "Kumquats. It's a small fruit. I always use fruits to determine the size of the babies. Week eleven they'll be the size of Brussel sprouts and at twelve weeks they'll be the size of a passion fruit! My favorite week though is week twenty-nine, butternut squash.

I love butternut squash! Oh, and week thirty-three! Pineapples! You'll have two pineapples in you!"

Pineapples? The heavy green fruit with hard pointy things sticking out of it? I must give Kaden a look of horror because he stops her from continuing. "That's great. Can we get those pictures you mentioned?"

"Sure thing." She prints them and wheels me back to the room. My eyes don't leave the pictures of my two Kumquats. Jesus! I'm going to need to find another way to describe them. I can't spend the next seven months calling my babies fruits! Holy shit! I'm having two babies!

"Yes, we are." Kaden smiles at me.

"Huh?"

"You said you're having two babies."

"I said that out loud?"

Kaden laughs and nods.

After the doctor comes in and confirms what the ultrasound tech already told us, he lets me know he's going to keep me on fluids for a few hours to make sure I'm hydrated. Apparently being pregnant with twins ups your HCG count and can cause you to have even worse morning sickness. He prescribes me nausea medication and prenatal vitamins.

After I'm released from the hospital, Kaden goes through the pharmacy drive-thru to pick up my prescriptions then takes me to get something to eat. After we're seated, Kaden orders us both waters.

"Anything look good?" He looks up from his menu to me.

"Everything...nothing...I don't know. I'm afraid whatever I eat will make me sick."

He hands me a pill for nausea. "You have to eat. Even if it's something small."

I take the pill with the water the waitress delivers. When she returns to take our orders, I order chicken noodle soup and a piece of chocolate banana cake, then change my mind when I wonder if a banana is on the list of baby sizes. "Actually, I'll take the cheesecake."

"With strawberries?"

"No, no fruit. Thank you."

Kaden laughs, then orders a grilled chicken sandwich with a side of vegetables.

"I'm sorry I haven't texted you all week."

"Where have you been?"

"At a hotel. Working out at the gym there. With Alex taking his honeymoon this week, I took the week off."

"I don't want you to forgive me and marry me because I am pregnant."

He reaches into his pocket and pulls out a rectangular box. "Open this."

Lifting the lid, I see two silver puzzle pieces. They're put together and have an engraving across them. One reads: **YOU ARE MY MISSING PIECE.** The other reads: **YOU FIT ME PERFECTLY.**

"I saw them in the storefront yesterday and had them engraved. You're my missing piece, baby."

"You bought these yesterday?"

"Yes, obviously before I knew you were pregnant. I planned to talk to you today after the party. I just couldn't figure out how I felt about all of it. But I knew I loved you. I love you so much, baby. No matter what. And I'm sorry for leaving."

Kaden gets out of the booth and comes around to my side of the table, scooting in close to me. "You were assaulted and I put my anger above your feelings and wellbeing. Can you forgive me?"

"Yes, I missed you so much. And I'm quitting the club. I just want to focus on our babies and on us and Tristan."

Kaden grins and gives me a kiss. "I would really love that, but only if that's what you want to do."

"It is."

He takes my keys out of my purse and slides the keychain onto my keys. "So, you always have a piece of my heart with you."

"I love it."

"There's actually something I have been meaning to talk to you about. You know the recreational center will be breaking ground hopefully next month."

"Yeah, I can't wait to see it all done. It's going to be amazing."

"The guys and I were talking and we thought you would be the perfect person to run the place. You'll have help of course. Liz will be handling the accounting side, and we'll have to hire people and reach out to those who wish to volunteer, but you mentioned you would like to work with kids so I thought maybe you would want to work there."

"Kaden, I would love to manage the rec center. I have so many ideas. The different sports and programs we can offer. While I was teaching, I saw so many kids wish for after school activities that weren't offered because of budgeting. I'm so excited."

"Perfect. The place won't be up and running until the beginning of next year, but we want to make sure we're doing it right along the way. We can sit down and go over the plans, see if there's anything we need to add or change. Sound good?"

"Sounds amazing."

After we finish eating, we go to Liz's to pick up Tristan. The party has ended and Tristan and Bella are in the living room watching Ultimate Fighter on the television.

"How'd it go?" Liz whispers.

"Kaden knows."

"Okay, good. I wasn't sure whether to say anything outside. I'm so glad you're okay!" Liz pulls me into a hug. "How did he take it?"

"How did who take what?" Kaden comes over and puts his arms around me absently rubbing my belly as he nuzzles his face into my hair, giving me a kiss under my ear. I sink back into his arms welcoming the feel of his body against mine after a week of being without it.

"How did you take me being pregnant."

"You're pregnant?" Tristan comes into the kitchen with Bella following him.

"I am. What do you think about that?"

"I think that's awesome. I hope it's a boy, so I can have a brother."

"You can borrow my brother if you want," Bella offers.

"You don't like your brother?" Cooper asks.

"Of course I do! I love him. But if Tristan needs to practice, I don't mind lending Nathan to him."

We all laugh. "That's very sweet of you."

"Well, it might be a boy and girl," Kaden says, snuggling his face back into my neck.

Tristan looks at us confused.

Liz gasps.

Cooper laughs.

"You're having twins?" Liz looks down at my stomach.

"Apparently so."

"Well, that makes sense. Why you're so sick and your tiny belly is already protruding!"

"Yeah, I'm only like ten weeks. We aren't going to tell everyone until I'm out of the first trimester, but there are definitely two little ones in there."

"Aww...If I remember correctly isn't ten weeks a lemon?"

"Oh no! Not you, too!"

Kaden cracks up. "Nope, it's a kumquat."

Cooper laughs.

"What's a kumquat?" Tristan asks.

"Okay, I don't know what's up with you all and measuring the size of a fetus by fruits, but my babies are not freaking kumquats!"

Everybody laughs.

Thirty-Four

KADEN

"UM, WHAT ARE THESE?" ASHLEY IS STANDING IN THE backyard, staring at my four-wheelers like they're personally offending her.

"Baby, you've never seen a four-wheeler before?"

"Oh, I've seen them. I'm just wondering what so many of them are doing back here and why my son is sitting on a mini-one."

It's a three-day weekend and the entire gang is over for a barbeque. I'm assuming by the look on Ashley's face, she hasn't been to the detached garage in the back to see all my toys, four of which are four-wheelers. Since Tristan is too small to ride a regular one, I had a Honda 90 delivered for him, along with a chest guard and helmet. He took one look at that machine and jumped on it ready to go. But now looking at the death glare Ashley is giving me, I'm thinking that maybe I should have mentioned it to mama bear first.

"Can I ride on the back of Tristan's?" Bella squeals.

"You should ride on the back of mine, Bella," Marco cuts in. "I'm older and can drive better. You'll be safer with me."

"Since when can you drive?" Caleb grills Marco.

"Well, I haven't yet, but I'm older and almost thirteen."

"There's no way Marco is riding that death-trap by himself." Hayley is standing next to Ashley and if I don't do something quick the women are going to overpower us.

"The guys will each take one, and Marco and Bella can ride behind one of us. Tristan's got his own, though. He has to learn how to ride." When Ashley's eyebrows go up in defiance, I jog over to her to defuse the situation. "Baby, I'm going to be with him the entire time. It's an automatic so he doesn't even have to shift. He has head and chest gear. I wouldn't let anything happen to him."

I give her a small kiss on her lips, but it doesn't work. The tears well up in her eyes just begging to be released. "B-but he's m-my baby."

"Yes, he is, but the babies in there"—I point to her stomach—"are making you a tad emotional."

If looks could kill, I would be a dead man.

"Are you saying my concerns for my child aren't real? That I'm only worried about the well-being of my only son because you knocked me up and I'm carrying two babies in here?"

I hold my hands up, palms out, silently waving the white flag, but it's too late. She's revved and ready to ride.

"And even if I am a tad emotional, don't you think it's a bit rude to point it out? It's not my fault my hormones are all over the place. Maybe you should have thought about this when you insisted I get rid of my birth control. Now my son is sitting on a death contraption about to go riding through the millions of acres of woods where he can get lost or hurt."

Damn, I love this woman. I feel a smile grace my lips and quickly try to reign it in before she catches it.

"So....does that mean we can't go riding?" Bentley whines. Kayla smacks him.

Ashley huffs and storms off, but I chase after her. Yeah, yeah, I'm pussy whipped. I'll be the first to admit it. "Wait, Ash." She stops and turns glaring at me. "If you don't want him to ride on his own, he can ride on the back of mine. I'm sorry, baby. I don't want you stressed."

I'm granted a small smile, warming my heart. "Ugh! He can ride. Just be careful, please. I'm going to go start on the side dishes for lunch. I can't be out here and watch this. It's going to give me a heart attack."

I look back and forth between Tristan and Ashley trying to decipher the code of what she just said knowing if I make the wrong choice, my ass will be in the dog house tonight.

"Tristan, we'll practice with your new four-wheeler later. You're on the back of mine, bud."

I hear a soft giggle behind me, then tiny hands come up behind me. "Good decision. You'll definitely be rewarded tonight."

"HOLY SHIT, BRO! THOSE TRAILS ARE SOMETHING ELSE."

"Yeah, we need to go again, and soon."

"I can't believe after all these years, we've never gone mudding after a good rain."

We spent the good portion of the morning and early afternoon riding the trails that line up to my backyard. Once we returned and got cleaned up, the ladies had lunch ready to go. Ashley can make a mean homemade cornbread casserole.

I look around and take a moment to thank God for everyone at this table. Everybody is chowing down and talking. The kids are laughing. We're all healthy and happy.

"You okay?" Ashley looks at me quizzically.

"Yeah, I am. Thank you." I bring my lips to hers, and what starts off as a quick kiss quickly turns into something more. Suddenly there's a piece of food hitting me in the side of my head.

"Hey!"

"Quit making out like teenagers at the lunch table." Cooper laughs.

Ashley leans over and whispers into my ear, "Later."

That one word has my dick twitching.

Thirty-Five

ASHLEY

"MOM, YOU LANDED ON PARK PLACE, AND DAD HAS A HOTEL on it. You owe him…"

"Fifteen hundred." Kaden waves his monopoly card in the air excitedly. I would like to smack that smirk right off his damn face.

Let's have a family game night, they said…

It'll be fun, they said…

Fun, my ass! While Tristan and Kaden are holding all the damn deeds to everything that matters, I have like two hundred bucks left and own Oriental freaking avenue!

"I need to go to the bathroom real quick! Don't let Mom steal my money." Tristan runs out of the room to the bathroom.

"Hey Ash…"

"What?" I glare at Kaden, knowing I'm about to lose. I hate losing. And for the record, I am so done with family game nights.

Kaden moves closer to me, giving me a kiss on my cheek, then bites down softly on my ear lobe. The act sends sparks right to my core.

This pregnant woman is horny twenty-four-seven these days.

"If you give me a blow job behind the hotel I own, I might consider your debt paid."

I laugh out loud, throwing my money onto the board. "I'm out."

"Oh, c'mon, baby. I'm sure we can work something out."

"How about you put Tristan to bed while I take a shower and then we can meet in bed to negotiate?" I squeeze his semi through his jeans.

"Tristan!" he yells. "Time for bed." Then he turns to me. "I'll meet you in bed, and you better be naked."

"FUCK. YES!" KADEN IS LYING IN BED WEARING NOTHING BUT a pair of briefs watching TV when I walk out of our bathroom naked, as he requested.

I wave the Park Place deed in the air. "So, I apparently owe you fifteen hundred dollars. I'm here to work off my balance."

When I get close enough, Kaden moves to the edge of the bed, then grasping my hips, pulls me toward him, so his face is level with my protruding belly. I'm now fourteen weeks pregnant, and while you would think a month wouldn't make a difference, when you're carrying twins, it does.

After placing several small kisses on my belly, Kaden looks up and smiles at me. "I love you."

I entwine my fingers into his hair, then lean down to give him a kiss. "I love you, too."

Squatting in front of him, I quickly pull his briefs down so his beautiful dick pops out.

"Get up here." I look up in confusion.

"I don't want my fiancée sucking my dick tonight. I want to make love to you." Grabbing me under my arms, he lifts and places me on the bed.

"Do you know what today is?" Kaden starts raining kisses all over my face: my cheeks, my forehead, my lips. Then he moves downward to my neck and collarbone.

"Sunday?"

He laughs as he moves lower to kiss each of my nipples, causing me to stir.

"Yes, it's Sunday. But it's also three weeks until we get married."

Holy moly! I can't believe it! In three weeks, Kaden Scott will be my husband.

"I need to make love to you as many times as possible before then," he says with urgency.

"Why? What will happen once we're married?"

Kaden looks at me like I'm stupid before he breaks out into a huge grin. "I'll never be able to make love to you as my fiancée, again."

"You're so silly!"

He gives me a kiss on my belly. "Hey there, little ones. Hopefully you have no idea what is going on because I am about to make sweet, sweet love to your mama."

He looks up at me and winks, soaking my non-existent panties in the process. Then he does just as he promised, and makes sweet, sweet love to me for hours.

Thirty-Six

ASHLEY

"YOU LOOK BREATHTAKING, SWEETHEART," MY MOM GUSHES like it's the first time she has ever seen my wedding dress.

"I'm just so glad Sandra was able to get the seamstress to bring it out more. I need to hurry up and get married before my belly grows again!"

We're sitting in one of the rooms at the amazing wedding venue Kaden and his mom picked out. Parkside Mansion is gorgeous on the inside and outside. The ceremony will be held out back under a huge white tent, which will shield the blazing Colorado sun, and the reception will be held in their ballroom.

Most of our guests flew in yesterday, some early this morning. Since it's a tradition for the bride and groom to not see each other the night before the wedding, the girls planned a spa day for us yesterday with lunch. It was the perfect bachelorette luncheon. The guys all stayed at Bentley's cabin and spent the day skiing, returning this morning.

Earlier this morning, Kaden's mom brought me by the venue so

I could see everything before the wedding. She told me that it will all feel like a blur once the wedding gets started so she wanted me to take it all in now. The outside is simple. White wooden back chairs that lead up to the front where we will say our vows. Light pink petals are littered along the walkway and upfront.

The ballroom is filled with large circular tables with light pink linens all covered with sterling silver vases that are filled with fresh gardenias. It's all simple and elegant and I love it. The linens even match the bridesmaids' dresses.

"Oh, Ashley, you look beautiful!" Hayley comes over and gives me a one-handed hug since she's holding something in the other. "This is for you, from Kaden."

I take the wrapped box from her hand and unwrap it. Inside is a puzzle box with the image of what the puzzle will be when it's completed. It's a picture of Kaden, Tristan, and me holding up the sonogram we got last week at my appointment where we found out the sex of the babies.

"A thousand-piece puzzle?" Kayla laughs. "That's more like work than a gift."

"No, it's perfect.

Inside the box, there's a note on top of all the pieces.

Ashley,

Love is like a puzzle, hard to piece together, but beautiful when all the right pieces are put together. I can't wait to spend my life putting all our puzzle pieces together, baby. I love you.

Love always,

Kaden

"Don't you cry! You can't go messing up your makeup until he at least sees you!" Rose pulls me into a hug. "Thank you, my darling girl. You took my broken grandson and pieced him back together."

"What did you get him?" Hayley asks. I feel the blush hit my cheeks.

"I did a boudoir photo shoot…"

"Nice!" Kayla exclaims, and all the women giggle. I look over at Rose, embarrassed that I just admitted to doing a sexy photo shoot for her grandson, but she just smiles and winks.

"You ready?" My dad opens the door, extending his hand to me. "Yes, I am more than ready."

Once we get to the backdoors of the mansion, Bella and Tristan walk down the walkway first. Bella is the flower girl and Tristan is the ring bearer. Next, Hayley, Liz, and Kayla all walk down the aisles escorted by their husbands. Once they get to the end, the wedding march begins and my dad walks me down the aisle.

As my dad kisses my cheek giving me away, Kaden takes my hand in his. "There are no words, Ash. You look gorgeous."

"Thank you. You look handsome yourself. Thank you for the puzzle."

"Do you know what it took to make my dick go down after seeing those pictures of you right before having to come out here?" Kaden whispers, making me smile.

We stand in front of the Ordained minister and say our vows to one another. We've created our own vows but decided to keep them simple—beginning and ending them the same. I couldn't memorize mine to save my life, so I pull the paper out of my dress. Kaden chuckles.

"I, Ashley, choose you, Kaden. To stand by your side and sleep in your arms. To be the joy to your heart and the food for your soul. To learn with you and grow with you. I promise to respect you and cherish you as an individual, a partner, and an equal. I vow to support you, push you, and inspire you, and above all love you, for better or worse, in sickness and health, for richer or poorer, as long as we both shall live."

I take the ring Tristan hands me and put it on Kaden's finger. He looks down at it for a moment then back up at me with unshed tears in his eyes.

"I, Kaden, choose you, Ashley. I promise to choose you every day, to do the hard work of making now into always. To laugh with you, cry with you, grow with you, and create with you. I promise to protect you and above all love you, for better or worse, in sickness and health, for richer or poorer, as long as we both shall live."

Kaden takes the ring from Tristan and slides it onto my finger.

"Kaden and Ashley Scott, I now pronounce you husband and wife. You may kiss the bride."

Kaden bridges the gap between us and kisses me. Everybody claps and cheers.

After we take way too many pictures, we make our way to the reception where the deejay announces us as Husband and Wife.

After we enter, we're called to the dancefloor for our first dance. Kaden insisted since he was planning the wedding he would also plan the song for our first dance. *Then* by Brad Paisley comes across the speakers and tears hit my cheeks.

"May I have this dance, Mrs. Scott?" Kaden puts his hand out for me to take and I nod because words can't be spoken.

He pulls me into his arms and my face goes to his chest as he softly sings the lyrics of the song to me. When the song ends, Kaden stops moving and lifts my chin so I'm looking him in the eyes. "You're my whole world, baby. My missing puzzle piece. Thank you for making me the happiest man in the world."

We spend the rest of the night celebrating our wedding with our family and friends. I dance with my father and father-in-law several times, as well as with all the girls. The night is amazing and I couldn't ask for anything more.

As the night comes to a close, Kaden lets me know the valet has pulled our vehicle up. He has a surprise for Tristan and me and is driving us to it tonight. We decided since Tristan was off school for a week, we would bring him along with us, and honeymoon family style.

"Thank you everyone for joining us." Kaden, Tristan, and I wave to everyone then get in the car to head to the secret destination.

"The wedding was amazing. Thank you." We're driving down the dark highway to wherever it is Kaden insists we will love.

"I'm glad you enjoyed it, baby. It was fun planning it with my mom, but I'm glad I don't ever have to plan another one." He squeezes my hand. I turn in my seatbelt to check on Tristan and Kaden stops me. "I can see him in the rearview mirror. He's fine. Don't even think about taking your seatbelt off."

I turn back around and reach down to grab my iPad to read, since

I don't know how long we'll be driving for. When my head pops up, I see a set of bright lights coming toward us as Kaden's hand hits my chest to protect me.

There's a flash of something, I don't know what, but it looks like beautiful angel wings, and then everything goes black.

Epilogue

KADEN

Nine Months Later

"I MISS YOU SO DAMN MUCH. HELL, WE ALL MISS YOU. BUT I know you're up there with Gabe and Gabby looking down on us, watching and protecting us all."

"Of course she is, Kaden."

I turn to see my beautiful wife standing next to me.

"I'm just glad my grandmother got to meet the twins before she passed away."

"Me, too. Thank you for giving me a few minutes at Gabrielle's grave alone."

"Of course. You ready to get back to my parents and the kids?"

"I sure am."

We get back to my parents' house, and after searching the house, find them on the back porch. Morgan and Emma, our twin girls are both in portable swings and Tristan is sitting in front of them, just watching them. My mother and father are sitting at the table, drinking iced tea and eating lunch.

"Tristan? What are you doing, bud? The twins are only three months old. You know they sleep a lot."

"You told me to watch them. This is the first time you both left them. I had to make sure to watch them good."

"He hasn't left that spot since you both left. He takes being a big brother very seriously," my mother says.

"You're the best big brother," I point out to Tristan, making his face light up. I sit next to him, looking at my beautiful little girls, remembering the night I thought for sure I would never get to meet them.

The bright lights.

The crunching sound.

The screaming.

The silence.

For the briefest moment, I thought for sure fate was fucking with me and presenting me with the most sick, twisted form of déjà vu. The ambulance was called, and when we got to the hospital, I wasn't allowed in the back with Tristan because legally, I wasn't his father. The nurse broke the rules and let me know Tristan had a couple bruises on his head but was otherwise perfect.

Ashley was rushed back to be assessed, and after a thorough check, had nothing more than a broken arm. The babies both had perfect heartbeats and the doctor said everything looked good. It was a close call, but for whatever reason, we were all protected. Ashley swears Gabby and Gabe were our guardian angels, looking down and protecting us.

The next day, since the hospital insisted on keeping the two of them over night to be monitored, we made it to our destination. I purchased a cabin near Bentley and Kayla's so we could continue our tradition of skiing during the holidays. We spent the rest of the week at the resort taking it easy, and once we returned home I doted on Ashley the entire rest of her pregnancy.

After the accident at the hospital, and the doctors refusing to talk to me about Tristan since I wasn't his legal guardian, Ashley and I filed the papers with the court for me to legally adopt Tristan, only to find out the papers that asshole Tyler gave her were fake. I hired a PI to locate him, and we found out he was killed shortly after taking the money from Ashley—a fight gone bad. Since he was no longer living, it made it easy for me to adopt Tristan, officially making him my son four months later.

Two months after me legally becoming Tristan's father, Morgan and Emma made me a father of three. They graced us with their presence on September second via Caesarean.

Once the twins were six weeks old, we brought them to Denver to meet my grandparents and I'm glad we did because a few days later, my grandmother passed away in her sleep. We stayed for the funeral and flew home a few days afterward. Now we're back for Thanksgiving, since we're planning to go to Breckenridge for Christmas.

Morgan stretches her tiny arms and Tristan jumps up to make sure she's okay. He is not a fan of them crying at all.

"She's okay, bud."

"Mom, I think she's hungry. Grab her a bottle."

Emma starts wiggling as well. "Mom, wait!" Ashley looks back at him from the doorway. "Emma needs one, too. Hurry before they cry."

I look over at my wife and smile, and she holds back her laugh. "Sure thing."

Both babies start to whine, waking up more, ready to be fed. "Dad, grab Emma, and I'll pat Morgan."

When I don't pick her up quick enough, Tristan says, "Dad, now!"

"Tristan, you know it's okay for them to cry, right?"

He looks at me like I just told him he would never be allowed to fight again. "Okay, okay. Got it."

I pick up my sweet princess, talking softly to her as she continues to stretch. Before the crying starts, Ashley hands me a bottle and I pop it right into Emma's mouth.

Ashley picks up Morgan, and once Tristan is situated sitting Indian style with a nursing pillow in his lap—we bought it just for him to hold the babies so he could feed them—Ashley sets Morgan down and hands Tristan the bottle. Morgan starts to whimper, but Tristan puts the nipple into her mouth before it gets loud. "Whew, that was close," he says, dead serious.

We all look at each other, holding in our laughter.

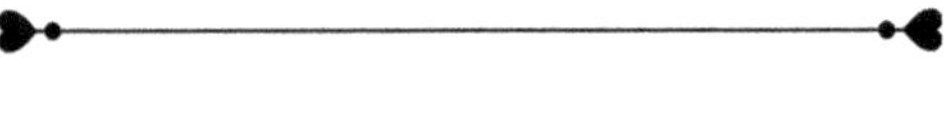

ASHLEY

I LOOK AROUND AT THE PEOPLE IN FRONT OF ME. TRISTAN is feeding Morgan, softly patting her head, and Kaden is feeding Emma.

The night of our wedding, when we got into that car accident, I knew we would all be okay. Many people don't believe in ghosts and angels, but after that night I'm not one of them.

When the car hit us, I know what I saw, two pairs of angel wings flying above. I believe Gabrielle and Gabe were watching us from above that night and protected us, and nobody will ever tell me any different.

When we came to Denver to visit Kaden's family, I insisted on needing a few minutes alone with Gabrielle and Gabe at the cemetery. I needed to thank them for shielding us and protecting us from harm's way. Kaden doesn't really believe it or understand. I don't blame him. Unless you saw the wings the way I saw them, it's hard to convince someone to believe.

I sit down in front of the two headstones and place a single rose on the top of Gabrielle's. "Hey there, I'm Ashley. Although you probably know that, since you're up in heaven looking down on us. I just wanted to say thank you for protecting us. I want you to know that I'm going to make sure Kaden is always happy. I've seen the pictures of you two and know how much you loved each other. Your love is one people wish for their entire lives and I promise to live every day loving him the way you would have. Thank you for being our guardian angel that night."

Turning to Gabe's headstone, I place a set of boxing gloves. "Thank you for protecting us. Your daddy misses you every day. Soon you'll have a couple of siblings. I'll make sure they know you saved them that night."

"Hey Ash, you ready to go home?" I shake myself out of my memory and see both babies are fed and smiling. Tristan is staring at Morgan in awe and Kaden's parents are both smiling at us.

"Yep, I sure am."

Kaden and I both stand. He hands me Emma, but before releasing her, pulls me close to him, giving me a kiss. "I love you, baby."

"I love you, more."

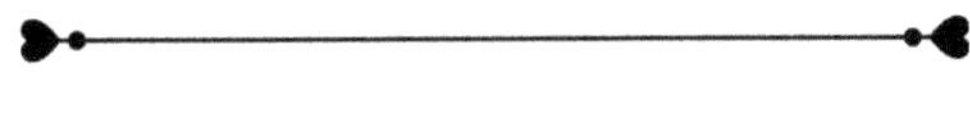

KADEN

Eight Years Later

I'M SITTING ON TOP OF THE PICNIC TABLE IN THE BACKYARD staring at my wife's ass while she lays out on her towel in the grass next to Hayley, Kayla, and Liz. They're all talking quietly and every now and then I hear my wife giggle. I love that fucking giggle. They all stand at the same time. Hayley walks with Ashley toward the table where Caleb and I are sitting, while Kayla and Liz walk toward Bentley and Cooper who are dicking around on the four wheelers.

"Hey Dad." Tristan throws the wet towel at me from the four wheeler he's cleaning. "After dinner, can you drop me off at Bella's to study for our finals."

"Yeah, sure, but why didn't she come over for dinner."

"She needed to study...just like I do."

Caleb is sitting next to me texting on his phone, looking frustrated, but I can't think about what has him annoyed when my wife is getting closer to me in her tiny bikini. Even after having three kids, my wife's body is banging.

"I'm going to go start dinner." She gives me a chaste kiss before walking inside.

Hayley sits next to Caleb. "Everything okay?"

"Yeah, just texting with Marco. I don't think we're going to win this battle, Hayles."

"I'm going to miss him like crazy, but Caleb, we have to let him go and spread his wings. He'll be twenty-one in six months."

Giving them a few minutes to talk in private, I follow my sexy wife inside the house.

"Ash," I call out.

"In here."

I find her in our room changing out of her bathing suit, but before she can put her feet into her shorts to put them on, I grab her by her hips and pick her up placing her on top of our dresser.

"Hey."

"Hey." She giggles. "I need to start dinner."

"How about I just eat you instead?"

"Hmm...that would be great, but what would everyone else eat?"

"Fuck them." I spread my wife's legs and pull her to the edge of the dresser, my tongue darting out straight to her clit.

"Kaden, we have company!" The last word comes out in a long moan and I know I've got her.

"Fuck them," I repeat. I start to tongue fuck her, circling her hard nub, then gliding my tongue up and down her slit. She moans louder.

"Shh...Ash. We have company," I mock her words.

"Fuck them," she growls as I bite down on her clit. Her hands go to my hair and she pushes my face into her pussy needing more. As she moans my name, I bring my hand up to her inner thigh, fingertips brushing her pussy lips. Inserting one, then two fingers deep in her, my wife begins to buck in pleasure. "Play with your nipples, baby," I say before I continue to devour her pussy with my fingers and tongue. A few minutes later and Ashley is praying to the gods as she comes all over my face.

Not even waiting for her to come down from her high, I stand, grab her off the dresser, and turn her around, bending her over the edge of the dresser. My cock slides right into her slick pussy and I still for a second, willing my dick to cooperate so I don't come in seconds.

"Kaden, what are you waiting for? Fuck me." And I do. Grabbing the curves of Ashley's hips, I pound into her pussy from behind. The edge of the dresser keeps her in place as I fuck her hard. With the mirror in front of us, my eyes find hers, which are filled with lust and love—the same way I feel. Reaching around the front of her, I massage circles on her hard nub. Already sensitive from her just orgasming, she squirms and moans, her eyes never leaving mine.

When her moans get louder and her pussy clenches tight around my cock, I know she's close. I pick up the pace, pounding deeper and harder. Seconds later, Ashley's eyes roll back and her lids close briefly. The vision alone has me coming right behind her.

We both stand there for a minute, me still inside her, both of us catching our breath. Then I lean down and give her a kiss on her shoulder. She gives me a small smile that always makes my heart rate pick up.

This woman is my missing puzzle piece and I'm so damn blessed to get to spend the rest of our lives, putting our puzzle together.

"KADEN, CAN YOU GO OUT BACK AND TELL ALL THE KIDS TO wash up for dinner. And please tell Tristan not to walk through the house with mud all over his boots again." Ashley's in the kitchen cooking dinner and Hayley is sitting on the counter talking to her while she cooks. Kayla and Bentley are bringing dishes out to the picnic tables, and Cooper and Liz are somewhere around here.

"Sure thing." I walk out back to see Emma and Tristan washing down their four wheelers with the help of Nathan, Liz and Cooper's son, and Chloe and Faith, Bentley and Kayla's two little girls. The rain came through yesterday, which means today was the perfect day to go mudding.

I look for Morgan and see her, Lilly, and Mackenzie sitting in the grass gossiping just like mini versions of their moms.

Lilly is Liz and Coopers seven-year-old daughter. Liz found out shortly after Ashley gave birth to the twins that she was pregnant. After cussing Cooper out for knocking her up once again, she got excited that she and Ashley would have kids less than a year apart. Lilly, Morgan, and Mackenzie are all inseparable.

"Hey dad, can you bring us to Lilly's house when you drop off Tristan?"

"No way! We aren't babysitting you guys. You can hang out here with the rest of the circus. We have actual studying to do."

"Your brother needs to study for his finals. He only has three years left before he goes off to college. He needs to keep his grades up."

"Dad, can we go to the gym tomorrow?" Emma yells.

"Sure."

"Ugh! I don't want to go to the gym. You know I hate it there, and so does Lilly and Mackenzie. It's smelly and gross." Morgan crosses her arms over her chest pouting adorably like a mini-version of Ashley.

"You don't have to go. So, stop pouting and go wash up for dinner."

"Damn, I'm hungry," Caleb says, looking up from his phone.

"Everything okay?" I ask him, sitting down.

"Yeah, I'm just worried about Marco. I get he needs to find his place in the world, but can't he find it while training at Cooper's gym?"

"The training facility in San Diego is a good one, and he'll be staying with people he knows. He'll be fine," Cooper says, sitting next to his wife.

"After his last win, he thinks he's rolling in the dough. He doesn't understand how quickly that paycheck will run out," Caleb says.

"Then he'll learn," I point out.

We all sit at the table and start scooping up the food. Ashley is an amazing cook.

"Mom, Dad said I can go to the gym with him tomorrow." Emma shovels piles of food onto her plate then starts digging in. While both girls look like mini-versions of Ashley, Emma without a doubt has my personality and love of fighting. She is always begging to go to the gym with Tristan and me.

"Okay, sweetie." I give my wife a wink and she rewards me with a smile in return.

I look around the table at my wife, our three kids, and our friends that are more like family, and thank God once again for the people in my life. I will never understand how, that horrible night, Ashley, Tristan, and our babies weren't taken from me, but I stopped questioning how this world works a long time ago. I've learned to count each and every blessing and to be thankful for each day we're given. To love those around you like it's your last day, and never take a single moment for granted. To this day, Ashley swears it was Gabrielle and Gabe who saved us and, although, I sometimes give her a hard time about it, I would love to believe that was the case.

The End!

About the Author

Reading is like breathing in, writing is like breathing out.– Pam Allyn

Nikki Ash resides in South Florida where she is an English teacher by day and a writer by night. When she's not writing, you can find her with a book in her hand. From the Boxcar Children, to Wuthering Heights, to the latest single parent romance, she has lived and breathed every type of book. While reading and writing are her passions, her two children are her entire world. You can probably find them at a Disney park before you would find them at home on the weekends!